Hope fr

by

Karl Manke

Author of

Unintended Consequences

The Prodigal Father

Secret, Lies and Dreams

Age of Shame

The Scourge of Captain Seavey

Gone to Pot

The Adventures of Railcar Rogues

Harsens Island Revenge

Re-wired

Available at authorkarlmanke.com

Curwood Publishing, LLC

Publisher: Curwood Publishing

Cover Design: Kirsten Pappas

ISBN: 978-1-7338029-1-8

Curwood Publishing

All of Karl's books are available at authorkarlmanke.com

After You Are The Reason I Write

March 22 2025

Karl Manke was born in Frankfort Michigan. He has spent most of his life in the small Mid-Michigan town of Owosso, home to author and conservationist James Oliver Curwood. He and his wife Carolyn have twin daughters and five grandchildren.

A graduate of Michigan State University, the author has been self-employed entrepreneur his entire working career. Discovering an inclination for telling a good story, he spends much of his free time fine-tuning the craft of writing.

Dedicated to my twin daughters, Kirsten and Gretchen

PROLOGUE

Startled awake by an uncompromising struggle for air, Peggy Fortine sits straight up in bed, grasping at her neck, tearing at an imperceptible object tightening its grip around her throat. Accompanying this strange phenomenon is the distinct bad smell of alcohol and cigarette breath, the unmistakable odor of sweat, and the guttural sounds from her seeming assailant—all invisible. Her sympathetic nervous system sends her hands slashing out with the hopes of warding off this unseen assailant. Literally thrown from her bed to the floor, the darkness of the room conceals what she imagines is the appearance of her attacker. No sooner does she hit the floor than she feels the distinct sensation of a blunt instrument striking her skull, and then another and another. She is surprised that she is still conscious. With no notice, she's suddenly left alone. There's no sound to interrupt the silence other than her own heavy breathing. Not certain what she has just encountered, and not certain what she may yet be facing, she musters the courage to turn on the lamp beside her bed. Much to her surprise, there is no one in her room besides herself. Even more perplexing, there are no visible injuries anywhere on her body. Her mind hits a dead end.

Was this a dream? She attempts to reason her way through this unreasonable encounter. Everything in the bedroom is as neat as she left it several hours earlier. Her clothing is still laid it out for tomorrow, just as she left it. Her dorm room door is still closed, and her window shades are still drawn, with no evidence that anything has been tampered with.

Not getting the satisfaction that her whole being is screaming for and finding it impossible to return to bed, she makes a cup of hot tea and hopes this devilish experience will explain itself. Nothing is forthcoming. With dawn approaching and a strong aversion to return to the bed that produced in her so much realistic bewilderment, she chooses to curl up in her chair. Sleep once again has its way, and she's soon dead to the world.

A full morning sun quickly turns the night into a different certainty. With the daylight easing her tension, Peggy's thoughts turn toward the here and now, and she lets the early morning debacle remain a weird, unexplained anomaly.

CHAPTER 1

Life Stories

Everyone's life is a story. Some are good stories, and some are bad. Bruce Fortine began life as everyone does, with a certain amount of God-given talent, but by the time he was twenty years old, he had already dropped out of high school; impregnated his girlfriend, Sylvia; and lost his job because of poor attendance. Now, he's currently into the twentieth year of a life sentence for a robbery gone bad that resulted in a murder conviction.

The fallout of his dereliction resulted in his young girlfriend finishing out her pregnancy alone. She delivered identical twin girls she named Peggy and Julia and found herself alone, with no aid from family on either side. Her story doesn't look very promising.

As the difficulties of raising two babies on the welfare system increased, Sylvia, often out of desperation, supplemented that support with occasional contributions from the assortment of men she allowed into her life. This proved not to be well thought out. Most times, it's ended just short of a dangerous threat to herself and her daughters. In addition, alcohol abuse has run a rampant course through the life of this mother, affecting not only her wellbeing, but also her daughters' security as man after man has laid a lasting mark of abuse on their mental development. Often, they have been forced to lock themselves in their bedroom to protect themselves from the unsettling intentions of their mother's drunken live-in.

Peggy and Julia have buttressed each other through their mother's never-ending blunders in bringing treacherous men into their lives. In spite of their father's incarceration, they've romanticized the notion that things would be much better under his protection, if only he were available. All of their visits with their father have been at their mother's discretion and at best a mere hour long. For various reasons, there were only a handful of these visits over the years. Regardless, each sister has entertained how much better her life would have been if only they'd had their father at home.

The Fortines live in a northwestern Michigan village with only a handful of residents, situated on the shores of Lake Michigan. Their father had moved their mother there from downstate before they were born. The idea was to isolate himself from the scrutinizing eyes of her parents. Her parents didn't waste words in attempting to sway their daughter away from his controlling behavior, but like so many young girls, the more they criticized him, the more determined she became to prove them wrong. When he was sent to prison for the cold-blooded murder of a young station attendant with a wife and baby, Sylvia remained rebellious, refusing to ask her own dysfunctional family for help. Over time, she has developed a sense of community with her misery, remaining isolated some three hundred miles from her roots, always assuring herself that she'll manage her life better the next time and that she's done with men—only to find herself involved with another loser.

At this time in her life, Sylvia's gotten involved with one more slacker. His name is Harold Gilles. He's a laid-off construction worker sucking out as much unemployment as he can before he's forced to go back to work. She met him several months ago at the bar where she works. They have discovered a common interest capable of holding them together: they both like to drink. His singular athletic capability is that when he's drunk, he can—with both feet flat on the floor—leap to the top of a barroom table in one single effort.

Because his given name is "Harold," one would think he would go by "Harry," but he's been tagged with simply "Gil." He's in his middle-to-late forties. Never one to overdo getting a haircut or shaving, he is rather scruffy in appearance and considers his "six-pack abs" to be the kind that a six-pack can sit on. He has no shame in appearing shirtless—and still brags about how he still wears the same size pants he wore in his teens—despite the fact that his overhanging beer belly totally hides his belt buckle. Even so, he has no problem considering himself a "ladies' man."

Gil moved into the area a number of years ago from Michigan's upper peninsula. The Gilles family were known scofflaws. Illegal drugs, moonshine, burglary, wife beating, and abusing children are just a small sample of the kinds of violence they enacted within their community. Gil's mother deserted the family when he was twelve and ran off with a Finnish copper miner. Because of his father's behavior, Gil never blamed his mother for leaving.

His father was a hard-drinking Irishman who beat him when he drank too much; this increased tenfold after his mother left. He always knew Gil preferred his mother over him and would punish him as a result. After a beating, Gil waited for an opportunity to get even. The opportunity arose one day when his father was drunk. There was no one else in the house. His father was at the top of the stairs. Gil realized he could give him a push. The old man went crashing down stairs, banging his head, arms, legs, and back on every step until he came to rest in a pile of broken bones at the very bottom. Gil stood at the top of the stairs, reviewing the situation. The instinct for violence had become a mainstay in this home. Making his way down the stairway, careful not to slip on the blood covering many of the steps, Gil concluded that if his father were ever to recover, he would probably kill him. If his father wasn't dead yet, that Gil would have to make sure he was.

His father lay moaning but not moving. Gil stood over him, shaking. A mixture of fear, loss, relief, and a few indescribable emotions surged through him. His father had shot an old dog one time to put the critter out of his misery; the best thing to do now was to put the old man out of his misery. At thirteen, Gil lacked the adult knowledge of how to do this. In looking around, he spotted a clothespin—the type one squeezes open. After toying with it for a few minutes, he placed it on his father's nose, pinching it closed. He sat watching for a few more minutes. When the old man began to gasp for air through his mouth, Gil's frustration grew, and he had to come up with another plan. It's been said that "frustration is the wet nurse of savagery." He finally settled on removing his socks and stuffing them into his father's mouth. It didn't take long before there was no indication of life left in his father. The coroner determined the cause of death was an accidental fall following a period of intoxication.

Gil has many relatives on both sides of his family, but because of the family dynamics, their fighting is too much to deal with. He hardly knows them and hasn't felt the slightest loss in leaving. Being the youngest of six, once in a while, he'll wonder if any of his older siblings are still living. He became aware his mother had died of lung cancer a few years after he left. He regrets his mother's plight, but that's usually overshadowed by his resentment over the fact that she left him alone and unprotected. *Why didn't you take me with you?* has been his underlying thought. The year his mother deserted the family, he was thirteen. This was also the year he began his own drinking career; he hasn't found a good enough reason to quit since. Most of the time, it's a miserable, desolate life, but at least life's laws of cause and effect make it comfortably predictable.

Gil had made his way into this village shortly after he had been freed from a later charge of attempted murder. It seems he had awakened to a neighbor burglarizing his house and attacked the man with a hammer, leaving him paralyzed and confined to a wheelchair for the duration of his life. Because of Gil's previous record—starting as a juvenile and extending into his adult years—he was lucky to beat the charge. Shortly after this incident, he left to make a new start rather than push his luck and ended up ordering a beer from Sylvia in the Midway bar and grill. Sylvia has always been drawn to the "bad boy" image in her choice of men—Gil proved not to be an exception.

Gil lives in a single-wide thirty-four-foot house trailer tucked into a wooded area on the edge of town. It's a washed-out, greenish tone that may have been a cutting-edge color twenty years ago, but today, it typifies its owner as a tasteless renegade. Its leaking roof has led Gil to fashion a makeshift roof held up by stilts, covering it end to end so it appears as though it's parked in its own garage. The tires, thoroughly rotted, are still in place but jacked up off the ground. The trailer is now resting on cement blocks strategically placed on each of the four corners, which have become its permanent foundation. Straw bales surround the trailer's perimeter, functioning as a substitute for skirting and acting as a windbreaker.

The inside is barely livable. A distinct musty smell mixed with the odor of stale cigarette smoke prevails even in the coldest weather. The linoleum-covered floors are warped giving them an undulating appearance. Empty beer cans comingled with weeks-old fast food wrappers and overly filled ashtrays adorn much of the counter space. In the bathroom, the toilet and shower have a layer of rust that has taken years to accumulate. Humidity has warped the paneling that covers the walls, which are only adorned with a three-year-old, faded Playboy calendar featuring the nude of the month. His bed lacks sheets, so only a single soiled bed covering lies twisted and carelessly cast aside on the bare mattress. He has a TV, but something went wrong with it months ago; since he can't fix it, it sits unused. He hasn't been to a movie in years, and aside from Clint Eastwood, he has no interest in these new actors.

He drives a four-year-old Ford pickup truck; its bed carries a mixture of empty beer cans, bags of garbage (which are usually surreptitiously deposited in gas station trash cans), and various used truck parts.

Other than going to the bar, his other passions include what he refers to as "collecting" (others refer to it as "hoarding") and fishing. The most elaborate possession he owns is a fifteen-year-old, twenty-six-foot cabin cruiser outfitted for salmon fishing in the Great Lakes.

Most people couldn't or wouldn't live their lives this way, but Gil can hardly be classified as "most people." Today, he's somewhere in his mid-to-late forties but could easily pass for someone much older.

Despite his irresponsible living, Gil has always been the first to volunteer when help is needed. On the surface, he's likable enough, even with his sloppy first impression. Consequently, his eccentricities are often overlooked.

CHAPTER 2

A Storm

Because of the life course this mother and father provided for their daughters, one could easily predict a negative outcome for their prodigy. Regardless of how much these delinquent parents have left these sisters to fend for themselves, the girls have empowered one another in side-stepping many of life's countless landmines. At nineteen, not only are both girls strikingly beautiful, but they have also graduated at the top of their class. There is another unusual aftermath for these identical twins; they've each developed outside interests. The result is a separate life away from their mother and, to a lesser extent, away from each other.

Julia has developed a love of the outdoors and outdoor sports, while Peggy has excelled in indoor sporting events such as volleyball and basketball. They also paint to fulfill their love of the arts. After taking an art class together, they discover they share a common interest in painting depictions of various kinds of beautiful butterflies. Despite most young women their age having the usual array of rock stars adorning their bedroom walls, these girls have a display of butterfly paintings they've painted themselves.

Their bond of mutual support that has held them together through so much in their lives remains in place, but today, they're further confronted by the realization that despite being identical twins, they are, nonetheless, separate people. Deep in their psyches, each has known a day is approaching that will force them to reexamine their relationship. These unspecified circumstances always bring a silent fear within them.

After a June graduation, they've both managed to find summer jobs. The area is rife with tourists during both summer and winter. In the summer, the lakes and rivers provide recreational boating, fishing, and all other activities associated with the warm northern Michigan climate. In the winter, the nearby ski slopes promise that winter is never so severe that one can't enjoy it. Since they each qualify for educational grants and student loans, they hope to earn enough spending money through the summer months to last through much of their freshman year. Peggy has settled for a waitress job in the same bar where her mother works. She has been accepted at a major state university. Her desire is to become an elementary school teacher. Julia, on the other hand, has given in to her mother's panic over being left alone and, for the time being, has settled for a nearby junior college, which enables her to live at home and commute. She has done well enough in high school sciences to consider becoming a pediatrician. It's not uncommon for young people who have had a struggle-filled life to want to avail themselves in working with children. Julia is no exception.

Today is a sunny June morning in northern Michigan, where temperatures are hovering near the high eighties. Julia has been fortunate to have gotten a job working at a local camp. Her job description, much to her delight, is to coordinate outdoor activities for eighth-grade girls. This includes hiking, bicycling, overnight camping expeditions in the nearby dunes, and being a lifeguard for swimming activities.

Jim Samples is a year older and is her supervisor. It's no secret the two of them have had their eyes on each other since they've begun working together.

"I love these kids, but sometimes I want to choke them," says Julia, speaking to Jim of her young vacationers.

He looks at her in disbelief. "I don't believe I just heard you say you want to choke someone."

"Well, I don't really mean I'd choke anyone. It's just that these girls are so catty and mean to each other."

"I've never been able to figure girls out at any age, much less anything about this bunch specifically," says Jim with an air of satisfaction regarding his male stupidity.

Not willing to let him gloat over a remark she regards as stupid, Julia says, "That doesn't surprise me one bit, Jim Samples. You always have had a thick head when it comes to knowing anything about girls."

Because of Julia's less than fulfilling experience of men, Jim is finding it challenging to muster up a conversation with her. He's taking this discussion with her as a win, even if it means that she regards him as stupid.

Having broken the ice with Julia, Jim says, "Well, let's try another tack. How'd you like to go sailing this evening?"

This abrupt invitation has caught Julia completely off guard. Not willing to appear as though she can't think on her feet and is as stupid as he is, she fights an inward struggle that prevents a thoughtful answer.

"I have nothing definite planned. I'd love to," she says, hoping the tightening muscles in her throat won't choke her words before she can get them out.

Jim Samples had been a high school senior when Julia was a junior. He had flirted a little with her when they were both on the track team, but that was two years ago. She still regards him as cute, but on the other hand, she is certainly not willing to let him become aware of this. In doing so, she hopes her coyness will give her an upper hand. If there is anything that she's learned from living with her mother's failing relationships, it's to not let a man walk on her in any way—physically, mentally, and especially not spiritually.

Back in high school, Jim had been attracted to Julia's sassiness. He found it delightful, but as high school goes, diversions and distractions are the norm, and he went with different pursuits. However, this is no longer high school, and he finds the distractions have become much more manageable. Lately, Jim finds his attention turning more and more to Julia's movements. She's slim, leggy, and genuinely blithe but not mindless or immature, so Jim finds her attractive.

With the afternoon waning, they're both expected to be engrossed with camp activities, but again and again, they find their minds excited in recalling their agreement to meet that evening. Consequently, they're finding their tasks are becoming the distraction.

Julia is on a hiking expedition up into the dunes with her eighth-grade charges. The girls are chattering incessantly among themselves with the inordinate use of the expletive "Oh my God" to dramatize even the least of everyday occurrences.

Meanwhile, Julia's thoughts begin to wander unfettered. *I wonder if he'll notice those lumps on my hips if I wear my yellow bikini? But then, I think my tan looks better in yellow.* This is the kind of important stuff that she knows has to be settled before this evening.

Jim also has a group of young boys on a canoe trip paddling down river. He's made it clear there'll be no shenanigans to disrupt the safety of the group. The idea is to teach them boating courtesy and water safety. Nonetheless, within a half hour, the overriding temptation of adolescent boys to use their paddles to create a splash war is in full motion. It isn't long before every canoe is involved and nearly every occupant is in the water. Thankfully, the water is only waist deep and not likely to become a safety issue.

Jim's thoughts toward this evening's rendezvous are primarily centered around whether Julia will notice his overly developed pecs. It's no secret he finds physical challenges motivating. He's never too far from a workout bench with the makeshift gym he's put together in one of the camps unused storerooms. He considers himself a serious bodybuilder and has worked hard at lifting weights, sculpting his pecs so he can flex them one at a time as though they are performing a dance.

The hour finally arrives, and they rendezvous at the sailboat. Neither of them feels they are presenting themselves exactly the way they had hoped, but they're nonetheless excited to get the evening underway.

Jim has been working at this camp since he was a young boy and has developed skills on the water others have missed because the opportunity was never available for them. The boat Jim has on hand is a seventeen-foot sloop with a medium-sized V-berth to stash stuff. Since he began to work at the camp, he has sailed this boat hundreds of times without serious incident. The boat is moored offshore and requires a small skiff to reach it. The purpose of this is to avoid dealing with a dock and a sail when trying to catch a wind.

For the time being, both are engrossed in the moment, enjoying the good times. Julia has forgotten about the small pads adorning her hips, and Jim is no longer obsessing over his physique. For now, they are immersed in each other.

The small skiff has successfully carried them to the waiting sloop without incident. The larger craft has been tied to a buoy that serves both to anchor and secure it from drifting off. It's only a matter of minutes before Jim has the sloop untied, the rigging unleashed, and the headsail raised. It takes only a moment for the waiting breeze to fill the sail, allowing them to begin tacking toward a small inlet, after which they'll let the wind and the current jettison them into the waters of the Great Lake Michigan. As the wind catches the sail, the boat leaps forward like an anxious dog on a leash. Satisfied with the conditions, Jim lets out a substantial whoop.

"What d'ya think, Julia? Can you handle being the first mate?" asks Jim, supplying her with a cap emblazoned with FIRST MATE and himself the one that says CAPTAIN.

She places the cap on her head playfully, giving him her sexiest first mate pose. He can't help but feel a sense of happiness seeing Julia respond in such a carefree and lighthearted way. It tells him she isn't always as guarded as she sometimes seems.

The lake is choppy—but then, that comes with a good wind. The best thing about the sloop is that it's capable of sailing into a wind as well as with the wind. Like most athletes, whether runners or cyclists, Jim chooses to head into the wind on the first leg of their jaunt in hopes of enjoying the exhilaration of a fast wind at their back on their way back. This tacking method causes an ample amount of lake water to splash into the craft. Handing Julia a small pail, Jim jovially declares, "First duty of a first mate is to bail water!"

Looking at the pail with a look that says, *"This ain't what I signed up for,"* she halfheartedly takes it anyway and begins the bailing process.

When she's done, Jim has one arm busily adjusting the tiller and the other casually draped behind Julia. She leans into him, savoring the solidness of his muscular body against hers. Lost in the exhilarating moment, mother nature is having her way. They are perfectly content to stay this way, taking each other in.

Suddenly, Jim notices the wind is picking up much more vigorously than it did a half hour ago, when they'd first entered the lake. Looking off to the west, he's startled to face what is confronting them: the foreboding formation of flat anvil types of clouds. This tells him they're about to face a full-blown thunderstorm—lightning and all. His demeanor quickly changes from the carefree captain of a half hour ago to the perilous look of one facing an unrelenting threat. Jim is well aware of the dangers of being on the water during a lightning storm. Lightning will more often than not strike the tallest object in the neighborhood. In this instance, it's his boat on an otherwise flat surface of water. There've been instances where lightning has blown the hull completely off a small craft, sinking it in seconds.

The telltale change on Jim's face suggests something out of the ordinary is occurring that Julia is not completely aware of. She is tuning into his concern rather quickly. He has a foreboding look that's changed his whole demeanor. This abrupt change stirs a sense of unrest bordering on panic within her.

"What can I do to help?" she asks over the sound of the now raging wind.

Jim doesn't answer. His mind and body are working vigorously to turn the sloop around and make their way back to port. Judging from the size of the seas, he calculates that they'll take the brunt of the fury before he can safely return. Up until now, they have not been wearing the lifejackets required by the camp rules (yellow bikinis and over-developed pecs don't look as good under a lifejacket), but now is not the time for looking good. Within seconds, Jim has retrieved the jackets from the stow cabinets. He struggles to put his on with one hand while the other is fighting with a tiller that has developed a mind of its own.

The first clap of thunder is directly above them. It's terrifying, and especially terrifying to someone like Julia, who has never found herself in such a helpless situation due to weather. Abandoning all other concerns, she falls to the bottom of the boat, still struggling to get the hang of how her lifejacket is supposed to fit, all the while looking straight up at the raw churning of thick black clouds. Her only thought is, *Lord only knows, this is a truly life-threatening calamity.* The swirling wind seems to be hell-bent on giving their little boat over to the mounting waves' desire to swallow it. When the craft is in the low trough of a swell, all that can be seen is a wall of water.

Well aware this is not the time for fear and seeing Julia helplessly lying on the bottom boards, Jim quickly extends his hand, aiding her back to her seat.

Now Jim becomes aware of another looming problem. "Julia, I need you to take this tiller. I need to get this sail and mast pole down fast. Can you do that?" Jim asks, extending a hand again to steady her to the aft seat. His voice is not frantic or rude; rather, it's firm and commanding. With a flash of lightning, Julia leaps to her feet and hurries to the tiller.

"Just hold it steady until I can get this rigging down or the lightning will beat me to it." Working as fast as he can, Jim manages to complete the task without being thrown overboard.

Wanting to get as much metal off the sloop as possible, he next tosses the anchor over the side, as well as a gold chain and crucifix he's wearing around his neck. He motions to Julia to do the same and rid herself of silver rings on her fingers and ears. "Lightning will jump to anything that will assist it in making its way to the water, and that includes jewelry worn by us," says Jim, throwing over his watch.

Barely rid of that fear, Julia is taking note of the positive actions she sees Jim taking to ensure her wellbeing. In these uncertain circumstances, it's giving her an unbelievable degree of comfort. As quickly as he finishes this task, he begins tossing things out of the small V-berth and motioning for Julia to get inside. With the next clap of thunder, she doesn't have to be asked twice. She dives into her newly carved out cave of safety. Glancing up from the bottom of the boat, the first thing she is aware of is Jim's muscular legs straining with his every action. As her eyes travel upward, she becomes even more aware of his well-managed movements orchestrated to defend them against the storm's ravages. Even though his actions are fast and furious, she is strangely comforted by his seeming expertise.

The last thing on Jim's mind is how cool his actions may look to Julia. What has become paramount is that his every action has a purpose. His unrehearsed response to the motions of the storm proves to be the only thing standing between them and scuttling, followed by certain drowning.

Julia remains huddled as far back in the small V-berth as she can cram her body. It's as though the deeper into the recess she can retreat, the safer she'll become. She finds it difficult to brace herself against the lake; it tosses the boat skyward on every upsurge, only to slam the bow downward on every down-surge.

Jim has an eye on every wave that is breaking—not only in front, but also on each side. His hand tightens around the tiller as he fights to prevent the small craft from positioning itself in such a way as to have one of these crashing ten-foot swells hit them broadside—which would capsize this boat in a second. The storm's seeming anger against Jim's efforts to ride it out parallel the rage of a rodeo bull thwarting the efforts of its rider to tame it. With the sea's refusal to retire, it's as though it's personally taking offence at this mere mortal daring to challenge its fury. Instead, the intensity of the waves striking them strengthens to fifty knots, forcing the tiller out of Jim's hands long enough to allow the next wave to hook the craft like a claw and spin it completely around. This repositioning no longer allows the bow to cut the force of the waves and has placed the aft plank to take the full brunt of the water's driving force. This flat surface not only allows the water to break over and flood the decking, but also propels the boat headlong toward shore.

Jim believes that if he can manage the sloop, he will not only save their lives, but also keep the vessel in one piece. The craft's safe keeping is at risk as it takes on unwelcome water, making it less buoyant. With less buoyancy, it's certain to smash against a series of boulders bordering the shoreline, submerged only a few inches beneath the pounding breakers. Any attempt to maneuver against hazards will put even a skilled sailor at the mercy of fate. Some of these rocks are slanted in various positions—none of them friendly to a boat's hull.

With the storm's hurricane force not changing for the better, Jim braces himself and hopes for the best but expects to deal with the worst. At this moment, a huge wave snatches the half-submerged sloop, uprooting it as though it were nothing more than a cork bobbing along in its path, catapulting it several feet above all these precarious, submerged rocks, and lodging it twenty feet up onto the beach, where it's no worse for wear.

With this unexpected turn of events and with the rain beating on them, Jim and Julia remain, still frozen in the same positions: shocked, expressionless, and unresponsive. They're still not certain what has just occurred, but in the same moment, they become aware of their seeming safe deliverance from what seconds before had appeared to be the surety of death—or at the very least, serious injury.

With their lives out of danger for the moment, Jim's full attention turns to Julia. She is attempting to free herself from what only moments before was considered as a safe room and has suddenly turned back into what it was designed for—a small, cramped storage compartment. Her long, water-soaked, tanned legs, all slick and shiny, are the first part of her frame to emerge, followed by a torso cloaked in an orange life preserver hung up on a latch that's preventing her escape from this prison. The next sound is the hollow resonance of a woman's voice reverberating well above the roar of the storm. It echoes with a mixture of fear and anger and sounds as though it were coming from inside a barrel.

"Get me the hell out of here! I'm trapped!" is Julia's protestation. Not only is she trapped, but the boat has taken on enough water to nearly fill her compartment.

Still in a daze, Jim is suddenly jerked into the present. He deftly unsnags Julia's life jacket. The rest of her emerges along with what had once been a well coifed hairdo; it now looks as though she's styled it with a grenade. She begins to shiver as Jim helps her to her feet. Desperate words fly out from his lips: "Julia, are you okay?"

Julia is relieved by Jim's successful effort to free her and more relieved to discover they are safe on shore. They shamelessly hug each other.

"I'm freezing!" Julia exclaims.

The beached sloop appears to be much larger and much more imposing than it did while they were being tossed about by the storm. This doesn't prevent Jim from rifling through a compartment to pull loose some much-needed rain gear to wrap around a still shivering Julia.

"Thank you," she offers with the ghost of a smile and breathes a sigh of relief. Sitting back down on the same seat she had been seated on during simpler times, she says, "Thank God, we made it."

With Jim standing in front of her, Julia recognizes something awakening in her that has never been there with any other man in her life—an element of trust. Along with her entry into this phase of her life, she has vowed not to become her mother. She had hoped this awakening would just be a matter of time; on the other hand, she never expected it to be on a disabled boat stranded on a beach in the middle of a thunderstorm. Realizing this levelheadedness is coming to life within a man she has known her entire life gives her pause; consequently, she doesn't have a clue what her next step should be. It's all happening fast and scaring her. *I should be enjoying this more somehow. What the heck should I be doing next?* she asks herself. All she feels is a strange sense of peace that's coming from an unlikely source. For no other reason than the lack of a frame of reference for her feelings, she sits quietly, absentmindedly pulling her fingers through her knotted hair.

Jim has finished studying the condition of the beached sloop and has returned to sit in silence. With both of them wrapped up in their own thoughts, the pause becomes uncomfortable. As he sits, silently facing her, she has the sudden crazy thought that he may try to kiss her. Not knowing what her response should be, she quickly stands up with the intention of avoiding the confrontation by busying herself with rolling up the cuff of her oversized rain pants. When he doesn't attempt this, she gives a little sigh of relief but remains guarded.

Jim is deep in thought about how he's going to get this boat off the beach. It's a good twenty feet from the water's edge. The images of the struggle he had in keeping the sloop from capsizing and giving them over to the ravages of the lake remains fresh in his mind. It's a nightmare he can do without, but it refuses to loosen its grip. Nonetheless, this new problem continues to invade his attention. *Somehow, I gotta get this heap back in the water.*

The dark clouds and wet wind are giving way to a brilliant sunset. The storm has wrung the moisture from the air, lending an earthly sense of comfort to what had earlier been experienced as a wrathful exhibition threatening their wellbeing. Now what's left is a beautiful rainbow stretching across the eastern sky.

After taking inventory, Jim realizes their phones are both lying in the bottom of the boat in six inches of water— totally incapacitated. He spends the next few minutes scouring through any emergency provisions that have been assigned to the boat. This takes several more minutes of silent contemplation. Decisively, Jim faces Julia with a less than happy demeanor. "The way I'm seeing it, we have a couple options. We can walk the five or six miles back to camp, which will be mostly in the dark, or we can wait here to see if we are missed in the hope that they'll be looking for us. If we choose the latter, we can make the boat covering into a makeshift tent and camp here for the night."

This kind of decision making is not Julia's strength. Nevertheless, she is determined to put her adult hat on and offer a thought. "I don't relish walking that far in the dark. Besides, every rescue instruction warns people not to wander off, but rather to stay put."

"I agree with you. We need to stay put. Other than worrying everyone when we don't show up before dark, we'll be okay. The only problem is that we don't have anything to start a fire," laments Jim.

Listening to Jim and rustling around inside a small handbag she's carrying, Julia proclaims, "Will this help?" In her hand is a small butane lighter. "I used this to light a fire to roast marshmallows with my girls this afternoon."

"Well, ain't you the Girl Scout," says Jim, sporting the biggest smile he's had since they began this jaunt.

Now that they're on the same page, picking a spot for their camp occupies the next few minutes. A scrubby bunch of Scotch pines lining an area in front of a large dune has caught their attention. What catches Jim's eye is a dead white birch tree. This tree is comprised of a mass of creosote—great for a quick, hot fire. Its bark guarantees an easy, quick ignition— even when it's wet.

With a makeshift tent, a blazing fire, and a canopy of stars overhead, they talk into the night until Jim falls asleep. Julia is suddenly aware of her loneliness. She looks up at the clear sky at the twinkling stars. "Well, at least you guys have each other." Without her watch, it's difficult to know what time it is. The darkness is foreboding enough to discourage her from leaving the safety of the canopy to tend the fire alone. All she knows is that she's cramped and cold and would give anything to be in her own bed. With one last glimmer of hope, she turns her ear toward the lake in hopes of hearing a rescue boat. At last, resigned to the probability that their rescue isn't happening tonight, she huddles herself into a little ball and accepts sleep.

CHAPTER 3

A Dilemma

It's well after dark. Peggy is becoming more and more concerned that her sister is not home and that her cell phone responds with a "not available" response. Concerned but not alarmed, she carries on with her nightly routine with the expectation that her sister will be making an appearance any moment. After trying to call Julia's cell a few more times, Peggy finally asks her mother, "Mom, did Julia tell you any of her plans other than her hooking up with Jim Samples for a sailboat date?"

"Well, if they got the same storm we got, they're probably floundering around out on the lake somewhere," says Sylvia. Her lack of worry about the welfare of her daughters is something Julia and Peggy have grudgingly adjusted to.

Peggy pauses for a moment. She is well aware of the thunderstorm that passed through, but she thinks that her sister would have called if they were experiencing difficulty.

"It doesn't make any sense, Mom. Julia's cell phone isn't accepting calls," says Peggy with a worried sigh.

"Maybe the damn thing fell overboard," says Sylvia with her normal lack of apprehension. "Besides, that Jim guy she's with should have a phone she could borrow if she wanted to call you bad enough."

These are not the comforting words from the mother Peggy has always hoped Sylvia would somehow transform into.

Another hour passes without an explanation. Peggy is becoming more distressed. She has called the camp, only to hear they have no idea where Jim and Julia are. Peggy returns to her mother only to discover that she's well on her way into an alcohol oblivion.

"Mother, you have to stop drinking long enough to help me find out what's happened to Julia," she tells her mother.

"She's probably out with Gil? He's always had his eyes on you girls." Sylvia slurs. "You ain't the only pretty ones in this family, ya know. I ain't exactly chopped liver."'"

The look on her daughter's face at this suggestion is not surprising. Sylvia's drunken jealousy has so blinded her that she's convinced herself that Gil is probably having an affair with Julia. The truth is, the girls have always placed Gil in the slimeball category with all the other men they've seen come in and out their mother's life. Sylvia has resented her daughters' accurate judgements for the most part and doesn't mind sticking it to them when she gets a chance—usually when she's drinking, which is all the time, lately.

If a hard stare was a bullet, Sylvia would be dead. Peggy is incensed that her mother would even suggest that Julia is having anything to do with Gil. "Why do you always accuse us of coming on to Gil? If he were the last man on this earth, neither of us would hook up with him."

"Yeah, well, I've seen different. I see how you swing your butts around when he's here, and how he ogles both of you, so don't tell me you ain't puttin' on a show."

Hardly able to contain her disgust, Peggy shouts, "Why do I even ask you for anything to do with my sister's and my wellbeing when I know you'll fail us at every turn?" With that said, she storms out of the house and gets in her mother's car, only to remember it hasn't run in a week. Gil promised her he'd work on it, but he's been too drunk to get anything done. Out of total frustration, Peggy pounds her fists on the steering wheel and begins to sob. "Why, God, why?" is all she can conjure up. Very seldom has she had to face life's trauma alone. She's always had Julia. Now that support is being threatened. Not knowing where else to turn, she musters up a new resolve. Returning to her mother, she grabs the beer from her mother's hand, walks to the sink, and dumps it.

Stunned at her daughter's impudence, Sylvia lashes out, shouting, "You little bitch! Just what makes you think you have a right to dump my beer?"

With a voice a notch above her mother's, Peggy shouts back, "Whether you like it or not, for once in your life, you're going to do something other than drink your way out of helping us. We need you right now, and by God, you're going to help us. For all we know, my sister is someplace out on that lake. You're going to get your ass over to your Mr. Wonderful's dumpy trailer and get him to get his boat out and help us find my sister!"

Slurring her words and flicking the ash from her cigarette, Sylvia says, "This has always been how you and your sister overreact to everything by attacking your mother."

Seeing Peggy's reaction to this statement, Sylvia butts her cigarette and throws her hands in the air, saying, "Okay! Okay, I'll go with you to Gil's. I don't know what we're gonna do in the dark, but we'll have it your way."

Gil lives about a mile away. Sylvia hasn't walked this far in years. They walk in silence other than Sylvia's incessant smoker's hack and cursing Gil for not getting her car fixed. A half hour later, they are stumbling along Gil's driveway, hoping they don't fall headlong over a broken-down lawn mower or some other treasure Gil dragged home. A yellow glow in a nicotine-stained window suggests their trek has not been in vain. Peggy doesn't wait for her mother to make the first move; she begins to bang on Gil's door with both fists. There is no response. This doesn't discourage her; she begins to kick it as well. Sylvia is standing by, willing to let things go for a few minutes. Then she reaches under a familiar rock next to the entrance and produces a key. Saying nothing, she nudges Peggy out of the way, inserts the key into the lock, and opens the door. This key has been provided especially for Sylvia.

Stepping into the trailer, she finds the usual litter of empty beer cans and Gil passed out on the couch. Sylvia has enough sobriety from her walk to have some of her wits about her. Shaking him, she says, "Gil, wake up. I gotta talk to ya for a minute." She gets no response. "Damn it, Gil, wake your sorry ass up. I gotta ask ya somethin' important." This time, he stirs a little as one would when faced with an unwelcome intruder. "Who the hell is buggin' me?" Gil asks, struggling to sit up and open both eyes.

"It's me. Sylvia," she says.

"Oh, hi, baby, what ya up to?" he slurs, wiping the drool from his mouth. It's obvious that he's in no condition to make a rational judgement about anything.

Peggy has been standing in the background, willing to let her mother make the initial introduction, but now the conversation is going in a direction where only two drunks can make it go. Not able to put up with it another second, Peggy steps around her mother and approaches Gil. The presentation of this tall, athletic young woman with an angry demeanor has a more sobering effect on him than anything so far. The look on his face is one of total confusion. Peggy is one of the last people he expected to see in his trailer.

"Gil, my sister got caught out on the lake in that storm we had earlier, and she hasn't come home yet." Cutting right to the chase, she continues, "We need your boat to go and look for her."

Gil is actually stunned to hear Peggy's voice. This is the first time she has ever spoken directly to him. With a mind still fogged with the dregs of the bottle, it takes him a second to process all that's occurred in the last two minutes.

"What the hell are you talkin' about?" he asks, squinting his eyes in yet another attempt to catch on to what's happening.

Realizing to a fuller extent with what she is dealing with, Peggy takes her time in going into the details of Julia's and Jim's jaunt on the lake.

Hoping to normalize this weird situation, Gil lights another cigarette. As he listens, that part of him that yearns for approval in contrast to his drunken everyday life is kicking in. It gives him a sense of being needed, even if it's by people who normally can't stand him. Still listening to Peggy, he heats a cup of day-old coffee and lights yet another cigarette. This is his normal routine to bring his mind and body together. At last, he says, "If we're gonna light this candle, we gotta get goin'."

With a slight smile of relief, these are exactly the words that Peggy has been hoping to hear. In the next few minutes, Gil cleans the passenger side of his pickup. He pulls out every kind of tool, fishing tackles, empty beer cans, and an assortment of rags soiled by everything from truck grease to mustard. Hesitant to sit next to Gil despite his suddenly charitable nature, Peggy lets her mother enter the truck first. Within fifteen minutes, they have arrived at Gil's boat. It's berthed in a small marina with old wooden slips that have seen better days. They sway and bob with the water as much as the boats attached to them—but they serve Gil's purpose, and the price is right.

Using the headlights from his truck, Gil wastes no time giving his boat, *The Rat Trap,* a once-over. Looking at Peggy he declares, "I know yer chompin' at the bit to get started, but we only got a couple hours 'fore daylight. Ain't no sense in gettin' started 'fore we can see where we're goin'." With that said, he lights another cigarette and pulls a can of beer out of a small refrigerator and sits back in a galley chair as though he hasn't a care in the world.

Peggy can't muster up enough disdain to show how much she considers Gil to be a dredge of humanity. Long ago, she and Julia quit attempting to analyze their mother's choice in men. Without fondness, she recalls a time when she caught Gil stooped over, peering through a bathroom door keyhole while Julia was taking a shower. He excused himself by saying, "I have to use the facility and was only checking to see if it was occupied." Asking him, "Wouldn't it have been nobler had you merely knocked." The girls agreed that would have been too simple for Gil; besides he fits the pervert mold along with all the other characters their mother insisted on exposing them to.

Watching Gil drop an entire package of salted peanuts one by one into his can of beer and gulp by gulp retrieve them is more than Peggy can endure. Then to sit and watch him chew them puts his eccentricities over the top.

Leaving her mother and Gil to talk their stupid drunk talk alone, Peggy has decided to wait in the truck by herself. There is not enough tea in China to bring about the day that Peggy is willing to sit and make small talk with this man.

With no other choices, her worry has turned to prayer. Despite not being in touch with God other than in times like this, her first thought is to bargain with God as though He is some celestial auctioneer auctioning off her sister as if she were no more than a bargaining chip He needed to get something from Peggy. She's considering offering herself as a nun if God will spare Julia. Because she isn't Catholic, she begins to think that the whole process may be too complicated. Attempting to put all this together is making her tired. The next thing she is aware of, is her mother shaking her awake. "C'mon, wake up! This is all your idea, and Gil's got other things to do."

It's barely daylight. She has a strong need to relieve herself. Recalling what she had viewed of the toilet facilities on Gil's boat, she comes to a quick conclusion. *Under no circumstance am I going to touch anything in that toilet.* Instead, she spots a covered cabin cruiser of sorts behind the marina. Hoping for a minute's worth of privacy, she casts an eye around to ensure she isn't seen. Satisfied, she makes a decision to sneak behind it and do her business. Soon after pulling her clothing down around her ankles, she finishes in time to see a familiar form stand behind another of the many blue-tarped boats leering at her. Seeing he's been found out, Gil chuckles a little, saying, "Well, I didn't know you was over here, little lady—s'cuse me."

Peggy hates him with all the contempt she can marshal. But for now, she needs him. It's as though Gil determines the cost of his services by how much of the person asking, he can devour in satisfying his own twisted appetites. To consider bringing circumstances like these to her mother's attention is useless. At the same time but in a different way, Sylvia also needs Gil; she will either not believe her or ignore the situation. Maybe her growing loneliness has so dominated her person that she has sacrificed even her own prodigy to its hunger. Knowing she can hate him later and with the bond between Peggy and Julia being so powerful, Peggy makes the decision to love her sister more than she hates Gil. She puts the incident aside and quickly readies herself to begin the search.

Gil's boat is just as unkempt as he, his trailer, his truck, and his yard are. There is the stuff that could be considered worthwhile—fishing poles, nets, tackle, and downriggers—all mixed in with clothing that at one time became wet and discarded, empty lure boxes, the quintessential empty beer cans that are Gil's footprints, and an assortment of wadded fast food bags (as though wadding them was the only step needed to discard them). When confronted with the mess, his only defense is, "I ain't no polluter. I don't throw nothin' overboard." If there were one more notch below what is described as "minimalist," Gil's picture would be there as its founder.

Peggy sense of urgency has only increased with her sense of guilt over falling asleep. "*I know Julia will do anything to survive. I only hope she is still okay.*" Unfortunately, it's a thought she doesn't believe her present company shares. Whether the alcohol is merely a symptom of an underlying sickness in her mother or she is disengaged because of the alcohol, Peggy realizes this whole effort would not be taking place if it were left to her mother to bring together.

Once their search is underway, Peggy has chosen to sit on the aft bench, which is as far away from Gil as she can get without being in the lake. Meanwhile, Gil has taken his place behind the wheel above in a fully outfitted tower as he throttles the cabin cruiser between break walls designed to keep the waters still while boats are entering or exiting Lake Michigan. Once they're in the lake, he lifts a pair of large binoculars and scans the horizon. With the binoculars still in his hand, he says, "If you want to find your sister, you're gonna have to help. I can't run this boat and be lookin' through these things at the same time." With that, he hands the binoculars to Peggy. As much as she would like to not have to depend on Gil, she knows there is no other choice. Grabbing the binoculars and bracing herself with her knees, she stations herself against the boat's sidewall to begin her part of this rescue process.

CHAPTER 4

A Rescue

Julia has had a fitful night. Her sleep pattern has been turned upside down by this untimely peccadillo. Several times, she has awakened in the night to see if by chance her phone has dried out enough to make a call. Disappointed, she tries to fall back to sleep again, but always with the strong feeling that Peggy is also stirring around over this incident— it's like she can feel her sister's energy. Initially, Jim has been a source of comfort with his upbeat reassurance. He's convinced when given a chance to be reviewed, this incident will prove to be merely a blurb on their journal of life experiences, but for the present, it's giving Julia a spin. She's fraught with anxiety and tension that isn't easing with Jim still sleeping so soundly. In her apprehension, the thought has occurred: *I wonder if he's dead*? This leaves her feeling even more alone. Catching herself, she whispers, "Think, think." It seems as though there are demons around her trying to torment her sleep and bring her to a level of uselessness.

Another hour has lapsed, and Julia is still wide awake. It's barely dawn. She looks over at Jim, who's still sleeping on his side with his hands between his knees. She's heard him snore a few times—at least relieving the fear that he's dead. Finally, one of his snores causes him to gasp and cough enough to wake himself. It takes another minute for it to register where he is and the circumstances that caused his sore back. It all flashes back very quickly. He hasn't stood up yet, and his gaze is already flashing from one place to another. Somewhere between shouting out an order and an alarm, he makes the insightful observation, "Our fire is nearly out!" Immediately on his feet, he broadens his perception, adding, "Now that it's daylight and since we want to do our part in being found, we need to get a smoky fire going."

Julia is taking comfort in not having all the responsibility of creating the success behind a rescue, but she is more than willing to do her part. Without another word, she heads into the stand of pines and begins to gather anything that's blighted, rotted, or in early stages of decay and burnable. Viewing their intentions as anything other than getting rescued would be a miscalculation. They haven't said a word to each other since the task began—they don't need to, as each is well aware of their plight and their need to work together. Within fifteen minutes, they have revived the fire to nearly a roaring inferno as it easily eats through the dampness of the wood, creating just the kind of smoky situation they want.

With one eye on the fire and the other on the lake, it isn't long before Jim spots a dot of something moving about a mile out from the shoreline and maybe five miles up the coast. Keeping his eyes focused on discerning what direction this dot is moving, it soon becomes obvious; it is getting larger, so it is moving in their direction. With the assurance that it is indeed a small vessel, he calls for Julia to take notice.

"Ohmygod, do you think they'll see us?!" she exclaims with the tenor of a cheerleader. She is definitely excited. There is something very positive about this sighting. She can just feel it.

At about the same time back on the Rat Trap, Peggy's binoculars are focusing on what appears to be smoke drifting off the beach some distance ahead. For the first time during this escapade, she excitedly climbs the ladder to Gil's perch and taps Gil on the shoulder while pointing to the whirling smoke on the distant shoreline. Quickly focusing his attention toward the hopeful target, he turns the wheel immediately to reposition the boat to meet the new objective.

Julia and Jim are taking notice of the repositioning maneuver the boat is making. Both are visibly encouraged. A big smile broadens across their faces. It's expressing an inner elation that hasn't been anywhere near the surface with either of them. It's an emotion that's been put on hold and replaced with anxiousness.

Within five minutes, it's become obvious to Peggy and Julia that their concerns are over. Gil is busy keeping an eye out for submerged rocks. He's approaching the shoreline with the tenuousness of one who knows how mean these stalwarts can be to the bottom of a boat. Meanwhile, Jim is sharing his concern by motioning him not to come any closer. Deciding to monitor the situation, Gil cuts the engine and drops the anchor. He gauges the water depth at about five feet, which is safe enough for the moment. With clamor of the engine removed, they're able to communicate across the fifty or so feet of water between them.

Compelled to further share the submerged rock information that Gil is already suspecting, Jim shouts out, "Don't risk coming any closer. I'm going swim out and come on board."

No time is lost with Julia. Before an answer can be returned, Julia is already out of her rain gear and in the water, making her way to the anchored boat. Her arrival in her yellow bikini has Gil totally torn between ogling her struggle to get aboard and listening to Jim share some further pertinent information. Either way, his attention apparatus is overloaded.

Just as suddenly, Jim is in the water, and just as quickly, he also makes his way across the short distance. In the absence of any agreeable sort of towel on board, Peggy's relief is so great to see her sister that she is already stripping herself of her jacket to wrap Julia against the onset of a chill. In the absence of a breeze, the sun is also eager to warm their chilled bodies. So happy to be freed from the anxiousness associated with their plight, both Jim and Julia are oblivious to any discomfort associated with Gil's floating scrapheap.

Sylvia finds herself left on the sidelines by the overwhelming welcome Peggy and Julia have for one another. More inclined to find fault with her daughters and less accustomed to sharing motherly affection, she struggles with how to assert a parental standing. When other people are in the vicinity, Sylvia has perfected the concerned mother role. Nonetheless, the girls have always had the feeling that their mother views them as unchosen inconveniences. However, Sylvia manages to put together some words that would be credible if they were coming from any other source.

"Julia, you had me worried sick. Why didn't you call?" As usual, Sylvia's response sounds hollow to both girls—they've heard it all before and are able to compare it to the tirades she explodes into when they're alone.

Julia halts her jubilation long enough to respond out of deference for a mother whose past behavior she has no respect for, saying, "We would have if our phones hadn't drowned."

Jim has never met Gil until today and is readily going into detail about how they battled the storm. Gil is listening with one ear but eager to give his own account of how it was back in the first year when the salmon were legal to catch.

"Guys come out here in anything that floats, from small bass boats to canoes. I swear I saw some dumbass in a bathtub with a trollin' motor. A storm blew up like the one you was in, but these guys never seen fish this big an' stayed out 'til they couldn't get in. The lucky ones got beached by the waves. The unlucky ones got dead. There was at least two hundred boats up an' down the shore. Most of 'em was all broke ta hell. They had to get tractors with cat tracks to come out an' pull 'em outta the sand."

It doesn't take Jim long to figure out Gil to be a story topper; whatever story you tell Gil, he'll try to top it.

After an assessment of the equipment needed to adequately retrieve the sloop, it's agreed to do this on another day. For the moment, the concern has changed from a rescue to getting some food and water.

CHAPTER 5

Negative Response

When she awakens the next morning, it takes Julia a second or two to realize where she is. Reaching over, she finds Peggy is still sharing the other half of her twin-sized bed. She feels a pleasant sense of comfort. As little girls, they always shared a bed. At that time, it was out of necessity. Sylvia has never been cognizant of them outgrowing anything, much less a bed. It was during their freshman year in high school when they added the second twin bed and sleeping apart soon became the norm, but after the harrowing experience the night before, they found it very easy to huddle together, like they did when little.

Sitting up, Julia pulls the sheet up under her chin, bringing with it a flashback to how lonely she had felt without the comfort of her sister during her ordeal. The distress of this past nightmare is hitting home. It's turned the whole episode into the reality of them separating to different colleges; they have no memory of not sharing this same room. At times, they look forward to the separation, knowing it will eventually need to happen, but at times like this, they are happy it hasn't.

For the moment, Julia lets her mind wander around the room, wondering what it will be like to be here alone. It's only a matter of weeks before Peggy will be several hours away at college, and she'll have this whole room to fill by herself. There is no secret they have been one another's confidants for as long as they can remember. They have shared every small detail of their lives. Whether it's the intimate nature of their feelings toward the opposite sex or they are making wrong decisions, they confess their secrets to each other.

Julia is also examining the scratches on her legs from her sister's razor-sharp toenails digging into her legs all night. This reality reminds her less sentimental self of how she and her sister have had to make adjustments to their individual foibles. To begin with, sleeping in separate beds solved a lot of problems. The nature of their relationship has gradually changed from an emphasis on needing one another, to one of support; it's just reassuring to each to know their bond will make the adjustment to the "where and when" it's needed.

Peggy is also awake and making her own assessment of this sleeping situation. Unable to turn in the small bed, her neck is stiff from lying in the same cramped position all night. Looking at her sister as only twins can, she rolls her head while massaging her neck and saying, "I'm way past this. I need my own bed."

Without further discussion, they break out in a knowing laugh and hug each other with the clear understanding they will always be there for each other in both their discomfort and happiness. With each sister turning her back, their feet hit the floor on opposite sides of this instrument of comfort turned instrument of torture. In doing so, it's as though they have affected another unconscious, nonverbal agreement to exercise the freedom to express their right to begin their own separate lives.

Meanwhile, the camp is shorthanded. When they discovered its sloop had been beached, they called every available able-bodied person—man or woman—to assist in getting the boat off the beach. The sloop is much too heavy to pull off the beach by hand back into the water. Consequently, Jim has made arrangements with a contractor in town to bring his Caterpillar tractor to the site. They need to reposition the boat so as not to cause it to flounder against the rocks lining the shoreline. Nonetheless, the camp continues to need supervision. This situation has rendered special allowances for Julia to bring Peggy to the camp to fill in for the missing personnel. Since she is needed at the camp only in the morning hours and isn't needed at the bar until later in the day, it's the perfect scenario. She finding this outdoor venture exhilarating. Julia introduced her to "day camping," which includes hiking, eating lunch along a dune trail, and interacting with a group of seventh- and eighth-grade girls. Peggy discovers this little side adventure is exactly what she's wanted. She can't help but imagine herself integrating into a group like this as their teacher. They're at an age she recalls being, and she remembers how much she grew from her school experiences. Her hope is that she can also contribute to the next generation's development. It's the very thing she needs at this moment to whet her appetite to begin her life after high school.

This summer is decidedly a turning point for Peggy. This little glimmer of another life after high school is the determiner to make this the best summer she can imagine. She's finished with her camp experience and has decided she's going to revisit at least one of the sporting events she excelled in during high school. This summer, there is a morning beach volleyball league. "Perfect!" is her reaction. Most young women wouldn't find this the "perfect" way to spend their last summer before going off to college, but between her grades and athletic grants, she really only needs to earn spending money. To add to her list of things she is hoping to explore, she decides to wean herself from her cell phone, texting, television, and using her mother's car. Instead, she has vowed to read at least two novels, run a mile every morning, go to the gym, bicycle where she needs to go, and be in the best physical shape in her life. She hasn't been on a date since her senior prom and is happy not to be tied to some guy she'll leave in the fall anyway.

Most girls her age would not choose to live their lives this way, but they're not her. She and Julia have always been private people. They have each other and very seldom find it necessary to reach beyond their sisterhood.

Then out of the blue on a warm July summer day, Peggy receives a letter from her university inviting her to partake in a summer training program for their volleyball program. Her choices are limited to saying no and risking losing a slot on the team or acquiescing and losing her last summer at home. This is the first time in her young life when she's been presented with such a frustrating decision.

Julia has joined her sister this morning in a run before her duties at the camp begin. "I think you need to think with both your head and heart. If you lose a spot on the team, it will mean your grant may be pulled, and your dream to become a teacher will be in the toilet," says Julia.

Peggy has slowed her stride from her normal competitive pace to one where she is able to speak. "I know you're probably right, and as much as I hate to admit it, I'm scared."

Julia is slowing the pace even more as she mulls over her sister's concern. "I'll go with you to help you settle in, if you like." Pausing for a moment for a second thought to form, she adds, "I just know you need to go."

"I know that. It's just this letter blindsided me. I was hoping to have the rest of the summer to adjust to the idea of leaving, and now I feel I'm being pressured to change my schedule."

"You'd probably go through the same crap if you'd followed your schedule to the end. You're just meeting your scaredy-cat before you wanted to."

"I know you're probably right. What am I going to do without you?"

"That works both ways, sister. We'll figure something out—I hope."

Just as they are rounding a curve, Julia catches a flash in the corner of her eye. It's a pickup slowly easing its way around them. Both girls have the same reaction. *"Oh God, no, it's Gil!"*

Before they can shout out their thought, Gil has run his window down. "You ladies are lookin' fine this morning. Can I give you a lift somewhere?"

They both know they share the same thoughts when it comes to Gil. *Creepy! He's just plain creepy!* Hardly able to bring together words strong enough to dismiss him, they merely wave him on.

This isn't the reaction he wants. "What's the matter, ladies? I'm good enough to save yer asses from drownin', but now yer too damn good to ride with me?"

Sensing his sudden hostility, they attempt to avoid any further confrontation as they veer off down another side street, leaving Gil to talk to himself. The squeal of his tires tells them this dismissal isn't sitting well.

Nervously, they watch over their shoulders half expecting to see Gil's truck dogging them again. He's not the type that takes rejection easily. "I guess we'll never understand what Mom sees in that creep. He grosses me out," says Julia.

"I think Mom gets upset with us because we don't accept him but how can we like him when all he does is peek through keyholes at us or watch us going to the bathroom?" replies Peggy remembering her most recent encounters. "All's well that ends well" is a saying that comes with the confidence that an encounter is avoided—even if it's only for the moment. Even though he isn't following them any further at the moment, knowing Gil the way they do, they fully expect he'll continue to pop up in their lives.

Sylvia has never left a relationship, no matter how abusive it was. The men either die, end up incarcerated, or in a couple of cases, leave the state before a warrant can be served. Living with their mother often finds Peggy and Julia protecting themselves from her decisions as one would an enemy. They've learned to balance their allegiance to each other's safety along with their loyalty to their mother despite her disastrous relationships.

Finishing their run, Julia and Peggy take turns showering and prepare to go their separate ways for the rest of the day. They curtail they're conversation regarding Gil as they hear the familiar stirrings coming from their mother's bedroom. Watching their mother go through the same ritual morning after morning still gives them pause. As Sylvia makes her way out of bed, she's accompanied by a raspy cough and throaty voice, which come with years of smoking Pall Mall unfiltered cigarettes. Her alcohol withdrawal shakes are not quelled until she pours herself a beer mixed with tomato juice and gets its effects into her system. Often, she'll throw a raw egg into the mess and refer to it as "breakfast."

Other than Peggy's and Julia's room, the rest of the house has a slight yellowish nicotine cast to it. Begging their mother to stop smoking has had the same success as asking her to stop breathing as she rarely takes a breath without either inhaling or exhaling a cloud of smoke. Convinced their mother is still beating the odds and is out of the woods one more time, Julia leaves for her camp job. Meanwhile, Peggy prepares herself to cover for her mother yet again. It seems her mother's drinking is preventing her from making it on time to open for the lunch crowd. Begrudgingly, because her mother misusing her, Peggy leaves on her bicycle, allowing her mother to take time to recover as best she can. Since the bar doesn't open for another half hour, she takes her time. Arriving at the Midway, she hardly expects to see Gil waiting in the parking lot. Taking a calculated moment to think while locking her bike, she hopes Gil will stay in his truck and leave her alone. It's too much to expect. Without looking up from her task, she feels Gil's presence.

"Where's yer ma?" he asks with the same goofy grin he always wears.

One of the novels Peggy has found herself drawn to this summer is a story by Nicholas Sparks titled, *The Best of Me*. In particular, she finds one of the characters that gives her a chilling reminder of Gil. The grin Gil portrays is the same type that Sparks' character Ted renders: *"When he grins at her, there is a gleeful malevolence about it, like he can't decide whether to strangle her or kiss her, but thinks both would be equally fun."*

Not wanting to have any more conversation with Gil than is necessary and certainly not wanting to be alone with him in the bar, without losing a step, she quickly brushes by him. Inserting her key in the door and preparing to lock it behind her, she says, "She'll be along. She had a last-minute phone call." It's all Peggy can think of to say, and really more than she wants to engage with him. She can tell by the look on his face that he doesn't appreciate her abruptness. She doesn't hear his words, "You little bitch," as she is safely behind the door.

It's only been a couple hours since her and Julia's encounter with Gil while on their run. They see Gil as the type of man who expects that out of gratitude for his help, he should be allowed into the inner circle of the recipient's life. Peggy would have used the devil himself if it would have aided in locating her missing sister; Gil was as close to the devil as she needed to go. As far as developing any further relationship with Gil, there is no place in the mind of either Peggy or Julia to make this come to fruition.

During this pre-open period, Gil is able to get a free beer from Sylvia because she knows he needs it, especially if they had spent the night before drinking together. To have Peggy lock the door on him is not sitting well with him. He can feel his whole body being washed over with a wave of anger. Along with it is the sharp sting one feels with the bite of rejection.

"That little witch and her haughty sister need to be brought down a peg or two. Just 'cause they're good lookin', they think they're too damn good for me," laments Gil, mumbling under his breath as he heads back to his pickup to brood and wait for Sylvia. Once settled, he's content to sit and chain-smoke. Camels are his smoke of choice, adding a bit of yellow-brown stain to his only remaining front teeth. His feelings toward either of these young women is more often a strong attraction mixed with his anger. It's the same feeling he had beginning as a young kid in school when attractive girls disregarded him. It's as if any rebuff to his advances is a personal affront to his whole manhood. To this day, he's still never been able to work out an agreeable way to get past the feeling.

After another half hour of frustration, Gil finally spots Sylvia. Her familiar clunker is making its way into the bar parking lot. She has also spotted him and pulls in next to him. Not willing to wait for a greeting from Gil, Sylvia begins with, "No thanks to you and your promise to help me get this beast running, I finally got it started."

Gil feels himself being pulled into an incriminating conversation. Sylvia's good at it, and he usually gets the worst end of the deal. She knows his weaknesses and pushes his buttons at will.

"Yeah, I know, but I been busy," says Gil, trying as best he can to defend himself from any further inquisition.

If Sylvia's demeanor is any indication, it's obvious that she's displeased with Gil's reply. "Why ya sittin' out here, anyway? Why ain't ya inside like normal people?" asks Sylvia.

"'Cause that crazy kid of yours locked me out!"

Sylvia pauses for a moment as though a searching thought had just entered her mind. 'Yeah, I overheard 'em sayin' you was out stalkin' 'em earlier this morning."

In defense, Gil's voice goes up a notch, practically yelling, "I was mindin' my own damn business when they come runnin' up my road wigglin' their little asses in their little runnin' shorts. All's I did was offer 'em a ride."

Sylvia turns her head letting her eyes rest against the bar as though it contained an answer to an impasse. It's apparent her thoughts are in a logjam. Without another word, she exits her car, slamming the door behind her and makes her way to the bar's entrance. Once inside, she spots Peggy, who is busy taking an order. Their eyes meet. Quickly finishing, Peggy senses something is wrong.

"Are you feeling any better?" is her first question to her mother.

Sylvia nearly ignores the question by asking one of her own. "Are you ready to tell me what's going on?"

Peggy looks perplexed. Twisting her head to the side with a questioning squint, she asks, "Ready to tell you *what?*"

Sylvia is quiet but her eyes tell a different story. Lately, she is nothing but unpredictable. It's evident she is struggling to keep her voice even but it's apparent there is something simmering below the surface. "You know *what!*" says Sylvia. It's all she's willing to say and storms off behind the bar.

Peggy is trying to keep her voice down so as not to include the customers in on a family discussion. Following her mother, with her hand on her hip, she says, "Just what is it you're getting at, Mother?"

Sylvia's demeanor has changed again from a simmering anger to one of nearly a weeping obsequiousness. "Oh, don't pay any attention to me, I'm okay. I'm just having a rough time lately," she says turning to place some dirty glasses in the sink.

Not willing to let it go, Peggy turns from disgust toward her mother's behavior to one of concern. "Mom, what's this all about?" asks Peggy in a voice that contains an apparent bewildered tone.

Sensing there is something about this she can't explain, in the next moment, Sylvia is back on an even keel. "I don't know, maybe it's my period," she says. There is a definite superficial, nearly sophomoric tone to her answer.

At this moment, in all his manly glory, Gil walks into the bar. Immediately, Sylvia's demeanor shifts, back to her strange behavior. Her eyes dart back and forth from Gil to Peggy as though she were on the track of a discovery. It's as though some image is strafing across her mind. Then just as quickly, she has her normal deportment and goes about the chores that need attending.

Gil waste no time sidling up to the bar. Peggy is trying her best to treat him as though he were just another ordinary customer. What she hates about him is his flippant attitude toward the feelings of her mother, herself and Julia. *"He's such a chauvinist pig,"* is her predominate thought.

"Gimme a shot and a beer," solicits Gil with a less than polite tongue.

Without a word, Peggy turns to fill Gil's order, only to once again be met by her mother's strange look. It's apparent she's been watching. She immediately drops her gaze. Saying nothing, Sylvia continues washing glasses.

At this point, Peggy isn't willing to let her mother's odd behavior go unchallenged. "Do you want to tell me what's bothering you?" she asks.

Sylvia is quiet. It's apparent she's all nervous about something. When she finally speaks, her voice has lost its edge. "I don't know. I wish I knew myself, but I don't."

Peggy is getting a little tired of trying to read her mother's strange moods. Because of the other bar patrons, Peggy realizes that for the time being, it's necessary to be satisfied with her mother's reluctance to elaborate any further. Instead, Peggy finds another task to take her mind in another direction.

With Peggy out of the way, Sylvia has ceased her dish washing and made her way down the bar to where Gil is sipping on his beer. Looking onto this foreboding girlfriend standing directly in front of him cutting him off from his own reflection in the mirrored backbar, he's getting the feeling again that he's done something wrong. He sure as hell isn't happy to see her and by her look, she shares the same feeling. At that moment, everything about her look tells Gil that all she wants to do is drag him out into the street and kick his sorry ass. In turn, it's taking all Gil has to stifle his urge to backhand Sylvia. She's a popular waitress, and he knows he'd suffer some severe repercussions if he tried. The next thing that's heard is Gil's voice penetrating the normal din of the bar. "Don't be stickin' yer nose into my business, woman!" With that, he slams the rest of his whiskey down his throat along with his beer chaser, banging both empty glasses down on the bar, he storms out the front door, fires up his pickup and squeals his tires down the street, fishtailing the backend from one side of the road to the other.

Those that know Gil know he's not quite right upstairs. He's becoming harder and harder to keep in line. This is one of the reasons he hasn't gone back to work. He's usually considered as an accident waiting to happen—especially when he's drinking—which is nearly all the time. He's more than capable of scaring the crap out of people with his drunken shenanigans. On the other side of the coin, there are very few people left in the community who haven't enjoyed Gil's willingness to lend a helping hand when they've needed it. Because of this attribute, most people are willing to turn a blind eye—providing no one gets hurt.

For reasons still unknown, both were in an argument and both settled it—even to the satisfaction of those stander-byes forced to either listen to the fray or find another bar. For those already in their cups, they feel they know exactly what was transpiring and are ready at the drop of a hat to give their opinion.

With Gil out of the way, and happy not to have to watch him fawn over every skirt that walks through the door, Sylvia is soon back to her old self. She is popular among her male patrons especially when setting drinks on their table always making certain she shows plenty of cleavage. One thing she has learned is what makes men tick. She knows if she gives them what they want that she can get about anything she wants. Many, many times it's kept the rent paid and an old car on the road.

CHAPTER 6

Romance in the Air

Jim Samples is hardly able to live down the "beaching" episode. After many years of boating experience, he has vigorously prided himself in his navigational skills, but this incident has left him rattled. Accordingly, it's invited some lighthearted teasing on the part of his co-workers. The last thing he wants to give in to is that any of this ribbing affects him. He is also mindful that nothing is going to make this episode go away until his tormenters tire of it. Consequently, he takes the ribbing without reacting, continues to do what he needs to do and quickly moves to his next task, all the while secretly hoping everyone will forget this unnerving event.

The only person not involved in Jim's razzing is Julia. She is well aware that his careful responses to their situation were death defying; that his meticulous thinking was what saved them both from becoming little more than another of Lake Michigan's casualties. The fact that the sloop ended up on the beach was a small enough price to pay for their lives.

What Julia remembers is how unselfishly and valiantly Jim fought to ensure not only her comfort during this perilous event, but also her life. *"I almost wished he had kissed me,"* when she recalls how she gave him the impression that she didn't want that to happen.

This incident has moved their relationship up a notch. Since it involves a deeper understanding of one another, it has proven to be just a little too much togetherness to remain merely a casual thing. They have shared a profound experience that very few people live through and come out victorious. There is nothing that will bring out the best or worst in a person than to face a situation threatening their own life.

Jim, on the other hand recalls how calm Julia remained and how she didn't panic when things weren't looking so good and the gratitude she had showed for his persistent concerns. It's become his single-minded desire to continue to press forward with their relationship.

This afternoon, Jim is doing what he does every chance he gets—he's working out with his weights. (With Jim there is a fine line between passion and obsession for his undertakings. Some days he has aspirations to become a competitive body builder and other days, he imagines he will be ready if he's ever called on to lift a bus.)

Julia is aware of his penchant to work his body through a regimen of exhausting exercises. In truth, she really doesn't care why. To her, it is nothing more than a frivolous activity that can be interrupted if she chooses to do so. This afternoon, she has silently crept up behind him, finding him lying flat on his back on his weight bench. His eyes are closed as he takes deep breath after deep breath. His fingers grip and regrip his weight bar as he searches for the sweet spot. He's preparing to make his heaviest lift of the day. Sucking in his final load of oxygen, he attempts to detach the big load from its perch. At this very moment, without being detected, Julia sneakily places both her hands on the bar, adding just enough weight to prevent him from budging the thing. She can feel his renewed effort as he accompanies it with a grunt that only weightlifters emanate. Frustrated with his failure, he opens his eyes to discover a grinning Julia hovering over him.

"Well, you little shit!" These are the first words that come to mind. "So, you're the one holdin' me back. I thought I'd lost my mojo!" says Jim, now sitting up on the bench. Julia is making a lighthearted smirk once she sees his reaction. This little bit of mockery is enough for Jim to respond by jumping to his feet with the full intention of playfully grabbing her. Still laughing at her ruse, Julia reacts by attempting to jump away. Right away, Jim realizes his hand is wrapped around hers. Becoming aware of it takes no more than a split second. He's suddenly mindful that her hand feels much smaller and very feminine. The other thing he notices is that she is not trying to free herself. Instead, her whole behavior has shifted from one of naughtiness to one of submission. His breathing and heartbeat have continued to be intense, but instead of flowing out of a physical effort, it's as a result of this very beautiful and very feminine young women resting her hand in his. Julia's reaction is also out of the blue. It's as if a welcomed warmness has waved over her and is taking possession of her spirit. Separately, their minds are racing as to what to do next. Without another moment of thought, Jim has released her hand and pulled her against his bare chest. He feels her collapse against his body. He gently cups her face in his hands, barely touching his lips to hers. Her reaction is to release a long sigh and throw her arms around his neck, firmly pressing her lips to his. This, in turn, finds Jim's hands directing themselves to that small hallow spot in Julia's back just above her hips, then pulling her yet closer. The embrace is long. All that is heard is the heavy breathing emanating from both of these newly enlivened paramours. This being their first kiss, they can hardly bear to release the other. No sooner does one begin to release the other and the other prohibits it by rekindling the whole action all over again.

What finally brings them out of their affectionate exhibition is the giggling of a group of their young charges. The kids, not believing what they're viewing, place both hands across their mouths in an attempt to smother their giggles. Not sure how to react to being caught, Jim and Julia quickly disengage as if each had been shot through with a lightning bolt of panic. Each of them begins to talk over the top of the other in an attempt to convince these young voyeurs that they can't trust their lying eyes and need to accept an alternative explanation. Julia clears her throat for the umpteenth time hoping to have an epiphany to explain to these witnesses a plausible lie. Jim's mind has also kicked into defense mode. Seeing Julia blinking in confusion spurs him to take control. After all, it's a happening in which he played a major role. It also initiates another opportunity to defend her. To be economical with the truth is not going to be a problem with Jim if it gives Julia the breathing room she's trying to find.

"Don't read any more than that into what you may think you saw. You all know how touchy Miss Julia's back can be. I want you to know I've been trained to treat these problems with a high degree of success," says Jim with the wordy expression of a professional physical therapist. To prove his point, he once again grabs Julia and proceeds to hold her tight against him. Subsequently, he begins to manipulate his hands up and down her spine, reenacting what they had seen him doing just seconds ago. Seeing that he has the full attention of these youngsters, he's particularly attentive to how effectively he's baffling them as he continues to work his hands up and down Julia's back. The kids' behavior is slowly transforming from laughter to paying close attention to what one of their camp counselors is offering them as an explanation as to why he and Miss Julia were in that seemingly compromising position. Perceiving he has captured their attention, he adds as a precautionary note. "Kids, as you probably have noticed by now, I'm a trained professional. I don't want any of you to attempt anything you've seen me do here today at home, as I've spent years in training. Do I have your word?"

With the astute attention of only those who can be easily baffled, they all say, "Yes sir, Mr. Samples, we won't."

Satisfied after carefully viewing his audience for the possibility of divergent judgements, he gives his final statement, "Okay, you're all excused now."

Like most kids their age, they enjoy having an upper hand on adults but are happy when they don't have to be with it too long.

Satisfied that the kids are out of sight, Jim and Julia break out in what they hope is a well-deserved laugh. This does not mean they are totally at ease with one another, but it does spark open another chapter in their lives. Julia is certain that what has just transpired between them is something she has been awaiting to happen but like all of life's stories, this chapter begins with an uncertainty. They have known each other since high school and since it is a small school, their paths had crossed frequently, but in less than memorable ways. This summer is the first time they have done more than merely exchange a few words between classes. There has never been a time that Jim didn't think she was attractive, but this was not a singular observation. She and her twin sister were popular, the type of girls who would have no problem getting the boys' attention. It wasn't unusual to see their lunch table surrounded by young men hoping to be noticed by either of them. Julia, as well as Peggy, had both been involved in sports from grade school on and seemed to Jim to be as inaccessible to him as some sexy movie stars. They had their own world and he had his.

Today things have changed. There isn't a throng of other males vying for her attention. He's discovering that she isn't anything like he had imagined. She's much more demonstrative with her feelings than he had given her credit. She also has a hint of "the mischief," which he had never seen in her and discovered with his weight lifting episode where he had become the recipient of one of her playful stunts.

This isn't all he's noticed—her hair always has a glow giving her a radiance that envelops her whole person. Often times when he is busy doing other things, she dominates his thoughts. What he finds so surprising is how much easier it has been to get to know her than what he had imagined. Even when she is doing nothing more than merely looking at him, he can almost feel her touch. What he had never expected with Julia is that in just being himself, he could find it this easy to be content. This is the kind of relationship he has always hoped for, but never guessed it would be available so soon—and in his own backyard to boot. To imagine this is not love would only make any other explanation pale to the way he feels toward Julia at this moment. And to say that Julia is not on cloud nine would be an understatement. This last year of school, she involved herself in strictly academics and sports—both highly structured. This is the first time since her seventh-grade crush on Tony Hornus that she has involved her thoughts so deeply with the opposite sex. As she timidly intertwines her fingers in Jim's, leaning in and out of him, she imparts an openness. Sensing that she wants a conversation, Jim begins, "What d'ya say we build a fire on the beach after work and roast some hot dogs?"

Julia is silent for a moment. It's nothing to do with Jim. Rather, she is wondering when she is ready to share their budding relationship with Peggy. At first, her inclination has been to conceal her and Jim's connection, but in a town this small, trying to conceal anything is akin to lying. In some towns, they whisper of these things; in this town, they nearly shout, "Hey, did ya hear about Julia Fortine and Jim Samples?"

As she mulls over her concerns and not desiring to appear unwilling, she's conscious of not allowing an unusual amount of time to lapse between Jim's proposal and her answer. "I think that would be fun," she declares still wondering how her sister is going to take her new interest in stride. The two of them have developed a nearly anti-man attitude because of their mother's disasters but Julia is beginning to feel her hostility melt away. This change is brought about only by the sincere attention of Jim Samples. It's a longing she recognizes as something that can only be satisfied through a male exchange. Since she has been without a father, this male affection toward her has awakened a craving that she has had no name for—it's a yearning she can't explain but it's always been there and she's finding that she likes it.

It isn't a long pause between the time he's posed the question and Julia answers, but when one is breathlessly waiting for a desirable outcome, it may as well be a lifetime. Just the way Jim has straightened his back and brightened his face with his prevalent smile tells how pleased he is with

Julia's response. In his exuberance, he grabs hold of her drawing her into himself once again. Julia, on the other hand, has had enough of her life scrutinized for one day and pushes Jim back, saying, "You just can't wait to get us in trouble again."

He studies her reaction for a moment. Satisfied that it's a not a rejection but a bona fide concern, he attempts to make light of it. "It's just that you're so damn cute, I can't keep my hands off you."

Julia looks at him with her mischievous grin. "Do you know what I'm thinking?"

"I'm scared to ask."

"I think you're a dope." With that, she gives him a good-natured push landing him back on his weight bench.

*

The work day ends and the long-awaited liaison between these mutual admirers is at last coming to fruition. In Jim's usual exacting way, he has come with a cooler filled with hotdogs, buns, mustard, ketchup, pickles and two bottles of ice-cold cokes. Julia has brought a warm approving smile. She has also made note that with their work schedule he had not had the opportunity to go to town to purchase all this stuff. This prompts the question, "I'm impressed with your efficiency. Where did you come up with all this stuff?"

A shifty grin suddenly appears. Behind it, a devious little chuckle springs forth followed by a lame attempt to mimic the expressions of Sergeant Schultz from the old *Hogan's Heroes* TV series. "Ve haff our vays, Snookie!"

Julia is mildly amused by Jim's attempt at hi-jinx, adding, "Yeah, that and you flattering poor old Mrs. Grace (the camp cook) out of half her pantry."

"All I did was let her know that you were going to be the recipient of this spread and she added a couple extra hotdogs."

"Jim Samples, you're such a bull-shitter, I believe you could charm the stars out of the sky."

"Vell put, my dear," he says, continuing his Sergeant Schultz impersonation, "But ve haf our vays to make you vork. Ve needs camp firevood too cook our hotdogs. Gets beesy!"

Rolling her eyes at Jim's attempt to amuse her, she begins a search for suitable drift wood for their fire. They find it easy to work together but then this is young love—the period where it is easy to become so infatuated with the other that it's difficult to imagine the other is capable of sin.

With their picnic lunch consumed, the daylight begins to seep away, the night begins to bring out its occupants. There's the sound of a hoot owl perched high in a tree somewhere back in the hardwoods claiming his territory. Their hoots can be heard for miles in the stillness of night. And of course, the incessant sound of small windless waves lapping in sync against the shore. Jim is supporting his back against a large piece of drift wood poking at the fire with a stick. As each poke of the stick encounters the crackling coals, it sends a spiral column of sparkling cinders into the air. Julia sits with her arms wrapped around her drawn-up knees, staring at the fire's orange and blue tones. Erratic in their nature, the leaping flames are creating a quiet mesmerizing like distraction in each of them. Realizing that neither of them have spoken in some time, Jim bridges their silence with an invitation, "You're sitting right in the smoke. Come over here by me Julia—it's much clearer."

As entrancing as this moment is, this winding down time catches Julia's mind wandering around the dysfunction in her home as it centers in her mother's bizarre behavior. Anxious to have another human to comfort her in her funk has an appeal. Happy for the invitation, and pleased to hear Jim speak her name, Julia stands only long enough to brush the sand sticking to her behind. As hastily as conditions offer, she makes her way through the limited scrap of beach the campfire has lit up. Finding a spot as close to him as circumstances allow, she graciously rests her head against his shoulder.

"You're so quiet, Julia. Tell me your thoughts," Jim requests.

"Oh, there's a lot on my mind with Peggy leaving in a few days. This will be the first time we've ever been apart," she answers.

"Yeah, it's definitely going to be different for both of you. I hope you know that I'll be here for you anytime," promises Jim.

"I appreciate your support. I know I'll probably need it." There is a sudden pause in her talk.

Not wanting to push Julia beyond her willingness to discuss her private life, Jim reaches into that domain long enough to assure her of his sincerity, saying, "I want you to know that whatever is going on with you—day or night—I'll have open ears."

Julia hears him, but for this moment, her mind prefers to linger alone. When she compares the problems that she is facing by living with her mother without Peggy's support with Jim's intact family, it gives her pause. With this dark cloud hanging over her, her thoughts continue to drift off alone. "*He comes from a normal family; how could he possibly understand the insanity Peggy and I have been living with our entire lives.*" In some understandable ways, Julia and Peggy have gotten much older than needs be before their time. Although, they've never felt they've walked alone as long as they've had each other. Notwithstanding their unholy circumstances, together, they've formed an imitable alliance. Now things are changing—and in Julia's estimation—not for the better. They are much aware that things are at a juncture where life is never going to be the same again. In truth, both of them expect their boats are about to be rocked.

Jim Samples comes from an upper middle-class family. His mother and father have been married for twenty- two-years; they have always been there for him. Both sides of Jim's family tree can be traced back to the early days of the American colonial settlers. His mother is an English teacher and his father owns a local hardware store. They regularly attend Sunday services at the First Presbyterian church, where Jim's father serves on the church council and his mother is on the altar committee.

In contrast, Julia's family has a spotted legacy. To say they are at best described as scofflaws is doing them a favor. On her father's side is a long line of convicted felons ranging from burglary, in the case of her paternal grandfather, to various county jail sentences for her cousins and uncles. Their crimes included writing bad checks, drunk driving, poaching, meth manufacturing, and wife beating. Even her aunts were charged with failure to appear in court for hearings and her own father is serving a life sentence for murder.

Sylvia, on the other hand, comes from a middle-class family that did all they knew how to do to break Sylvia up with Bruce Fortine (short of killing them both). Sylvia's father made no bones about referring to Bruce as "trailer trash" even though he didn't live in a trailer. Shortly after this denigration, he would discover his car had been sabotaged with all four tires flattened. Without proof, he would rant on how that worthless piece of "trailer trash" had dared to come and destroy his property.

Sylvia's parents had divorced and had plenty of their own problems without taking on Sylvia's. They clung to the hope that she would find ways of not adding to their overload of dysfunction, come to her senses, and give up her defiant ways. After her parents divorced, Sylvia lived with her mother until she got pregnant and her mother kicked her out. Prior to that, her mother had tried limiting her phone calls to just girlfriends, only to discover Bruce had put them up to calling her. He then would reclaim the phone despite being on her mother's blacklist. Bruce had also lost his driver's license due to driving under the influence and depended on Sylvia to drive. Her mother then pulled her driver's license in the hopes that the loss of a car would dissuade him. They would simply meet riding their bikes. Her mother, then tried grounding her only to find that while she was sleeping, Bruce had climbed atop an entrance way roof just below Sylvia's second story open bedroom window to surreptitiously make his way to her bed. After becoming frustrated beyond her ability to bring their relationship to an end, her mother quit speaking to her. Why Sylvia had been hell bent on crushing her future to be with Bruce Fortine has a family circumstance behind the decision that Sylvia has kept secret.

But back to Jim Samples. Jim possesses an uncanny ability to be sensitive to the needs of those less fortunate than himself if the need is presented. He has never regarded Julia as being the needy type. She has always presented herself as a self-assured woman. But now with Peggy preparing to leave there are some cracks in her armor. His natural inclination is to be available to Julia's needs. "I'd rather be with you than be doing anything else," he readily admits. "I can't stand to see you unhappy, especially if I know can support you in some way."

Julia, on the other hand, can't imagine how somebody like Jim, who seemingly has never had it bad could want to get embroiled in the depths of insanity that's living its way through her life. With this sobering thought, Julia remains guarded. "*I hope he doesn't find out too much too soon,*" is her overwhelming thought. Despite his zeal to live up to his offer that nearly equals the vows only a husband makes to a wife about being present "in sickness and health," she has her misgivings. He isn't exactly a stranger to Julia, but neither is he aware of the pits that he may have to pass through to live up to such an offer.

For now, the campfire's gamboling yellow and blue flames provide the most light, tuning the twisting shadows to dance along in perfect harmony. With the fire beginning to die, the moon slowly replaces its light with its own glow, honing the shadows yet again into an amicable backdrop. It's the perfect dreamy environment for making a romantic link. The stars are not only in the skies but also in their eyes. Their kisses and embraces grow much more intense as the evening progresses. The moon finally crests lending the landscape yet another of its exotic staging's. It's too soon midnight on what has been the quickest day of both their lives; time has raced by for these young lovers. Ready—but not ready—to let their petting take them to a deeper commitment, Julia is scared that things are getting out of her control, that a man is emotionally dictating where this is all going. She has been on her own all her life and has a nose for risk. All she can envision At this point, is a picture of her mother helplessly gazing with doe eyes as another man is stealing her spirit. She has vowed this is never going to happen to her. Glancing at her watch, she knows she is ready to go and is the first to speak, "It's after midnight and I need to be up in the morning to help Peggy get ready for college. Please take me home,"

This sudden ending to what Jim has envisioned would take a different course is bewildering. Up until a minute ago, he imagined that they were ready to turn the page on their budding romance and begin a new chapter, now for her to brusquely cut their petting to an abrupt end has him rattled. The temperature has dropped enough to begin to create a blanket of dew on the ground. In Jim's mind it has become more like a wet blanket to snuff out a blazing romantic moment. Trying the best that he can to allow Julia the time she needs without smothering her, he makes the most of respecting her wishes, "Sure Julia, I'm sorry, I didn't realize it had gotten so late."

Together, they quietly gather up their left-over picnic items—each with their own thoughts. Meanwhile, oblivious to anyone, the landscape is taking on yet another of its captivating settings as the dew gives off a silvery shine from the moon's reflection. There is another striking change neither had noticed—the air is filled with the light fragrance of honeysuckle from the nearby woods. After breaking off their zealous pursuit of a heightened version of romantic passion, they continue it in a toned-down version as they walk hand in hand back to where they had parked.

CHAPTER 7

Separation

Despite it being well past midnight when Julia arrives home, she finds Gil's truck in the drive way. She knows exactly what is going on. Her mother and Gil will be at the kitchen table in some stage of inebriation. Depending on how early they got started will determine what stage they are at the moment. The last thing in the world she wants to deal with is her mother's, or, for that matter, with Gil's stupid drunkenness. From past experience, Peggy knows having to deal with either of them about anything at this juncture ensures problems. Careful when she enters so as not to let it be known that she's home, she judiciously closes the door. Removing her shoes also eliminates much of the noise on the bare wood floors. Out of necessity, she has learned how to silently slip silently past the kitchen door unnoticed, but the activity in the kitchen never slips by. The cigarette smoke along with the pungent smell it makes when combined with beer, waft out, enveloping the entire house. Knowing which squeaky stair steps to avoid ensures she's nearly home free. Reaching the top of the stairs, she only has a few feet before she reaches the door to the bedroom she and Peggy have lived in almost since they were born. After opening the door, she is relieved to find Peggy alone and available.

Peggy is busy on the university's website, finishing all the details she needs to make certain that her dorm is ready and her grants and scholarships are in order. She's wearing shorts and a tank top: an outfit she feels free to wear when she's not at the bar, being ogled by nearly every man that walks through the door. Furthermore, it provides her the option to take a run if she feels like it. Besides, they've never been able to afford air conditioning. She and Julia have always shared this upstairs bedroom that is freezing cold in the winter and suffocating hot in the summer. Tonight, the room is tolerable as it cools down along with the falling outside temperatures. Julia sits quietly watching as her sister is careful to get all her "t's" crossed and her "i's" dotted. One careless or misplaced word can create a scenario that leads to having to start all over.

"What am I going to do when you're gone?" she says from across the room.

Peggy raises her head at the question, as a snarky little smirk comes across her face. "Oh, but you'll have Jimmy boy," she says in a sing-songy voice.

"Oh, do I hear a little jealousy?" replies Julia mocking her sister using the same sing-songy voice.

"Maybe. I always wondered which of us would break our 'no men' pact first. Actually, I don't mind you're the one. I think with Jim Samples you've got the cream of the crop from around here."

Leaning back on her bed, Julia is happy to have her sister reaffirm the similar thoughts that she is coming to. "I have to admit, Jim surprises me—he gives me hope that all men aren't losers. Working alongside him at the camp, I find he actually cares as much about kids as I do."

Comparing her own work place with Julia's, Peggy says as she closes her computer, "You're a lot luckier than I am. All I get is a bunch of creeps that believe their God's gift to women. Remember all those guys that we always considered as 'big men' on campus? Well, they never left that mindset. They still think their bigshots. All they do now is hang out at the bar trying to hit on me every chance they get. They still believe they're so hot that they're actually doing women a favor by hitting on them."

Listening to her sister, Julia comes to only one conclusion, "I'm glad you're getting out that hole. Now that the camp is over, Mom wants me to take your place." Her eyes drift down as though in thought, she then adds, "I will—but only as a last resort."

"I know she does. I know she needs the help, but I hope she can find somebody else." The concern Peggy has is clearly coming through her voice. Despite her mother's failures, she feels an obligation to her—but then not any less of an obligation for the wellbeing of her sister.

It's after one o'clock in the morning. They plan on being up and ready to go by eight o'clock. The drive is at least three hours. Peggy makes a final check around the room, as if there is at least one more thing she can take that might keep her world from changing. With her mind worn thin with all the emotions, it's time to stop thinking and go to sleep. Slipping into her very familiar bed, she reaches to turn out the very familiar light on her very familiar night stand. Looking at Julia sound asleep in the bed next to hers, she wonders if this is really the last night they will spend together. Lying in the dark room with the assurance everything is still in place is, at least for now, enough contentment to let herself fall asleep.

Morning arrives with Peggy and Julia anxious to get on the road. Gil had spent a good amount of time the day before getting their old car in good enough running condition to make the trip, with a bit of luck. Of course, in Gil's world everything is quid pro quo. To Gil, the proper payment is to invite himself to share Sylvia's bed for the night. Before leaving, Peggy peeks into her mother's bedroom somewhat hoping, but not expecting, that her mother will be cognizant enough to say goodbye. Instead, what she sees is a bed stand with full ashtrays, littered with empty beer cans, and two middle-aged adults in bed, buck naked, twisted in among blankets, snoring and snorting like a couple of ailing gas combustion engines. This is not an unfamiliar scene. It's one they've lived with their entire life; so much so that it's considered to be the normal behavior of their outlandish parent. Peggy watches for a moment, making a little *"Ummpf!"* noise as if to say, "Disgusting, but normal."

The morning is still cool, and the skies are overcast with a thin misty fog. This is typical weather for communities along the Lake Michigan coast line in the morning's early hours. As it pertains to these two identical twins, very little needs to be said between them as they continue to prepare themselves for their trip. Without consulting one another, they seem to have a mutual understanding what their next step is going to entail. Characteristically, they have independently chosen the same pink colored work-out suits. With never a question between them as to how this happens independent of the other, it has been their norm since they were old enough to dress themselves. Another of their fascinating habits has caught the attention of their friends—and is disconcerting to others; when one of them is asked a question, the other will answer. In many ways, their blended personalities create a much larger personality than each would possess alone.

Their older-model Subaru is replete with faded blue paint and plenty of rust. The hatch back portion is filled to the brim with everything Peggy believes is needed to set up housekeeping on her own. The girls don't remember which of their mother's boyfriends abandoned the car in their yard before he had to get out of town. Nonetheless, in spite of its age and outward appearance, it has been a godsend since financially. They would find it impossible to replace. In one sense, they hate Gil, but in another sense, they know it would be difficult to get along without his mechanical abilities. In truth, the only reason this heap of junk is still on the road is because of Sylvia's inclination to choose men with mechanical aptitudes. Unfortunately, in order to continue to move forward, much of their lives have been spent under the catch-22 syndrome of discerning between what they need and what they are going to have to pay in human cost. What is misunderstood about people in the poverty class is that it's not all taking; it's also giving—trading a piece of oneself to gain a need. It's been only by the grace of God and the strong bond between these two young adults that they've been capable of avoiding many of life's landmines. Eventually, between the two of them, they more often get things right, than wrong.

Without the need of a discussion, Julia presumes the role of driver. She automatically knows her sister is a bit to rattled to take the wheel with all of the other things on her mind. Peggy too, without discussion is already sliding into the passenger seat. Of course, their mother didn't fill the gas tank so it's necessary to stop at Mix's gas station before starting their downstate trek.

"You girls are up good and early this morning—got somethin' special goin' on?" asks Russ Mix. He's been in this garage since he was a small boy. His mother had presumably run off with another man leaving his father to raise him alone. This resulted in his father bringing him to work in the garage at a very young age. He's amiable and so far, he has always been a trustworthy friend to both Peggy and Julia. The girls have grown up with him from kindergarten through high school. As little girls, they often stopped at the station to have him put air in their bicycle tires. Eager to do this task, he had always hoped that he was impressing them with his man-like responsibility. Since graduation, he has assumed working full time, taking on even more responsibility. He's tall and dark-complexioned, taking on more of his mother's Indian looks than his father's German heritage. In high school, it had become noticeable to each of them how with each progressive year, in a rough sort of way, he became more attractive.

Answering in unison, "Yep, we're on our way downstate."

"I'm—she's—on my—her way to college." Again, they both answer in unison.

"You sure this jalopy is gonna get you there?" he asks.

"No, but we're praying," they both answered.

In his own amicable way in attempting to keep at least a toe in the lives of either or both of them, he says, "If you run into any mechanical problems, give me a call. I'll drive down and help you out."

Both girls look at one another with the same look of suspicion. They have watched their mother fall into these situations time after time—always owing some man a debt of gratitude for his efforts to keep her afloat for one more day.

With similar forbearances, they thank Russ assuring him they'll be okay. Eager to get on the road, they pay him for the gas and begin their trek.

The mist is lifting as they travel further inland. Twenty-five thousand years ago, the glaciers covered most of Michigan, cutting the prevalent razorback hills with distinctly deep, narrow valleys. Nowadays, the roads in this region attempt to follow the paths of least resistance where possible, but more often, they find the least expensive way is to follow a straight line, all the while dealing with the undulating nature of the terrain.

For the first hour, each is quiet, content with their own thoughts. Peggy is the first to break the silence. "You gonna be all right with Mom?"

"I'm sure gonna try. I know I'm going to miss you. I've never had to deal with her alone," says Julia.

They return to their silence.

"I'm going to miss you too, sister," replies Peggy after several minutes.

Suddenly, like a wave overcoming them, the reality of their decisions begins to hit home. Their faces are wet with tears. Julia is driving while shamelessly blowing her nose, and wiping her tear-filled eyes and tear stained cheeks. Peggy is not doing much better. A word need not be spoken. This pair of sisters come the closest as is possible to possessing telepathic powers. They always know what the other is thinking because it's the same thing they are thinking.

Without warning a deer jumps onto the road. Julia's eyes are still blurry but not so blurry that she isn't aware of what is standing doe-eyed ahead of her. Instinctively she slams her foot to the brake pedal. The car takes a hard pull to the left. She finds it impossible to keep her car in her right lane. Instead, she finds herself facing an oncoming car in the opposite lane. This event has caused the other driver to switch lanes. In the meantime, the deer has also decided to lunge to the other side of the road, slamming into the oncoming car. This set of events has timed itself so perfectly that the only fatality is the deer.

With everything coming to a sudden standstill, Julia sits transfixed, staring straight ahead with eyes blinking and both hands still gripping the wheel. Peggy has instinctively pushed both her hands against the dashboard as if to ward off any oncoming danger. Neither is certain as what to do next, instead, they sit pinned to their seat. Finally, brought to their senses by a hard knock on the passenger side window, Peggy is confronted by the desperate look of a woman asking, "Are you all right?"

Peggy is struggling to make her brain say some words. Her fingers respond quicker than her words as they find the electric window button. By the time the window is at the bottom, she is able to form the words, "Yes, we're fine. How about you?"

"I'm okay but my car isn't—and the deer is worse," says the near hysterical woman, "It's still flopping around."

By this time, Julia has exited their car because it seems like there may be something for her to do. After taking a quick mental review of the last two minutes, something about this whole escapade has her stumped. "*Why when I applied the brakes, did they pull us into the opposite lane. There has to be something drastically wrong with the brakes on this stupid Subaru,*" she thinks to herself. "*That damn Gil is out to kill us yet.*"

Another motorist must have summoned the State Police as they are arriving on the scene. After these folks are satisfied no laws have been broken, and the lady's car is towed, they leave everyone to get on with their business.

Julia has calmed down enough to resume her position behind the wheel and the girls are soon on their way once again. The conversation takes its natural course to rehash their near accident. Peggy is the first to question, "Why in God's name didn't you just hit that ridiculous deer instead of crossing lanes?"

"Believe me I tried. The more I pressed on the brakes, the more we were being pulled into that poor woman's lane."

It only takes them a second to put their singular thought into words. Together, they repeat what is swimming around in their minds, "That damn Gil is out to kill us!"

"Promise me when you get back home that you'll take this pile of junk and get Russ to look it over. I don't trust that damn Gil from me to you," says Peggy.

By noon they have arrived at Peggy's dorm. It takes the rest of the afternoon to get her stuff unloaded and in her room. By four o'clock they have said their goodbyes and Julia is back on the road for her return trip. It's the loneliest she can ever recall being. It's like the further she drives separating herself from her sister, the thinner her soul is becoming. Alone in her dorm room Peggy is undergoing a similar sensation. It's a new anxiety that has never found its way into either of their lives. It's taking all that Julia can do to keep going in the same direction and not turn around. *"Why did we think this was going to be a good thing,"* is the similarly thought banging around in both their head

CHAPTER 8

Mandy

Peggy and Julia have already been on the road a couple hours before Sylvia and Gil come around. These latter two are battling various issues surrounding their overnight lack of alcohol. The shakes and convulsive retching are so common with the two of them the first thing in the morning that it's become as common to deal with as getting dressed. They each have their own "cure" methods they swear by and know enough to stay out of each other's program until they're well enough to have an exchange. Regardless of what method they eventually put to work, it always begins with a cigarette in one hand while the other struggles with their chosen means of getting a bit of the hair of the dog that bit them back into each of their systems—hopefully in a manner that prevents them from throwing it back up. It's a miserable life, but they have developed a sense of community with it—besides it's predictable. After about a half hour of hacking, retching, and shaking, they've finally gotten enough booze to stay down to reach a point where they begin to feel like they may live. Once they get to feeling better long enough to believe they are better, they resume their normal drinking pattern.

"It's awful damn quiet around here, where's those brats of yours?" asks Gil.

Sylvia looks tense. She's giving Gil a frown. "What d'you care where they are, they ain't no concern of yours. Sometimes I think you got a thing goin' on for one of 'em." Sylvia pauses as she takes another drag on her cigarette before she butts in in an overflowing ashtray. It's as though in her pause she has something she's contemplating. "Hell, knowin' you the way I do, you probably got a thing for both of 'em," says Sylvia as she lights another cigarette.

Gil ignores Sylvia's remark. He knows it irritates her when he looks at younger women—especially when she sees him trying to flirt with her own daughters.

"You're always tellin' me how much you love me 'til you get what you want and then you treat me like dirt!" continues Sylvia.

When she gets in these moods, it's as though something gets inside her and won't let go. Gil doesn't have the expertise to try and psychoanalyze Sylvia every time she attacks him over something, instead, he tries to get out the door as quick as he can. He sees what is taking shape with her as he watches her flicking her ashes as though even her cigarette needed to be chastised. Once she gets on a roll with this kind of diatribe, hell's out for breakfast and there is no stopping her.

There is no question that Gil has an eye for the ladies and is an opportunist. He would readily have an affair with anyone that would have him, and that includes Peggy or Julia. He finds Sylvia attractive enough and certainly convenient, but his eye is always straying to the next skirt if it should happen to cross his path. To him, there isn't much difference between women. His idea of a relationship is a wham, bam, thank you, ma'am, and then he leaves until the next time.

Sylvia is becoming more aware as the years go by that at best her youth had been very temporary. She is no longer the young chick hanging in the bar with the full realization that she could have her pick of any of the young bucks that have tripped over themselves all evening to buy her another drink, or pay for the next month's rent. Now days, she's had to settle with the Gils of the world. She still has the naïve idea that looks determine success. She sees her daughters coming into their own as young beautiful women and herself in contrast losing what she values most. Life is playing a cruel trick on her. It just makes her pour another drink in the hopes of recreating reality—as though the passing years have made a mistake.

Her alcohol-soaked mind doesn't always guarantee that she can predict her own behavior. Sometimes, instead of feeling youthful, the more she drinks, the more she wants to pay back mother nature for what she feels has been stolen from her. This morning, all it has taken to set her into a tirade is for Gil to inquire the whereabouts of her daughters.

"So, I ain't enough for ya anymore. Now ya think ya gotta have my daughters," she says, standing in front of him braless, with a cigarette in her mouth, a drink in one hand, and a fist ready to swing at Gil. He ducks just in time to take advantage of her being off balance to get to the door and make his escape. Sylvia recovers in time to scream some four-letter expletives and pitch the remainder of her drink—glass and all—at his retreating back. The next thing anyone within hearing distance hears is the roar of an engine and the squealing sound of rubber meeting the pavement, as Gil succeeds in making the last leg of his escape.

With Gil gone, Sylvia makes her own survey of the house. Seeing an empty bedroom and the car missing, it begins to come back to her that this is the morning that Peggy was leaving for college downstate. *The little ingrate. She never even said goodbye.*

The next realization is that she can no longer depend on Peggy to cover for her, and she now has to get around to open the Midway for the lunch crowd herself. As she tries to get her mind and body to work well enough together to get a shower, get dressed, and be ready to open in an hour, her thoughts continue to imagine ways that she can get revenge against all the people that are wrecking her life. Her thoughts would make a normal person shudder, but for her, they seem like unfulfilled dreams. Like if it weren't for certain people causing her to feel bad, her life would be perfect. *"God has put them in my life because He hates me too."*

Next her thoughts turn to how she is going to get to work with no car and Gil gone. Not five minutes ago, Gil was near the top of her hit list; now she's wondering how she can manipulate him around enough to get him to take her to work. Remembering that this is not the first time she's had to tone down her anger to manage to get things done when she feels they need doing, she picks up her phone and calls Gil.

"Gil, honey, maybe I was a little nasty to you, I'd like to say I'm sorry for yelling at you the way I did. I've been under pressure lately with Peggy going off to college, can you come over so I can give you a kiss?"

This is all Gil needs to hear to make him believe he's won. It's not five minutes before he's pulling into Sylvia's driveway. His eyes are firmly fixed on the front door. He slowly exits his truck; he struggles to adjust his pants, which are well below his waistline due to his overhanging belly. Watching from an inside window, Sylvia calculates his every move. He has both hands in his front pockets but due to either too short of arms or wearing his pants too low only his fingers reach the inside of the material. Slowly and cautiously, he makes his way to the door. In her attempt at innocence, she meets him with her skillfully practiced sophomoric and humbled air. For those women who find themselves on the fringes of economic security, this type of behavior toward men holding something that they need, has always proven to be effective. Gil is not to be held as an exception. As nasty as Sylvia can be to him, she is capable of turning the tables in a heartbeat.

With a pretentious, sorrowful look, Sylvia puts her arms around Gil's neck, pulling him down to where she can meet his lips, and gives him her best unassuming kiss. She can tell by the lack of tension in his body that she has succeeded.

Gil couldn't be happier. He's certain that in his own life, he has done very few things that he considers wrong, but he's well practiced in pointing out the wrongs of the rest of the human race.

Another bond besides alcohol and misusing each other that he and Sylvia hold dear to themselves is their devotion to victimhood. Gil is certain that it's rich people that are holding him back from reaching his own wealthy place. Sylvia, on the other hand, has an anomalous attitude toward women. She has no female friends, nor does she trust other women. She finds having any type of relationship with the same sex challenging. They're seen as competitors for men's attentions. All of her efforts have always centered around hanging onto her relationship with men, regardless of how sick the connection may be. And as she is demonstrating once again with Gil, she has nearly perfected her manipulative skills.

"Gil honey, I am so sorry. I don't know what gets into me at times." Heading toward his truck, she hops into the passenger side with her words still flowing like warm syrup. "Come on, I'll buy you a beer and let's forget about it."

Gil is perfectly content to get things back to normal where he imperceptibly becomes Sylvia's wrapped up sycophant.

Within minutes they arrive at the bar. Sylvia is met by a waiting work crew ready to get the lunch crowd taken care of. Among these is a young woman who turns out to be the niece of the Midway's owner. Her name is Mandy. She readily informs Sylvia she is there to replace Peggy. Sylvia is immediately taken back. "Why wasn't I informed of this. After all I'm the manager, you'd think someone would have informed me.?"

The young woman says, "My uncle says I'm supposed to inform you and if you have any questions, you're supposed to give him a call. He said I could start today."

Sylvia can't help but begin to foster a resentment. The young woman is a very attractive twenty-something with a trim figure. If this were not enough, Gil is already googling over her. He hasn't been able to take his eyes off her since they arrived. He gives off a creepy look when it comes to staring at women, which makes them uncomfortable. His gawk is so intense that he becomes nearly impervious to his surroundings. Since Gil has never been able, in the slightest way, to be indiscreet, Sylvia sees exactly what is beginning to take place. She immediately passes him her dirtiest look. Gil notices Sylvia's displeasure, but he lacks the moral compass to realize in how many different ways he's become so offensive. Consequently, the whole process is taking another bite into their rapport. As is usual, the whole stupid fight-and-make-up course between these two begins all over again.

CHAPTER 9

One-sided Brake Job

Late in the afternoon, Julia arrives back in town. Her first inclination is to check in at camp. Jim is happy to see her back safe. Before she's out of the car and before someone sees them, they quickly look around to determine if it's safe to exchange a kiss. Not seeing anyone in a close proximity, they risk it.

"I sure missed you today," says Jim. He's being his usual considerate self as he helps her out of the car.

"To be truthful, I didn't have time to miss anyone. I'm lucky to survive this piece of crap of a car. It gave me fits all the way down and all the way back. I almost parked it along side of the road and risked hitchhiking back."

"Why didn't you call me? I could have easily come and picked you up," says Jim. There is no mistaking his sincerity.

"Thank you, Jim, but then we would have had to take time we didn't have to get this piece of crap back home," replies Julia.

She continues on for the next five minutes to go through all the stress she endured with the deer incident, negotiating the traffic in getting Peggy downstate and then the problem the brakes gave her getting back home again. Jim listens attentively. When he thinks there is a break in her talk, he interrupts to say, "Sounds like you've had a rough day. What say, I buy you supper?"

Happy to have the interruption, Julia declares, "You've read my mind. I haven't eaten since this morning."

Knowing the strained relationship Julia has with her mother, Jim adds, "The only place open in town is the Midway. How do you feel about eating there?"

"I don't care. I'm so hungry I think I could eat at Gil's trailer right now," says Julia with a tired sigh. They both add a little uneasy chuckle at this last proposal.

Taking her by the hand, Jim leads her to the truck parked next to the Subaru. He introduces her to a late model Dodge Ram pickup he found on the internet. "Julia meet 'The Ram', Ram, meet Julia'. The price was right and, it's in immaculate condition." After putting up with the broken-down Subaru for hundreds of miles, this offer may as well be to take a ride in the world's most luxurious vehicle. Julia with mouth agape, stands and stares at a shiny, jet black truck with enough chrome on just the grill to cover her entire Subaru. With all of the horrible car concerns she's experienced a smile appears, lighting up her whole face. "Jim this is beautiful. How can you afford something like this?"

"I'm signed up to take a union apprentice program with the power company this fall. When I finish, I'll be a master electrician. It starts at prevailing wage," says Jim with a satisfying grin. "I have enough saved to get me through until I start in September.

Making her way to the passenger side and hardly able to resist touching its high gloss surface, Julia runs her fingers the length of the truck. Jim is directly behind her, prepared to open her door. Once the door is open, she casts her eyes on the inside décor. It has the most luxurious interior decoration she can imagine in a truck. It's a light grey, smooth leather meant to perfectly accent the exterior black. Immediately brought to mind is the horrible interior of her Subaru with its split open, sun-faded dashboard, cracked windshield, and torn seats with their exposed yellow foam interior.

"I can't believe these seats and dashboard. They make my Subaru look even more like a junk heap," says Julia. With a continuous approving smile, she steps on the shiny steel step provided to make her entry. Even before she is ready to accommodate herself, the smell of the cab's leather bucket seats fills her nose. Finally, inside and seated, she continues to run her fingers over every inch of the cab's surfaces.

Jim couldn't be prouder. When he bought this truck, he had Julia's preferences in mind. The response he's getting is exactly as he had hoped.

After a little cruise around town to show off his new ride (especially now, with a beautiful girl sitting next to him), Jim makes his way to the Midway.

The usual cars are in the parking lot. It's a phenomenon of small towns to respect one another's parking spaces at bars, also a favored bar stool, as though it were a pew in church. Jim attempts to park in the less favored spots further from the door in the hopes of lessening the chances of having his new truck damaged by someone with a more than .02 breathalyzer count.

Once inside, and not certain the pecking order of the available seats, they choose a corner table. Sylvia is busy behind the bar and at first doesn't see her daughter come in. When she does spot them, her eye immediately turns from her daughter to this strange, but cute looking young man that's accompanying her. This is enough to have her involuntary begin to adjust her hair in the impulsive hopes this young man will find her attractive. Without a single question as to how her and Peggy's trip went, she begins with a flirtatious question concerning Jim. Never taking her eyes off him, she asks, "And who might I ask is this with you Julia?"

Responding to her mother's inquiry and knowing her mother as she does, Julia introduces Jim. "Mother this is Jim Samples, *my* boyfriend, Jim meet my mother, Sylvia."

Well aware that despite her efforts to emphasize that Jim is not just some random date she has, she knows her mother wouldn't have as much as a second thought to hit on Jim if she thought it would get her somewhere.

Jim immediately stands up, extending his hand to Sylvia. Without taking her eyes off this handsome young man, Sylvia responds by making certain she holds his hand just a little longer than usual.

Despite the uncomfortable length of time Sylvia is extending their clasped hands, Jim remains polite and cordial, saying, "It's very nice to meet you, Mrs. Fortine."

"Oh, please, just call me Sylvia," Sylvia quickly replies lowering her eyes in an obvious, open flirtation.

Julia has seen this look enough times on her mother's face when meeting a new man that she has no doubt that she considers Jim as fair game.

With the introductions over, Julia asks, "How about a menu, Mother? We're starving."

Still carrying the same approving grin, Sylvia finally takes her eyes off Jim long enough to respond to Julia's request.

"Sure, honey, let me get you started." Quickly returning from a waitress station a few feet away, she hands them each a menu, adding, "What would you like to drink?" Julia can't get over how syrupy her mother is. It's obvious to her she's attempting to make a good impression on Jim. Ordinarily, she would be berating her for taking the car, leaving her to make her way to work as best that she can.

Ordering a couple soft drinks, and taking a quick look at the menu, they place their order. Just as Sylvia is making her way to the fry cook with their order, Gil walks through the door. Looking around, he makes his way to his favorite spot at the bar. As soon as he's seated, his vision spans the entire bar. It's his usual pattern to check out what ladies have made their way, his way today. It doesn't take him long to spot Julia. As usual, his eyes linger a little longer—enough to make Julia feel uncomfortable. She doesn't have to look in his direction to know that he's staring, as she feels it. Trying her best to ignore him, she prays he doesn't come over to their table and try and impress her.

Jim knows Gil and his reputation. He also is aware of Gil's and Sylvia's drunken dynamics as their escapades are at times been more public than they've realized. In deference to Julia's feelings, he has kept what he knows to himself.

Their meal soon comes, and their conversation turns toward their upcoming plans for their future. "Peggy's the lucky one. She got out of here."

Jim contemplates her words for a moment, then makes an observation. "This is the first time you two have been apart. How do you think you're going to do with it?"

Julia looks at him with surprise, wondering how he came to be so perceptive. "It's going to be different. That's for sure. I already miss her. We always had each other, regardless of what would go on."

Jim is listening intently to what she is saying. When she has finished speaking, he says, "I know there is no one who can fill Peggy's shoes, but I want you to know I'm going to do everything I can to come close."

This is the most selfless expression Julia has heard from a male in her life. If it were coming from anyone other than Jim, she would have reservations but from her personal experience, she has a tendency to trust what he says.

"I don't want to come across as needy, but I admit I do appreciate your concern. I promise you, if I can handle the situation myself, I will," Julia says. "I want you to know I feel the same way. If there is anything going on in your life, I hope you'll feel free to share it with me."

Without making a big scene and between bites from his burger, Jim says, "You know, Julia, you're making it easy for me to love you."

This is the first time the word "love" has come up in their conversation. Julia isn't certain that she heard what she thought she has just heard. Now with a mouth full of French fries, she nearly blurts, "Did I just hear you correctly?" Not wanting to be the least bit presumptuous, she is willing to allow Jim a follow up with what he may have meant.

Jim is being just as nonchalant as he was when he made the statement a couple seconds ago. He's not attempting to say he may have used a poor choice of words, or that she may have misunderstood him. Willing to lay it all on the line and risk a rejection, he's willing to take the chance. Taking another bite of his hamburger, he makes some finger gestures that indicates he'll be able to speak when his mouth is empty. Finally, able to put some words together, Jim says, "I said that you make it easy to love you."

"Well, isn't that romantic?" says Julia, mimicking Jim with her own mouth full of fries.

"If you remember I tried the romantic stuff and you cut it short by telling me you needed to get home and help Peggy pack," Jim reminds Julia. "So, I figured I'd attempt another strategy." With a half a grin, he adds, "So how's this method workin'."

Julia's mind is suddenly slugged into overdrive. That eighteen-inch span between her heart and mind is leaving a blazed trail of emotions she's never experienced. Her heart has slammed full force into her mind. Her thoughts are rapid, leaving her at the mercy of a near frozen body. Her breathing has begun to take little short gasps as she attempts to put this whole new sensation into some kind of perspective. Her eyes are the first to indicate a change; they've welled with water. These aren't tears of sadness, rather a response to a deeper feeling of an overwhelming passion—called love.

Through tear filled eyes, Julia attempts to speak. Swallowing hard and in a barely audible, quivering voice, she says, "Oh yes, Jim Samples, it's working." Trying hard not to show how overcome with emotion she has become; she tries to cover it by taking another bite. Unfortunately, it's difficult to pull it off with tears streaming down her face.

Jim is paying particular attention to her response. It's one of bewilderment. Seeing her tears raises his confusion in his words, "Julia, I'm sorry. I didn't mean to make you feel bad."

"Oh, you big dope, you don't understand. You don't make me feel bad, it's just that I've never had a single person ever tell they had reasons to love me," says Julia trying to laugh through her tears.

"Your sister must tell you that she loves you."

"We never have to say those words to each other—we have an attachment that has never required words."

As long as the lid on this can of worms is slightly lifted, Jim takes this thought to one more level. "Your mother certainly must have told you that she loved you!?" Not certain where this question is going to land, he is surprised how quickly Julia's demeanor changes.

Julia takes a deep breath, exhaling softly. "Jim, love in my family is determined by how much Peggy and I gave our mother. It has always been a one-way street."

Jim is focused one hundred percent on Julia, watching her oscillate between weeping with elation because he's let her know of his love for her and her growing anger when her mother is brought into the discussion.

To make matters worse, who should come sauntering over to their table? It's none other than Gil, carrying his customary drink. Seeing him coming across the room, the thought passes through Julia's mind wondering if his fingers may be permanently frozen in the shape of a can since she has rarely seen him without a beer in his hand.

"Your ma told me you and Peggy took the Subaru downstate t'day. I ain't done puttin' the brake line on both sides. I jus' got the one done," Gil reports.

Not wanting to let Gil have the satisfaction in knowing of their difficulties and their near-death situation with the deer and another motorist, she calmly says, "Yeah, we figured that out, and I'm taking it in to Russ Mix tomorrow."

"Hell, girlie, you don't have to do that. I can fix that for ya," Gil says. The way he says this betrays the fact that he's miffed at being set aside as their mechanic.

Not in the least sorry she is upsetting Gil; she reaffirms her commitment to take the Subaru to Russ. At the same time, she gives Jim a little kick under the table. He's aware of her dislike for Gil and is able to decode this to mean she would rather leave than have any further discussions with Gil.

Once out of the Midway and back in the safety of Jim's truck, Julia lets her feelings come to the surface, saying, "I hate that man."

Wanting to take Julia's side in this difficulty with her mother's insistence on bringing this man into their house, he pronounces, "If he ever lays a hand on you, I want you to let me know." With another moment, he adds, "That will be the last time he'll ever do that." Like others in town, Jim has never thought much of Gil. He's always regarded him as a low life and now that he has an involvement with Julia, he thinks even less of him.

Julia speaks up. "Oh, he knows that Peggy and I are never going to put up with his crap. He's always been cautious in how far he's willing to push stuff."

"Well, at the moment, you don't have Peggy, you only have me," declares Jim with an edgy tone. The edginess comes from his worries about leaving Julia exposed to Gil's unpredictable drunken behaviors.

"He wouldn't dare lay a hand on me, I'd kill him," Julia affirms.

"Nonetheless, I don't trust him around you. He's too much of a whack job to know what his drunken mind can tell him to do."

There is no misunderstanding the concern Jim has for Julia's safety. She on the other hand has been dealing with these problems her mother drags home for years. There is little doubt in her mind that she can't handle the likes of Harold Gilles.

Jim has been driving without saying where his destination is taking them. Soon, it's become clear he's taken them to the top of a dune with the lookout over Lake Michigan. They're just in time, along with the red coral sky, to watch the last of the sun sink into the lake. Together, they both recite the old sailor's poem, "Red sky at night, sailors delight. Red sky in the morning, sailors take warning." Unabashed at the simplicity of their growing union, they meld into the warmth of each other's arms.

CHAPTER 10

Humpty Dumpty

With Peggy gone and Julia working at the camp, Sylvia is under pressure to assure the Midway owners that as manager, she can fulfill her obligation to open and close on time and is able to manage the staff. With her increasing misuse of alcohol, it's becoming more and more difficult for her to manage her own life much less the bar. As much as she resents Mandy, the boss's niece, voluntarily Sylvia is having to depend more and more on her to act as the assistant manager.

A major perk accompanying this budding relationship between Julia and Jim is that Julia no longer depends on her bicycle get her to work; Jim has assumed the responsibility to get her there each morning and get her home each evening.

On this particular June morning, Julia has already left for work, leaving her mother to fend for herself. Sylvia has managed to get enough of the warm beer down that she had in last evening's drunken state forgotten to place in the refrigerator. Her shakes are worse this morning than in the past, requiring a few more beers to calm her prolonged tremors. Hardly able to put one foot in front of the other, she manages to get herself dressed and behind the wheel of the Subaru. With a turn of the key, the motor responds with the amplified racket only a rotted-out tailpipe can create. Struggling with the gears, she succeeds in backing onto the road barely missing the mailbox, but immediately finding herself coming to a sudden stop along with a back-breaking jolt. She finds herself lying flat against the back of the seat looking straight up. She's backed down a six-foot drainage ditch on the opposite side of the road with the rear end of the Subaru resting against the ditch's bottom. Too drunk to know the full extent of her circumstances, she passes out with the car still running, hopelessly spinning its tires against anything in this ditch that it can connect with. Within a minute a passing motorist is knocking on the driver's window. Considering this is a small town, the motorist knows Sylvia from the bar. "Sylvia, are you all right?" Sylvia is out cold. With no answer coming forth, the man opens the driver's door. Seeing that Sylvia is unresponsive, his next concern is that she may have some unseen injuries. With no good alternatives, he opts to leave her where she is and dials his cell phone to the 911 number. In a matter of minutes there's a firetruck with three attendants followed by a police car.

True to their training, the attendants are careful in their efforts to remove Sylvia. She remains near motionless with the smell of alcohol emanating from her shallow breathing. It's also evident that she has wet herself. Other than these obvious indicators telling them that they are more than likely dealing with a passed-out drunk driver. Since they have no other way to determine any further injuries, the next step is to get her on a gurney and to the hospital.

Cal "Greeny" Pierce, the local constable is also on the scene carefully monitoring each procedure. "I think we got us a drunk driver," is his professional assessment. With Sylvia strapped on the gurney, the only thing left is to get her to the hospital. To verify Greeny's reckoning means that he must follow them to the hospital and order a blood alcohol test. The hospital is a regional facility and some fifteen miles away, which gives Sylvia time to begin to come out of her stupor. Her first realization is that she is in some strange surroundings. When she attempts to move, her next sensation is a sharp pain in her neck.

"What's happening to me? I don't understand all this."

Aware of her probable inebriation, the ambulance attendant takes a fling at giving her give reassurance. "You're okay. You've been in an accident, and you're on your way to the hospital to be checked out." Letting this information sink in before he goes further with his next question, "Do you feel any pain?"

"My neck hurts. What happened? All I remember is backing out of my driveway. Did another car hit me?" asks Sylvia.

Not certain how much information he should be giving her, the attendant changes the subject. "Where in your neck do you feel the pain?"

In attempting to lift her arm her arm to show him the location, Sylvia stops short. "AAAGGHHH!" is all she is able to say through the pain.

"Okay, just lie still. We'll be at the hospital in just a few minutes," he says while making an adjustment to an IV they've initiated.

True to his word the ambulance has made its way to the big emergency room double doors. Greeny is right behind them, displaying his official behavior. When he sees that Sylvia is conscious, he wastes no time in beginning his examination by presenting her with a field breathalyzer. He's already found her purse containing her driver's license and has it attached to an official-looking clipboard he carries.

Sylvia knows this routine fairly well. It's been a couple years since she has gotten in trouble with the law over driving while intoxicated. Attempting to side step this demand by indicating the pain in her neck is too severe and likely to aggravate her condition, she laments, "Every breath I take shots pain through my body, I can't do it."

Greeny doesn't argue for a second, he merely nods to the attending nurse. She in turn prepares Sylvia's arm to draw the necessary blood sample for testing. In a few minutes she returns handing Greeny the results. Taking a few seconds to examine her report, he turns to Sylvia who is being given a shot for her pain, saying, "Mrs. Fortine I'm placing you under arrest for driving under the influence of alcohol. As soon as your treatment is finished, you'll be lodged in the county jail until you can get a hearing and have bail posted."

Sylvia is sober enough to understand what is being said but not sober enough to realize the full implication of what she has just heard being said.

In a voice intermingled with a slight slur, Sylvia proclaims, "Yeah, I know ya gotta do what ya gotta do."

Holding up her driver's license between his thumb and fore finger, Greeny adds one more requirement: "Until the judge makes his determination, the law says you can't operate a motor vehicle. Consequently, I have to confiscate your license." Still not sober enough to realize the full implication of all this, Sylvia complies with everything Greeny lays on her.

"Don't worry. I ain't goin' anywhere," she acquiesces.

Greeny appoints a deputy to stay at the hospital to assure when the doctor is finished with his exam that Sylvia doesn't walkout. An hour later, she is released. Sporting a neck brace, she is quickly handcuffed, led to a waiting patrol car and driven the several miles to the county jail. Once there, she is processed and put in a holding tank to await her hearing. From all she has been led to understand, her hearing won't occur until sometime on Monday. This being Saturday means she has to endure some forty-eight-plus hours without alcohol. She's been stripped of her clothing and given a lightweight orange jumpsuit saying "COUNTY JAIL" across the back.

Within an hour of her confinement, Sylvia is beginning to feel the effects of alcohol withdrawal. It begins with mild shakes followed by a bit of nausea. These symptoms are as far as she has ever endured withdrawals without getting something down. Not certain what could follow, she sits on a concrete slab pondering her future with her arms wrapped around her drawn up legs with her chin resting on her knees.

She's finding it very disconcerting to experience the onset of sweats that are soaking her clothing. It's an uncomfortable feeling that she knows could be cured in a minute with a shot and a beer. Until now, her disposition has been compliant, but things are beginning to change. As time lapses into the evening hours, her condition continues to deteriorate. Her temperament is being over shadowed by imminent forces outside the realm of normal reasoning. They're forces that create hallucinations. She's seeing spiders crawling around the ceiling and down the walls and across the floor. When she swats them, they disappear? This strange phenomenon is causing her to become very agitated. Her jailers have brought her food that remains on her plate, cold and untouched. This in turn has caused her to beg her jailer for a drink disregarding the cost, which they, one after another, summarily disregard. Her nausea has turned to having dry heaves, as there is nothing remaining in her stomach to regurgitate. This soon progresses into severe stomach cramps.

"One drink and I know I'd feel a lot better," has become her only thought.

Evening has turned into night and her headaches are getting worse. She's finding sleep to be interrupted almost minute by minute which is causing her extreme anxiety and irritability. By morning, she's so confused that she has no idea of time or place. Without warning, Sylvia's body begins to stiffen. There is a glaze seemingly casting itself over her eyes. In the next minute, she has collapsed to the floor in a jerking and thrashing phase of a seizure she is undergoing. Within seconds, a jailer has entered her cell and is attempting to position her on her side as foam is trailing out of her mouth. In another minute, her muscles have all returned to a more relaxed state initiating a long sigh as she regains consciousness.

"Are you okay?" is the question addressed to her as she is being helped to her feet and sat down on the concrete slab which serves both as a bed as well as a seat. Sylvia attempts to mutter some words, but her mind has become so confused that she can't make her speech coherent enough to be understood. She only seems able to sit and stare with no evident cognitive powers. Soon another team is entering her cell. This time it's with a gurney preparing to return her to the hospital. Rambling incomprehensibly, she begins to get combative with the ambulance crew. To prevent her from hurting herself or anyone else, they are left with no other choice than to physically over power her and strap her down on the gurney. Having exhausted herself, Sylvia retreats back into a psychotic sleep that's filled with tormenting visions.

When she becomes aware of herself again, she continues to be strapped down but now it's in a bed with an IV flowing into her wrist. Not certain what is happening, her clouded mind is struggling to make sense of her situation. She closes her eyes as if when she reopens them, things will be clearer. Opening her eyes again, she thinks, *This may be a hospital. How did I get here? What's happening to me?*

The sound of a human voice catches her attention. In an unexplained way, it sounds familiar. It's coming nearer now. Looking up, she squints as one does when one tries to focus on something. Turning her head, a little one way and then another, she speaks with a weakened voice: "Is that you, Julia?"

"Yeah, Ma, it's me," says Julia. Her voice is flat and deliberate, free of any emotion that can be regarded as sympathetic. Rather, it's the voice of someone who is resigning themselves to an unlikely situation.

"Did you come to get me outta here? I wanna go home."

"No, I don't think that's going to happen."

With the aid of the drugs in her IV that are preventing her from going any deeper into DT's, Sylvia is becoming more lucid.

"No, I suppose not," she says as some of the day's events, little by little, begin to make their way back into her psyche.

Julia is at a complete loss for words. She has, at times, wondered how she would react if her mother died. Reviewing her feelings for the moment, considering the circumstances and the less than motherly role Sylvia has demonstrated in her and her sister's life, she could see herself viewing it as not much more than an inconvenience.

"Well, I just wanted to stop by and make sure you were okay," says Julia as she adjusts her little jacket as she prepares to make her exit.

Sylvia barely hears her daughter, as her mind is on other things. "Did they say how long they're gonna keep me here?" she asks.

Julia pauses at the door for a moment. "No, Ma, they didn't but it's my understanding that you're on your way to jail as soon as you're better."

Sylvia doesn't respond. She turns her eyes to the wall and stares at nothing. Her life is still crumbling, and she can't do anything about it. Her mind drifts into a poem she recalls learning as a child, "*Humpty Dumpty sat on a wall. Humpty Dumpty had a great fall. All the King's horses and all the King's men couldn't put Humpty Dumpty together again.*"

The heavy blanket of anguish is enveloping around her like it never has before. "*If I can just get a drink, I know all this would not be happening,*" is her sole thought.

CHAPTER 11

False Bravado

Julia's mind remains an emotional blank. It's skirting the edges of anger but for an unexplained reason hasn't gone over its edge—that is until she reaches the parking lot where Jim is waiting for her. Once inside the truck, she stares through the window for a moment. This is the first time she has not had Peggy to share her frustration over her mother's behavior. She feels isolated and alone. Her tears begin to fill her eyes, pushed by every emotion that she can name and by some she has no name for. Anger, exasperation, resentment, bitterness, sadness, isolation, all balling up inside her, each determined to highlight how thoughtlessly and uncaringly her mother has unduly victimized her life. She and Peggy have always had each other and together could shut their mother's behavior out. As long as they had one another, the lack of motherly love was tolerable. Now Peggy is absent, to some extent her absence is also causing Julia some unresolved resentments. These angers are toward life itself for seemingly abandoning her to face its harshness alone.

Jim has never seen her this way. In spite of not having a share in a lifetime of dark thunder clouds overshadowing her, his first inclination is, to comfort her. Up until now, Julia's relationship with Jim has been to prove her independence and self-reliance, not placing dependence, nor burdening him with her problems. Not entirely certain how to enter into Julia's private life, Jim cautiously watches for an opportunity. He desperately wants to become more involved with her but doesn't want to overplay his hand. For the moment, he is being quiet and letting Julia be alone with her frustration. He's satisfied to have his arm lightly around her—enough to let her know he's here for her. They stay like this for what seems like an eternity. After using every dry tissue in her purse, Julia finally stops crying. Along with her tears subsiding, she's left with an unaffected, blank emotionless feeling toward her mother that she's had more often than not in her life.

Regathering herself, Julia says in her usual way, "Jim, I apologize for burdening you with my crazy family problems." Her embarrassment is easily heard in her voice.

So far, Jim has been patiently awaiting the right opportunity to speak. Like sticking his foot into a tub of hot water, he cautiously tests the climate.

"Julia, I don't have the slightest clue how your family has coped with all of its problems over the years, but if you'll let me in, I want to be here for you."

Hearing him say these words further sinks the harpoon of embarrassment a little deeper into her person. It's a harpoon that has been largely ignored by people like Julia for fear if it were ever given the recognition it demands, it would overtake her whole person. Before she can discern what words she is about to speak, her mouth goes into gear. Lashing out, she laments, "All you people that come from normal families feel you can afford to condescend yourselves to us poor, miserable wretches on the bottom rung of society. Don't bother, we can figure things out very well ourselves."

Jim politely listens. With a little sigh of his own, he says, "You still don't get it, do you, Julia? The reason I'm sitting here with you today is because I see something in you that you don't even see in yourself. You make me feel alive— that's why I want you in my life. That "thing" that you possess—and only you possess it—is the reason I love you like I do. It makes me want to do anything I can to see you stay healthy in your whole person—mentally, physically, and spiritually. So, I'm asking—no, I'm begging: don't shut me out."

Julia hardly hears his words. She is already plotting her defense. "All you people that come from normal families have no idea what you're asking. Those of us that are surviving these crap holes we live in have learned how to role with punches. Stuff that you and your normal families have never had thrown at you." Julia is mouthing these words for the first time to anyone. It was never necessary for her and Peggy to discuss in words what they already shared clairvoyantly.

Jim is not to be put off so quickly. "What Pollyanna thoughts you may be harboring about the rest of us, who you refer to as "normal families," are a lot less accurate than you're imagining. Wherever this "functional family" exists that by comparison finds all the rest of us as "dysfunctional" is a mystery. We all have our problems and they're all different from family to family."

"Well, I don't see any of your family going to jail," snaps Julia.

"Well, I don't see your dad cheating on your mother," returns Jim clearing his throat. It's a nervous tick that shows up when he would rather cry. This is clearly the first time he's dared give his untimely home situation the light of day with anyone.

Julia is stopped in her tracks. By the look on Jim's face, she can tell this problem is clawing at his core. This is one of those times in her and Jim's relationship where she feels they are on equal footings. It's true she has been so buried in her own defective family that she never imagined anyone would be having domestic circumstances equally as disruptive as hers—specially Jim Samples.

In reality, Jim's dad has had an ongoing affair with a woman in the church choir. His mother found them together in a parked car down a farm lane on her father's farm. Rather than go through a divorce, they have agreed to live in different parts of the house. Jim has a younger sister still in high school. His parents have decided to stay together until she goes off to college next year.

For a moment, they both are quiet. Julia breaks the ice. "I'm sorry. I sound like a selfish, unappreciative brat. Here you are, willing to help me through my struggle while I've been so absent to you in yours. I don't know what else to say other than I'm really sorry to hear about your parents."

With a little grin, Jim says, "Does this mean that now we can commiserate together rather than separately?"

Julie is getting better at catching Jim's wry sense of humor. She shoots back, "Only if you buy me lunch, I'm starved.

"Let's see what's on the Midway menu today," says Jim. His measure of eagerness is reflected in the length of his ear to ear grin.

Once inside, they find a table away from the bar humdrum in an attempt to disconnected themselves from the regulars. These men and women have found the Midway to be the social center for those who enjoy the camaraderie of like mindedness—that is—to stay half in the bag as often as they can afford it. There is an ample amount of raucous laughter coming from any number of bar patron. Julia recognizes one in particular. It's the unmistakable rough throated guffaws of none other than Harold Gillis. It's obvious he's trying to get the attention of a woman seated at the bar. Without saying a word, Julia says a silent prayer, *"Please God, don't let him see me."* Unfortunately for her, God has other plans. The woman he's hitting on has countered his advances by ducking out to the lady's room. In the typical Harold Gillis way, his eye begins to rove around the room looking for another soiled dove. Spotting Julia, he can't make his way across the room fast enough.

"What's goin on with yer ma? I heard she's in the hospital and then their gonna put her in jail." Not giving Julia a chance to respond, Gil keeps right on flapping his lips with his usual bunch of conjecture he tries to pass off as factual. "That damn Greeny, he's got a lot to talk about. He's drunk most of the time he's drivin' around in his squad car. He thinks he owns the whole the goddam town." Still rambling on like he expects Julia and Jim are certain to share his hyperboles. After all, doesn't it mostly have to do with making

Sylvia into a poor, thwarted misunderstood child that just needs understanding? This is typical of Gil. It's his method to make victims out of people that have gotten themselves in trouble with the law—especially himself. As usual, Julia isn't buying anything Gil stands behind. He could stand next to Jesus Christ and she'd have her doubts as to his motives.

"Why don't you shut your pie hole and just go away," is her thought. But she manages to give him a minimal response. "Mom will live."

After going through these great lengths to demonstrate his undying allegiance to Sylvia, he realizes he isn't getting the grateful reaction from Julia he is hoping for. His next tactic is to strike out at her apathetic attitude. "Your mother has given you the best years of her life and this is the thanks she gets. You and your sister are a couple of snooty brats that need to be brought down a peg or two."

Jim has been sitting with his forearms resting casually on the table. He's been quietly listening to Gil's harangue against Julia. It's at this point, staring directly at Gil, he quietly, without emotion simply says, "Gil I think it's time for you to go."

Looking down at Jim, and with the voice of one responding to an intruder, Gil says, "I don't think I was talkin' to you sonny boy. I suggest you butt out and mind your own business."

"And I suggest you weigh your options and take my first suggestion that it's time for you to leave," replies Jim with the same quiet assurance of one who is confident he's able to back up his imperative.

"Yeah, and what's gonna happen if I don't?" questions Gil taking a big nervous gulp out of his beer.

"There's gonna be two hits—you and the floor," counters Jim in the same quiet, assured voice.

"Well, you little punk, you know who yer talkin' to?" blurts Gil as he takes a couple of steps to reach the other side of the table.

Jim is also on his feet. There is no doubt he's ready to counter Gil in which ever method Gil presents. Suddenly there is an arm extending itself between Jim and Gil. Not able to sit still, Julia has jumped to her feet along with a loud invective, "Gil, get out of my life. You're an idiot."

This fiasco is not going unnoticed. Mandy, the assistant manager, is on the scene with not just her arms waving to separate these adversaries but her entire body. Standing between them, with her voice several octaves louder, barks, "All right, this crap ain't gonna happen in here. You got disagreements? Take 'em to your house." By now, the entire bar is gathering around. When one considers most of these patrons have endured the same boring path day after day, this kind of behavior is actually looked forward to. A good donnybrook serves as a form of entertainment for these people. Ready to frustrate Mandy's efforts to nip this debacle in the bud, somebody from the crowd yells, "Let 'em fight."

Then another voice cries out, "Yeah, let 'em fight."

Soon the entire crowd is chanting, "Fight, fight, fight!" At the same time, two other men are moving tables to produce a space for the hoped-for rumble.

The look on Gil's face couldn't be more unsure. His eyes are darting from one area of the room to another, as though one of these places would provide him an escape route.

Jim is also uncertain what his role in all of this mess is going to be. Where, just a few minutes ago, he was quite certain how he was going to hold his ground has now turned into a circus. This kind of attention is so foreign to Jim that all he wants to do now is get out of here with this insanity behind him.

Julia is as frustrated as Jim. This kind of public attention is so far from her experience that all she wants to do is leave.

Julia's and Jim's eyes meet with the same message for the other, *"Let's get out of here!"* With this agreeing message, Jim grabs Julia's hand and they head for the door. Following them are a number of disappointed jeers, "Oh, come on, don't leave now." And others are throwing the "chicken" word around. Never the less, the two of them, with a singleness of purpose, make their way to the door.

Watching them go out the door brings a sense of relief to Gil. In his mind of minds, his fear was that this young man is probably capable of handing him his lunch. The next phase for men like Gil is to have his ego kick back in. In his mind, this ending is perfect. In spite of him knowing that on the inside he was shaking in his boot's but now with them gone a false bravado is emerging, he's posturing himself as having scared them away. At this point, Gil couldn't be happier. This exactly the way he had hoped this would end—victory without an effort, accompanied with plenty of bragging rights. To bask in the moment, he'd like to show off with victory lap if it were possible. Instead, he marches himself to the bar and downs a double whisky. It's the manliest thing he knows how to do.

CHAPTER 12

Lunch at Julia's

Having left the Midway under adverse conditions Julia and Jim are still hungry. Nothing less than a fifteen-minute drive is available for even a take out. Realizing there is an alternative choice, Julia takes control of this situation. There is something she feels she needs to do at this juncture anyway. It's the occasion that sooner or later has to be faced. With the present circumstances providing an open door to solve her quandary, and despite an uneasy worry accompanying it, she makes the ultimate decision, saying, "What do you say we go to my house? I think I can dig something up."

Still prickling from his encounter with Gil, Jim says, "I think that would be great."

This is a rare occasion. Julia and Peggy very rarely brought friends home when they were in school. There was always the fear of not knowing what condition Sylvia would be in, but there has also been an issue with the condition of their furnishings. Without exception, this house has been furnished with other people's castoffs. The girls always felt a sense of embarrassment over the level of poverty they actually lived in. If it weren't for summer jobs, they wouldn't have had a change of clothing. It's just been in the last few years where the girls have discovered the relationship between the men coming and going and how the rent was paid. Nonetheless, Julia has made the eventual decision. *"I'll let the cards fall where they may,"* is her final thought.

The first thing they are met with is the Subaru sitting in the driveway. Greeny had Bob Zachar use his wrecker to pull the foundered vehicle from the ditch and move it the twenty feet to its normal resting place across the street. The poor beast doesn't appear to have any further loss for wear than had existed before Sylvia's misfortune.

To take the edginess off the abnormality of having Jim in her house for the first time, Julia is watching his expressions. "It's not a penthouse but so far the rent's paid," says Julia. She doesn't want to come across as apologetic, however, she knows there probably isn't a thing in this house that Jim wouldn't throw out; accordingly, she can't help but be a little on the defensive side.

The ashtrays are overflowing, beer cans, from empty to half full, are sitting on nearly everything that has a flat surface. Julia is nervous in her anxious effort to stay ahead of her mother's clutter. Her relationship with Jim has reached a level where she is willing to lay her life's cards on the table—the good, the bad, the ugly. *"If he runs now, I wouldn't blame him,"* is her prevailing thought as she continues her clean up. Instead, Jim pitches in, emptying partially filled glasses down the kitchen drain and stacking the haphazard clutter of magazines and last week's newspapers, and especially not assigning a "better than thou" attitude to the task. In particular, the outstanding feature Julia is discovering in this new suitor, is how less than judgmental he is. Rather, his unvarying disposition is one of dutiful help ("Hey, Babe, where does this go," or, "Hey, Babe, this a keeper or a throwaway?"). Within fifteen minutes, they have organized the house to meet Julia's standards.

As they continue to work together, Julia takes a moment to reflect back on their day. They have endured and overcome a near calamity with Gil, they are presently working together in putting a lunch together, and they're doing everything with a smile. With all of this finished, they are finally able to sit and talk for a while. Something that's been on Julia's mind for some time suddenly comes to the forefront of her thoughts.

"Jim, do your parents know about me?"

She is sitting in a chair near a window. The afternoon sun strikes her hair giving it a soft glowing appearance. Ignoring her question, Jim can't help but be taken in by her remarkable beauty. Her question is playing a second fiddle to his first consideration; to take into account her remarkable qualities—physical, mental, and spiritual. He feels as though he is absorbing her total personae by just looking at her. For now, just her company alone has him in its grip. There is something about her that is difficult to put his finger on but it's as warm as the sun and he's basking in every second of it.

"Jim you haven't answered me!" Julia exclaims.

Still in his own little world, he stammers, "What? Oh yeah, you asked something about my parents."

"I asked you if they know about you and me—about us?"

"I'm not sure. My mother and I have more things to discuss than I have with my dad. I mentioned you a couple times regarding how you and I work together. She reads the sports page and knows about you and Peggy, especially your athletic accomplishments from the frequent write-ups."

"What do you mean, you're not sure? You've either told her about us, or you haven't."

Jim's mind is getting a hard-right hook, knocking him off his Pollyanna cloud. He's catching a little more of Julia's fiery nature than he's bargained for. He hardly expected that not discussing their relationship with his parents would turn into such a problem.

"It's not because I'm opposed to it, it's just that I haven't gotten to it," he admits. There is an unmistakable apology in the tone of his voice.

This admission makes Julia uneasy. Her paranoia concerning the difference in their social status is making her fear what problems may be looming because of it. It's almost as if Julia feels their relationship is on borrowed time; that she's waiting for the other shoe to drop that will bring it all to an end. *"I never had these problems when it was just Peggy and me. Why'd I have to go and fall in love?"* are her wandering thoughts.

Jim is insightful to her sudden change. Not understanding what is triggering it, he realizes she is stressing over something that only she understands. Nonetheless, he takes her in his arms, drawing her close, he can't help but catch the fresh smell of her hair, he kisses her softly. He can feel the limpness in her lips. She is struggling with something that has not surfaced in words—only in some underlying, nameless emotion that's draining her vitality. She isn't saying anything.

Looking directly at her, he cradles her face in his hands. "I don't know what it is that's bothering you, but I want you to know one thing for certain: I love you and expect to be here for the long haul, so when you're ready, I want you to share what it is that's upsetting you."

Julia responds with an evident struggle to find the words she's looking for. One major agreement she and Peggy agreed on is to never allow themselves the luxury of falling into a "victim" mentality. Julia can feel it trying to find a home with her when she compares her families standing in the community up against Jim and his family. Older adults have a different value system than young adults. Among their peers, Julia and Peggy are the principal ambassadors connecting others to their family. They have earned the respect and admiration among their peers, but among older adults, the parents are the principal representatives of a family. Every adult in the area knows Sylvia. She is not held to the same high standard by her peers as her children are among theirs. It's possible these status differences among the parents are not something Jim is aware of, but it is a part of Julia's life.

With the resolve to hold true to her conviction of beating off the "victim" mentality, with a sigh, she has something between a quake and a quiver in her voice finally chocking out a response, "Oh it's nothing. I'm just being stupid.

Not certain he should be satisfied with her self-assessment; Jim continues with his concern. His voice has a calming effect as he tries to give Julia comfort; from "what" he knows not.

"It would help if you could find a way to tell me what your concerns are about you and me and my parents."

It's at times like this that Julia misses Peggy. This is the first separation they've had since conception. Jim is wonderful in many differing ways, but for certain circumstances, only Peggy will fill the bill—and this is one of them. In her own pragmatic way, Julia is trying to shape her concerns into words. This effort is producing a clumsy aura surrounding it. Still warding off the unwanted victim mentality relentlessly banging at the door of her emotional state, she takes a deep breath. As she releases it, the hope that she can form the words she feels are needed, finally come to fruition.

"Jim, our parents are miles apart in their roles in our town. Regardless of your father cheating on your mother, it remains merely a rumor. This allows your family to maintain the outward appearance of sanity. Mine is just the opposite. Because of my mother's public indiscretions, my family has been held up to nothing short of national scrutiny." Julia pauses for a moment, rethinking what she has just expressed hoping it's not a rant. *"God, I hope I don't sound like a victim!"*

Jim is listening. His less than wholehearted reaction is noted. It's not surprising that he doesn't share her concern, but then this has always been a luxury taken by the upper class. They are in a position where condescension is a virtue if so chosen—but it remains a choice. Julia finds it an oxymoron to even consider "condescending" to something above her and seemingly out of reach, like Jim's family.

Taking a moment before he responds, Jim is studying her concern.

"I realize some of the stuff you're concerned with is important, and obviously, it's haunting you, but honestly, I have never placed you in a low-class category. It's true that I've felt compassion for you for having to endure the crap thrown at you, but I've always known you're a lot more than your mother's problems. I believe that you are an amazing woman to have developed into the person you are today—especially in light of your mother's lack of parenting skills. I'm not certain I would do as well."

In spite of the unavoidable condescending nature of his response, Julia is relieved by the blunt honesty of Jim's reply. Looking out of the window, she watches a Robin dutifully feeding its offspring. The whole scenario is one of honest obligation. Jim's words are rightly supporting a similar calling. She senses she has made a right choice to move forward.

Instead of answering right away, Julia takes another sip from her Coke, pulling herself together. She spends a few moments looking at this amazing boyfriend. She's beginning to form a trust bond with Jim that she never imagined could happen. She is involved in the most open conversation she has ever had with anyone other than Peggy, much less someone of the opposite sex. Her mouth feels dry. Each breath is felt as it enters and leaves her lungs. For the first time in her life, she is at a loss for words. Saying nothing, she turns her head staring out the window. Jim also falls silent following her gaze. The Robins are still there. Without forethought, exactly like the generations before them, they are following a script preparing them to enter the next stage life has in store for them.

Eventually, while sharing the worn sofa, they fall asleep in each other's arms.

CHAPTER 13

DT's

Gil is suddenly awakened by the obnoxious ringer on his cell phone. It's playing "The Pennsylvania Polka" at full volume. He's had it on it since he heard it played at the movie "Ground Hog Days," one of the only movies he's been to. It's nine o'clock on Monday morning. He struggles in his usual manner to clear his head and figure out how to decide to answer the call. He's nearly out of breath and blinking his eyes incessantly as though they will clear if only from blinking fatigue. Recognizing the number, he answers.

"WHAT!?" is all he is inclined to say.

"Don't be such an ass, Gil. I ain't got any money, and the judge will cut me loose if I can come up with two hundred bucks' bail 'til I can get a hearing. Otherwise, he's gonna keep me here 'til I get sentenced," laments Sylvia."

"What d'ya expect me to do about it?" asks Gil.

Sylvia is allowed only this one phone call. She is struggling not to say anything that that will offend Gil to the point of hanging up. She desperately tries to change her tone to the willing girlfriend Gil expects her to be.

"Gil, if you'll do this for me, I'll make it worth your while. I promise."

Still clearing his head, Gil calculates as best he can what money he has left from a sale he made the past week. Out of the five hundred he gleaned by selling an old bass boat, he counts out two hundred and sixty clumped-up dollars lying in a wad on his nightstand. He left the rest at the bar.

"All's I got is a hundred bucks," lies Gil.

"I can't make any more calls, but if you get a hold of Julia, she should have the other hundred."

"That little witch!" is his singular thought. He's still smarting from the incident in the Midway the previous day. He'd like to bring it up to Sylvia, but he knows every time he involves himself with her daughters, she comes unglued. Instead, rather than open that can of worms, he tells her, "I'll see what I can do."

Sylvia's few minutes allowed for her phone call is over. "Please Gil, you gotta get me out this damn hell hole!" are her last words before the phone goes dead on her end. He spends the next moment like he's paralyzed with the phone still stuck to his ear. It's as if he doesn't know what to do next. Finally, it occurs to him to put the phone down. His head is far from clear. Searching around, he finds a half can of warm beer, only to discover after a couple of good gulps that it contained a cigarette butt. He spits too late to remove anything but a filter tip. With a head that's still not clear, his next step is to pour what's left of yesterday's coffee into a cup and stick it in a microwave that has a little of everything that it's ever heated stuck to its walls. In a minute, he has the cup to his lips. Whether coffee actually has medicinal properties to sober up with or merely creates an awake drunk is a question that needs further study. Either way, Gil goes through his morning "sobering up" routine. Within an hour, he has enough together to get his pickup on the road heading toward the jail. Just as he comes to the stop sign taking him to the main road, who should be jogging across in front of him? None other than Julia and Jim. Unaware of Gil's destination, they give him a quick glance. Whether or not they expect him to try and hit them with his truck, they nonetheless pick up their pace to avoid even the chance of a confrontation.

Gil gives them a hard stare. His only comment is in a low mutter, "Ya little witch, yer gonna get yer comin's, and it may be sooner than you think."

With a head still lingering with yesterday's booze, Gil pulls around back of the City Hall and parks. The jail is located on its lower level with a rear entrance. It's not like this is the first time he's been here. He's very familiar with where he has to go and who he has to see to post bond. This is something he could probably do in his sleep. Knowing the routine, he sits in the lobby to wait until Sylvia is back in her civilian clothing and retrieves her belongings. This leaves him with nothing to do but stare at the stains behind the chairs where countless heads have rested against the walls, or contemplate the thick bulletproof glass separating the office staff from any chance encounter with a disgruntled civilian. It also is giving him time to recall his last episode with the law. Since he was in an alcohol blackout, he remembers nothing that led up to his arrest. But when he slept off his drunk, he recalls with clarity the bruises left on his body by resisting arrest.

Jolted back to the present when the big steel door separating the jail from the lobby suddenly opens. The jail matron is in the lead, and Sylvia is directly behind her. One look at her tells the whole story. She has the haggard look of roadkill. There are no words exchanged between the two, it's all routine. As soon as Sylvia is in the lobby, she is free and on her own, the steel door is then closed with the matron back on the inside. Gil also doesn't have anything to say. As soon as he sees Sylvia, he is on his feet, heading for the door. Anything he has to say will be saved until he's out of this miserable place. He can't get out fast enough. As soon as they are out of the parking lot and on the road, Sylvia lights a cigarette along with the imperative, "I ain't feelin' good. I gotta get a beer before I get sick. They kept me in the hospital only long enough to level me out. They're saying I got 'psychosis.'"

Gil knows exactly what she is talking about. He tried to quit drinking cold turkey a year ago, but he considered the withdrawals to be worse than his alcoholic condition. Stopping at a local grocery store, he quickly picks up a case of beer. By the time he returns to his truck, Julia is hysterical over a snake she sees crawling over the dashboard. Taking one look at her, Gil knows she's crossed over an unspoken line. He's well aware that a beer isn't going to get her back to any semblance of normalcy. As usual, when faced with any circumstance where he senses powerlessness, Gil automatically cracks open a beer. Sitting in the grocery store parking lot with a beer in his hand and listening to Sylvia begin to shriek is way beyond his management skills. Gil's immediate reaction is to close the truck windows. This maneuver is hardly enough to contain Sylvia's worsening behavior. Despite Gil's efforts, her behavior is attracting all sorts of unwanted attention, including store security. Within the time it takes Gil to drink half the beer he's hoping will give him the answer he needs to take care of the problem (Gil maintains that he thinks much clearer when he's drinking), a security guard is tapping on the closed window. Gil dreads the sight of any uniformed person with the authority to give him grief. Short of a full-blown panic attack, Gil presses the power window switch. The security guard, seeing Sylvia's crazy behavior and hearing her weird rantings more clearly, asks, "What's going on here, sir?"

Not certain how to answer, Gil says, "I'm not sure, sir. She just started acting like this. I think I need to get her to the hospital."

Before the guard can react, Sylvia is out of the truck, running hysterically across the parking lot and screaming, "They're tryin' ta kill me. Somebody, please help me! Don't ya see, they're tryin' to kill me!"

People are stopped in their tracks, not knowing how to react. The security guard is fast to respond. He is on a full-court press to overtake her, but not before she reaches the store entrance. Once inside, she continues her rant, throwing cans in every direction. Unrestrained, she continues making her way to the rear of the store knocking over grocery carts and bumping into several unsuspecting shoppers. Not detained, she nearly tears the freezer door off, locking it behind her. Still unfettered and inside alone, she continues her irrational behavior to throw anything loose at whatever she is imagining to be her tormentors.

The guard has been taken by surprise and has hardly been close enough to subdue Sylvia before she cloisters herself inside a locked freezer. All he can do for the present is to peer through the glass window and try to reason with her to open the door. By now, Gil, who has followed at a distance, has joined the guard in imploring her to open the door.

Impervious to any impositions other than those she's creating, Sylvia barely looks in their direction. With her safety in jeopardy and with no other choice, the security guard makes the call to 911. In less than a minute, the sirens are heard as they make their way across town. Five minutes have not been expended before a number of fully dressed firemen are assessing the situation. Greeny is right behind them, along with several ambulance attendants. Working with very little regard to damage made to the freezer, within fifteen minutes, they have removed the door. Sylvia continues her paranoid behavior. In total fear of her rescuers, she continues to beg them not to kill her. Realizing there is no reasoning with this kind of behavior, they quickly place Sylvia in restraints, tethering her to a gurney. Making their way back through the destruction and an ample supply of onlookers, the entire entourage follows the first responders to the waiting ambulance. After placing Sylvia safely inside, they turn on their emergency lights and siren to return her to the same hospital she has just left.

For the only moment of silence experienced in the last half hour, Gil stands alone with Greeny. For Gil, it's an uncomfortable silence. Without looking at Greeny, he tries to leave by making a simple goodbye gesture and walk back to his truck. Greeny has another objective. "Hey, hey, wait a minute, Gil. I smell alcohol on your breath. If you get in that truck and drive off this parking lot onto a city street, I'm gonna stop you and make you take a breathalyzer."

Gil stops in his tracks. He knew all along things were going way too smoothly between himself and Greeny to be true. In an attempt to be a smartass, knowing result, he turns back to look at Greeny along with a grin and says, "Why? You offerin' me a ride to the Midway? Do it, and I'll buy ya a beer."

Greeny, not having just fallen off the turnip truck, retorts, "Don't push me, Gil. You're standin' on thin ice as it is. I know I can give that truck of yours a safety check and find just about everything out of code, and you'll find yourself walkin' a lot longer."

Gil is smart enough to know when the hand he's dealt shouldn't be bet on. He chooses to fold, but not without chancing a smaller wager. Using his middle finger to push his sunglasses up his nose, he asks Greeny, "Did I get my glasses up far enough?"

Greeny knows exactly what Gil is doing. Allowing Gil the last word, providing it's a feeble attempt to make himself feel he came out on top, is a small price to pay to have him comply.

Within a couple minutes, Greeny is in his patrol car and Gil is walking the couple miles back to his trailer.

CHAPTER 14

One Won't Hurt Me

Learning of the bizarre circumstances surrounding Sylvia's odd behavior, the grocery owner has declined pressing charges. Greeny, on the other hand, has opened a new chapter surrounding Gil and Sylvia. When small town people bring their aberrant behaviors into the public sphere, they run the risk of losing their privacy. This ensures that any future happenings with these two will be looked at through a lens of suspicion.

Julia has received the news of her mother's demise via a phone call from an acquaintance who happened in the grocery store as the whole event unfolded. Julia is the first to admit she has a love/hate relationship with her mother. It's very difficult for her to separate the sinner from the sin; to love the sinner and hate the sin. By the time she reaches the hospital, they have her mother on anti-seizure medicine and Librium. It's put her in a near comatose state, but she hasn't had one of her paranoid episodes since they got her treatment started. A nurse aid named Jessica, a schoolmate of Julia's, is eager to give her an update on her mother's condition.

"She came in combative, but as soon as doctor gave her a shot, she settled right down and hasn't given us a minute's trouble since."

Julia is listening but really hasn't a clue as to what her mother's diagnosis is. "What has she got wrong with her, Jess?" her question is naïve and innocent.

"I'm supposed to wait until doctor talks to you, but if you act like you didn't know, I'll tell you what I know. She's got the DT's and some sort of psychosis."

Julia is listening just as naively as previously. "Jess, what the heck are "DT's."

Recognizing her advantage in medical diagnostics, Jessica further explains, "'DT's' are what a person gets when they drink like your mom does. They go into what doctors refer to as 'delirium tremors'. Like your mom was when she came in here earlier."

"I'm afraid to ask. What was she like?" asks Julia with trepidation.

Jessica spends the next few minutes going over the details of Sylvia's condition. It corresponds with the information she received from the phone call she had received earlier. Neither, she nor, Peggy have witnessed this behavior in their mother.

"My mother's behavior has always been a pain for Peggy and me, but it's really hard for me to imagine her acting *this* way," says Julia. The sadness in her voice tells how deep this incident is affecting her.

There is a soft knock on the door. It cracks open wide enough to let a familiar head peek into the room. Looking in the direction of the bodiless head peering around the door, Julia recognizes it immediately as Gil. It's obvious by his reticent behavior that he's out of his element. With hat in hand, he enters the room. Looking at the motionless body lying in a near comatose condition of his long-time paramour, Gil asks simply, "How's she doin'?"

Julia can hardly contain herself. If it weren't for looking bad in front of Jessica, she'd like to say, "*No thanks to you, she's nearly drank herself to death. Now leave!*" Instead, she tries to overcome her immense dislike for this seeming interloper. Not about to show any crack in her demeanor, she recalls her and Peggy's resolve not to become Gil's victim. Mustering up her courage once again, she renews her pledge to stand tall against Gil's intrusion. Straightening her shoulders, she says just as simply, "She's going to be fine."

The smell of alcohol is prevalent. It's obvious that Gil is well fortified. Drunk or sober, Gil's look is more often much the same—blank and unreadable. It's always dismayed Julia that she can never decipher him; she believes it's because he always looks confounded; like he's not getting it. Today is not an exception. He's not making any gestures that indicate if he's happy, sad, or mad, he's just being his vacuous self. Julia attempts to ignore him by turning back to her conversation with Jessica. He continues his vigil of standing and blinking while looking around the room as though he's lost something. As usual, he makes Julia nervous. A minute of him is a minute too much as far as Julia is concerned. Her eyes are on Jessica, but once again, Gil owns her attention.

"Why doesn't he get it?"—I hate him!" Julia thinks.

Finally, turning toward Gil, Julia says, "I'll call you if there's any change." Her voice is flat and blunt.

Gil gives her a little nod that says he hears her, but his mind is someplace else. Still with hat in hand, he slowly approaches the side of Sylvia's bed. There are lines of tubing entering her body from several sources, each supplying something attempting to reverse the too many years of abusing her body. She's pale grey, and unresponsive. In an unprecedented act of concern, Gil leans over and kisses her forehead. He stands for a moment, staring at her through moistened eyes, proving that even the most hardened reprobate can feel the probability of losing something taken for granted. Gil remains silent. Turning to leave, he gives Julia another little nod and disappears through the door.

As much as Julia would prefer to have him totally out of her life, she couldn't help but be perplexed with his abnormal behavior. In her experience, her mother and Gil were either drinking and fighting or producing unwanted sounds from the bedroom. This quiet, almost surreal bedside manner from Gil is unique. Not ready to see Gil as anything near a human being, she shakes off the picture he's attempting to leave in her mind and continues her conversation with Jessica.

"In all honesty Jess, what do you see happening with my mother?"

Jessica's pause is not something a worried daughter wants to see. These pauses usually lead to bad news.

"If you want honesty, I'll give you my honest opinion, if she doesn't stop her drinking, I see more hospital, more jail, and an early death."

This is what Julia and Peggy have been silently fearful of without needing to hear the actual words. With the words now spoken, the reality of this fear is hitting home with Julia.

"Isn't there anything we can do?" Julia asks.

Again, Jessica pauses. With this pause, Julia is preparing herself for the worst.

"You can try by getting her into a rehab center."

This kind of talk is totally foreign to Julia. She wouldn't know a what a rehabilitation center does any more than she knows what goes on in Moscow.

"How do we do that?" is Julia's next question.

"My experience with this stuff is limited. All we do is try and keep people alive long enough that they begin to keep themselves alive."

Having this conversation with Jessica is leaving her with more questions than she's had answered.

Checking her watch, Jessica realizes she is getting behind with her duties. "If there's anything I can help with just call me," she offers. With that, she is on her way down the hall to the next patient.

Alone in the room, Julia finds an empty chair that gives her a view of her mother. There are wires and tubes in nearly every orifice. Viewing all this, her stomach is doing flip flops and the sides of her head are beginning to throb. The anxiety and the stress are beginning to take their toll. "I've never felt this alone in my life," she confesses. Peggy is downstate at college and Jim is working at the camp; he was kind enough to lend her his truck. The longer she sits looking at her mother, the more empty and forlorn she becomes. Her phone is the only thing she has in her hand. Before she fully realizes what she is doing, she has placed a call to Peggy. Hearing the ringing on the other end causes her to sigh, *"What am I going to say?"* It's the only thought that has made its way into her head.

"Hello, Peggy."

"Julia, what's up?"

"Mom's in the hospital."

"In the hospital? Is it serious?"

"It's serious enough. They're saying if she doesn't stop drinking, she's going to die."

Julia spends the next half hour bringing Peggy up to speed with what's transpired in the past few days. There is no way Peggy can be of any physical help, taking into account the number of miles separating them, but the emotional support Julia is gleaning is immeasurable. Finally bringing their conversation to a close, they've agreed to keep in touch morning, noon, or night if they need each other for anything. With this task concluded, it leaves Julia to face the fact she's left alone with only herself and her disabled mother together in the same room. She's realizing she can't remember when she had spent this much time alone with her mother.

Several days have passed. The doctor has been successful in preventing Sylvia from going into the DT's any further than she already had induced herself. She's at a point now where she is able to sit up in bed and alert enough to have her attention clearly on the doctor's words.

"Sylvia, you were close to deaths door when you arrived here; you had one foot in the grave and the other on a banana peel."

Sylvia is feeling the impact of the doctor's words. Her passed weeks experience is still fresh enough to give her pause. "I know Doctor, I don't ever want to go through that hell again."

The doctor is evaluating Sylvia's overall behavior i.e. emotional attitude, attention span, physical ability, and mental aptitude. He's also measuring his own words as he's particularly watching for an attitude of an honest compliance. "You've had several days of medical attention, you're young enough to make a fairly rapid recovery providing you stop drinking. I might add your liver isn't going to take much more abuse before it can't recover." The doctor is making a careful observation on Sylvia's reactions. Satisfied they're still on the same page, he continues, "But I believe there's more to your getting well than just your physical condition."

Sylvia is still listening with what appears to be an open mind. The doctor knows what he is about to say next is going to be either welcomed or rejected. Looking at her square in the eye, and with his most convincing professional demeanor, he makes the leap, "It's my recommendation that you spend the next thirty days at an alcoholic rehabilitation center."

Sylvia is quiet. The only expression she has is one of no expression. The doctor is studying any signs in her facial appearance, body movements—anything that will give him clues as to what level of treatment he should next entertain. Like most health care workers, he is prepared for the worst but remains hopeful for the best. Sylvia, by a lack of demonstration in either speech or expression, is exhibiting a befuddlement. It's clear this option has hit her on her blind side. Since the doctor has never met Sylvia before, he can only rely on *general* human reactions. He is hoping, generally speaking that he can depend on the idea that her failed drinking career has beat her into a state of reasonableness. This is what a classic recovering alcoholic will profess. At this moment, the doctor is looking for Sylvia's level of defeat. If her defeat is sufficient, she'll be tenderized enough to listen to reason.

In the time it took Sylvia to hear the words of her doctor, her mouth goes into gear, "I can't do that—I got rent ta pay. I need to get back to work."

The doctor hears what she has to say but is prepared to provide another option, "How about we apply for an outpatient treatment program. This will allow you to work and get the help you need."

The prevalent fear that anyone in the business of caring for others is concerned with is the total rejection of the care package they are attempting to provide. On the other hand, attempting to work *reasonably* with anyone suffering with anything less than a bottom, is nearly a waste of time. Alcoholism, all too often, proves to be a very unreasonable disease.

No one has to wait long in this case. Sylvia is quickly changing her tone from compliance to resisting. "I don't think I need that Doctor, I'm pretty sure I can cut back on my own."

When these words are spoken, the session is finished. Any further talk about rehabilitation will only fall on deaf ears. The next discussion is centered around her release.

"Well I wish you the best of luck. If you should change your mind, feel free to come and discuss it with me. As for now, I'm releasing you as soon as you can get ready."

With that, he smiles, slaps his hands on his thighs, rises from his chair, shakes Sylvia's hand and continues his rounds.

Sylvia spends the next few minutes changing from her hospital gown back into her own clothing. Looking at herself in the mirror, she realizes how haggard and old she's beginning to look. Her hair is streaked with strands of grey, hanging on her shoulders with no style. It's been years since she's been to a styling salon. The lines in the corners of her eyes are much more prominent than they had been, her skin is pale and unresponsive, her waist is thickening—but then, up until now her main concern has been maintaining her alcohol levels.

Free from the shakes, with not one cell in her body is demanding alcohol to function and free from the thoughts of where her next drink is coming from, she decides she is going to walk the distance from the hospital to her house. Physically, she feels better at this moment than she has in years. Mentally, her mind is remarkably clear. The day is a beautiful summer afternoon. As she opens the hospital door, she is met by a rush of glorious smells from the flower gardens gracing the hospital grounds. A Cardinal is singing to its mate in a nearby tree. The sun feels warm on her skin. The humming sound of a mower somewhere in the neighborhood is a summer sound she has ignored and suddenly finds as a welcomed noise. The grass and trees have suddenly taken on a much healthier green than she can remember. She couldn't feel freer than she does at this moment. *"So much for the past; and now for today."* This is Sylvia's prevailing thought, as she steps into her world for the first time in years as a sober woman. She is astounded at how she has become so much aware of life around her that she has left largely ignored.

Deciding to make first stop at Beverly's Beauty Salon, Sylvia begins her trek. Three hours later, she steps back into the street with a haircut, color and style. Her nails and toes have a fresh coat of paint and her brows have been waxed. Free of the alcoholic toxins in her body and the toxic mind that comes with it, Sylvia hasn't felt this good since Buddy Stroub gave her the biggest Valentine card in front of her whole third grade class.

Her next step is to stop by the local health club and see what they have to offer in exercise and yoga classes. She's met by a buffed guy named Skip. He couldn't be more flattering to her animated ego.

"I see a diamond in the rough in you. You have the frame for something that can be sculpted into a more beautiful body than you already have," says Skip in a reassuring voice. "You give me six weeks of your time; you'll be amazed at what you've accomplished."

Sylvia is standing before a young man who has the physical sex appeal of a Greek god. Furthermore, she has his full attention. Now that she is sober, she believes her nirvana is right around the corner. She's willing to begin her new life with vigor of one who is experiencing a kind of rebirth. Considering since this is the first day of the rest of this new life, she signs up.

Now that she's had her hair and nails done and signed up for a body sculpting class, all that's left to do is to make her way back home. Anxious to get there, she picks up her pace. Ignoring the Subaru parked in the drive, she steps inside after nearly a week without smoking or drinking and is struck by the stale smell of nicotine still lingering in the air. She immediately throws open the doors and windows and begins a vigorous cleaning process. Her physical and mental energy levels haven't been at this high a level since her teen years. An hour later, exhausted but invigorated, she can't understand why she would ever let things get this bad.

The sound of a vehicle pulling into the driveway has caught Sylvia's attention. Without looking out the window, she recognizes the sound of Gil's truck. He sits for a minute as though he's surveying the area. Finishing a cigarette, he exhales the last of the smoke out his nostrils. Climbing out of his truck, he ambles over to the Subaru. It sits like a broken but defiant creature that demands to be kept alive if for no other reason than to taunt the drivers with no other choice other than to drive it. The grass and dirt are still in the bumper and tailpipe from being slammed into the bottom of the ditch. Sylvia watches him from the dining room window. She's successfully ignored the Subaru all afternoon. It doesn't fit her resurrection. Looking at it is like looking at a wound that has a thin scab over it. To have to deal with this piece of carnage from her past is like brutally throwing her off her pink cloud of recovery.

Gil looks up long enough to see her staring out at him. He makes a futile attempt to direct a weak wave back at her. She returns the same. He's replaced his cigarette with his incessant need to chew on a toothpick. With his fingers barely reaching the front pockets of his overalls cinched tight below a bulging beer belly, he ambles toward the door. Julia meets him. "Hey, how ya doin'," seems appropriate enough, since she doesn't remember when she saw him last. The events leading up to her stay in the hospital are still murky enough to not be readily recalled. Bits and pieces are slowly returning, but at their own pace.

Gil is well aware of where her drinking took her, but he's torn between a concern for Sylvia's wellbeing and losing a drinking buddy. "Damn, girl, you sure look nice," is Gil's salutation. It seems appropriate enough considering the makeover she went through earlier. Replacing the toothpick with another cigarette, he immediately sits down in the nearest chair prepared to light it. Sylvia speaks up before he has a chance, "Don't light that thing in here, I'm tryin' to air the dump out a little." Taking him by the hand, Sylvia pulls at him to get him out of the chair and outside to do his smoking. Reluctantly, Gil succumbs to her wishes. To make her point clearer, she's pushing at him from behind. Once they're outdoors, he makes a point to offer Sylvia a drag. She hasn't had a cigarette since she landed in the hospital days ago. It's not that she needs to smoke, but something in her head from an old, well-worn path speaks out. "Thanks, Gil. I haven't had a smoke in days." Taking the cigarette, she takes a long drag.

"I know you done somethin' ta help me 'cause I saw your name on some papers somewhere," says Sylvia. "I want to thank you."

"I got you outta jail."

"Jail!? I totally forgot I went to jail."

"Yeah. I got you out. Then you went to the hospital. You was bad," says Gil.

Sylvia's pink cloud of sobriety is quickly turning black, into some kind of looming thundercloud. Her whole demeanor is changing. All the good feelings she's had all afternoon are disappearing, buried under her old companions of fear and anxiety. Those dark alcohol induced blank spots in her memory are beginning to restructure themselves. Back in commission are the full-blown channels of worry and dread.

They're bringing up concerns she hadn't thought of all afternoon—like, *"Do I still have my job at the Midway? Am I going to have a car again—or for that matter, a driving license?"*

As if this were not enough, an unwelcomed vehicle has entered the driveway. To further add to Sylvia's growing anxiousness, it's none other than Greeny. For a larger paycheck, he has taken on the role of process server. In his hands are papers that can only bring more grief to Sylvia's ever mounting depression. Whether or not Greeny enjoys his job is seldom left for him to answer, as nearly everyone he engages has their own opinion. This opinion is supported by Greeny's ever present grin. The contradiction lies in his eyes—they have a firmness that doesn't back such a grin. These phenomena have left him with a vagueness that only he benefits in—in that people can't second guess him.

Awkwardly defenseless, they watch him march toward them with one hand incessantly adjusting a belt containing a pistol, taser, night stick, handcuffs and a few closed leather containers and the other hand with the dreaded court appearance papers. In this case, Sylvia will prefer the discharge everything on his belt can produce rather than take these papers. Remaining defenseless, Sylvia has no other choice than to await the inevitable. Greeny's last twenty steps are buried in Sylvia's psyche as indelibly as if he were coming to hang her. Even with the sun still shining bright, for Sylvia it's turned to a foggy day. Nothing short of a miracle is going to change the present. Unfortunately, no twinkling stars are in store for her, as Greeny, along with his incessant grin hands over her court papers. Little tear drops begin to fill Sylvia's eyes as she stands staring at this handful of disappointment. Regret—which can only be described as legion—is unmistakably overtaking her whole persona. Finished with his task, Greeny returns to his squad car. The process leaves Gil with his normal big dumb look. Neither Sylvia or Gil have any appropriate words to filter this happening to turn it into anything other than a downer.

Wanting more than anything to have this all go away, Sylvia says, "Can you take me over to the Midway, I want to see if I still have a job."

Within five minutes, they walking through the Midway door. Sylvia's familiarity with the din of voices that only a bar can produce along with the volume of several TV's broadcasting a baseball game, brings an apprehension. She has suspected all along the owner was surreptitiously having her train his niece to replace her as manager. Her uncertainty turns to certainty when she reads below Mandy's name tag, the words "MANAGER." Taking a deep breath, Sylvia says, "I suppose this means, I'm fired."

Mandy is surprised to see Sylvia. Looking her all over, she's even more surprised to see her looking as good as she does. "The last information I had was that you were in the hospital. Then I heard you went to jail, and then I quit hearing anything. My uncle called and told me to take over as manager."

"Yeah, I know I should've called, but regretfully, I was indisposed for a few days and was unable to get to a phone. Let me get a few of my things, and I'll get out of here."

Mandy says nothing for a moment and then, with a voice of uncertainty, adds, "I realize it will mean a pay cut, but we can always use a good waitress if you're willing to do that."

Sylvia doesn't hesitate with her reply. "I'll do that! Thank you. Thank you." She is relieved beyond words that she still has a job, despite her demotion.

"By the way, I love your hair," adds Mandy.

Unconsciously, Sylvia hand rises enough to adjusts some loose strands behind her ears, adding another appreciative, "Thank you."

Mandy also has a close eye on Gil. She hasn't forgotten the ruckus he created a few days ago. She has been around him enough to see him go through a few of his infamous moods, where he takes on the persona of some weird alien looking to bring the world to its knees, or imagines he's Casanova, hitting on anything that wears a bra. Seeing his sober deportment and the likeliness of him causing another problem negated, she goes about her work. This leaves Gil and Sylvia at ease and provides an option to stay a little longer.

Seeing the smile of relief on Sylvia, Gil turns to the only way he knows to celebrate such an occasion. Without forethought, Gil says, "How about we celebrate? How about a beer on me, my lady?"

Sylvia, *with* a moment's forethought, thinks, *"One beer is not going to hurt me, I'll just have the one and quit."*

Taken with Gil's seeming attempt at chivalry, Sylvia says, "Okay, but just one!"

CHAPTER 15

An Omen

Julia is just making her way home from work. Jim is driving her. They've stayed late at the camp putting together a program for the next day. As they enter her driveway, they encounter not only the broken-down Subaru, but also another recognizable pickup belonging to none other than Harold "Gil" Gilles.

The two slowly pull into the driveway all the while studying the situation in an attempt to put together a reasonable scenario for what they are seeing.

"What in the world would Gil be here for if my mother is still in the hospital?" is Julia's quandary.

The Subaru is jacked up in some manner of assembling or disassembling. There are parts, hoses, wiring, tools scattered completely around it. It's definitely Gil's trademark.

Fresh in Jim's mind is the confrontation he had with Gil not that long ago. "Maybe he changed his mind about getting his ass kicked," is Jim's summary.

"Oh, I hope you don't start anything with him. You never know what he may do. He's likely to have a knife, a gun—who knows what?" begs Julia.

"Oh, don't worry, I'm not about to sink to his level of stupid."

Julia looks at him suspiciously, saying nothing; her look tells it all.

"You prefer I stay in the truck?" he asks.

"Heck no. I'm not going in there alone with him roaming around."

Cautiously, they move out of the truck to make their way to an unlocked front door standing wide open. The first thing they become aware is the number of beer cans sitting on everything that will hold one. The next awareness is a familiar sound to Julia emanating from the bedroom. Jim is noticeably uncomfortable with what he is hearing.

"Well, I guess the mystery is cleared up," says Julia in an attempt to hide her discomfort.

"I don't know how you put up with this. You want to come to my house.? My mom will find a place for you to stay."

"Thanks for the offer but I've put up with my mother's antics my whole life," submits Julia, "I guess I can go another day."

"If Gil gives you any trouble, I'm only a phone call away. I can be here in less than five minutes," says Jim. The look on his face says his confrontation with Gil at the Midway is still an unresolved issue. After saying their goodnights, Jim reluctantly returns to his truck to leave Julia on her own.

*

In a different part of the state, Peggy is wrapped up tight in her college athletic training for the fall semester. This regimen is much more competitive than anything she's had to face at this point. She is faring better than Julia with their separation anxiety—and that's only because her schedule absorbs the majority of her time. Just having finished a 5K run, Peggy's cell tone is telling her she has an incoming call. Taking a towel to wipe the sweat from her face and hands, she answers, "Hello."

"Hi, big sister. This is your little sister. (Peggy was born two minutes earlier.) I'm just checking in. How's your training going?"

"It's going okay, I can't believe how good some of these girls are. I'm glad I didn't have to play against them in high school," reports Peggy. "What's going on at home?"

"Same stuff, only worse," response Julia. She spends the next few minutes filling Peggy in.

Peggy is far from being shocked. She takes a moment to study what Julia is relating and then, in a tone of regret, says, "I'm so sorry I'm not there to support you, sis."

"I miss you, too. So far, I've been doing okay. Thank God I've had a lot of support from Jim. Other than he and Gil nearly coming to blows, he's been wonderful," further adds Julia.

Referring back to Julia's rendition as to what went on between Jim and Gil, Peggy lends her opinion, "You've always been more forgiving than me. I've always regarded Gil as nothing more than a dirty old pervert. I'm the first to tell you there has never been any love lost between me and Gil. I'm with Jim on this one. Gil needs a good ass-whoopin'."

"You might think so as long as you're a couple hundred miles away but I gotta stay here and live with the results. Gil is so crazy that anything short of taking his life, I know he'll go to any length to get even."

Peggy has grown quiet on the other end; quiet enough to cause Julia to ask, "You still there?"

"Yeah, I'm still here," answers Peggy. Another pause before she gives cause for her moments of reflection. "I'm chewing on the thought of what we'll do if she doesn't make it. As much as we *should* be relieved for eliminating a pain in the neck that's been with us our entire life, and since she is truly *our* pain in the neck, we'd probably not know what to do without it."

Julia is on the same page with her sister. "Before she gets that far, the courts are going to have another go at her. She hasn't been sentenced yet. From what I understand, she may be ordered into long term treatment."

Once they've gotten past their mother problems and thoroughly stripped Gil of any redeeming value, they move on to discuss Julia's and Jim's relationship.

"Lucky you. Back in school, I always thought he had a stabilizing effect on his friends. Other than him trying to look like Arnold Schwarzenegger, I've always liked him," declares Peggy.

"Yeah, I know. I get the same kind of vibes from him. Just about the time I think we have some ancient curse haunting us, he seems to be able to put his finger on a solution. When Mom and Gil are driving me nuts, he's right there with his support—I just hope I'm not laying too much on him. But even without that, I like him a lot."

A couple hours have passed since this conversation began. With a solemn promise to continue to be there for one another, they end their chat.

Hearing a noise in the driveway, Julia peeks out her bedroom window to a welcomed sight—it's Jim. Quickly making her way past her mother's bedroom door to the sounds of two passed out drunks snorting and chortling their way through the night, she happily hops in the passenger seat. With a curious expression, she asks, "Not that I'm not happy to see you, but what are you doing?"

"I couldn't get you and your situation off my mind. I just don't feel right leaving you alone."

There is no question Julia is benefiting from the interest Jim is paying her. It seems each time they get together, they learn something new about one another. With each new discovery, Julia feels she is getting a glimpse of a Shangri-La that has alluded her. Not certain at times as to how much she should trust her feelings, she nonetheless, is beginning to care for him in a way she never imagined she could. After all, hasn't Jim revived her life in a way she never thought possible? When she's with him, she feels unshackled from the problems with her mother; at least for that period of time, they seem to be at a manageable distance. Some of Julia's best conversations are with Jim. He makes her feel like life has more to offer than just dealing with her mother's problems. He's also not afraid to compliment her when she's proven to be an asset in his life.

"Anyone who has dealt with parents like yours, who by any number of definitions, have abandoned you and your sister to deal with life alone—not to mention how well you've done—encourages me to believe that I can do the same with my family situation. I'm happy you're in my life," says Jim.

Because of their young age, these problems they're facing can be described as "difficult but workable." In many ways, the waves of life that are hell bent to destroy them, as they have to their parents before them, are already lapping at their backs. Many of their friends, with similar circumstances, are readily defining themselves as "victims," prepared to live their lives under its unsatisfied appetite to have more and more of each of them.

As is true of all of destructive forces, to give in to "victimization" comes with no effort. It's a very real and looming force among Peggy, Julia, and Jim. What begins as a whisper to "just give up" is becoming louder with the potential that they may overcome this voice and become healthy adults.

It can be assumed that neither of their parents grew up saying, "I think I'll become an alcoholic and destroy my life" or "I think I'll have an extra marital affair and destroy my family." Most often the lie that is acted on starts with a misconception that says, *"Not that I should share this advice with those of you I consider as common, weak people, but believing I have special powers given by God to defy the laws of nature to enable me to pee straight into the wind and not get wet—so I eat, drink, and be merry just to prove that I have these special gifts to defy any of these silly laws."*

As crazy as it sounds, these seeming innocuous concepts carry a power of their own capable of destroying entire nations leaving them to believe they have been victimized—not by their foolish decisions—but by some outside person, place, or thing. One of Jim's favorite sayings is, "If it's too good to be true, it probably is." Very few questions this logic but most are willing to play the odds that, *this time*, the situation warrants a stupid approach.

In their own way, without voicing it, Julia and Jim have found a way around the lack of parental stability due them, by being stable for each other. In giving of themselves for the sake of another has a power all its own. Its result is it will pull their hearts away from the influence of that whisper that grows louder as its demands get met to "just give up."

They are learning that their "getting" is a byproduct of their "giving." For Julia, this has been a long practice between her and Peggy but for Jim, he has a natural heart for it and only seems to need a recipient.

Now that the Subaru is out of commission, and Julia has no means of transportation other than her bicycle, Jim has an occasion to stop by. He is more than fine with this. "I couldn't get to sleep knowing that you're trapped over here with no car. I just had to check on you once more."

Julia has come to see this as Jim's norm. He has an over-developed sense of responsibility to control situations like this. "I'm glad to see you and believe me, I welcome your thoughtfulness. But I'm also ready to assure you that I can take care of myself."

"I wish I had more confidence in what you're saying, I just remember how much of an ass Gil can be to you. I believe him to be more vindictive than you know. I don't trust him—especially when he's drinking. And now, he's in the same house with you."

This is the only way of life Julia has known and has become common place. "I've got a lock on my door. Only Mother, Peggy, and I have a key. Besides, Gil knows I'd kill him if he ever tried to get in my room."

Jim is far from comforted by Julia's cavalier attitude. He looks as though he's ready to pull Gil out of the house and give him a thrashing. Julia gives him a smile and kisses him on his cheek along with the assuring words, "You worry too much. I'm a big girl, I can handle this."

For a moment, Jim is speechless. He is certain Julia is naïve about Gil, but has determined there is nothing he can do. With a sigh, he says, "Okay, Amazon Woman. If there is anything changing, I want to know about it."

"Don't worry. Everything is going to be okay."

Just as he feels some of the tension leaving, an ominous happening occurs. It's with some ordinary things that are part and parcel of daily life. A streetlight driving its beam through a swaying branch from the big maple in the front yard is creating an unsettling silhouette across Julia's face, giving it a Tragedy and Comedy theatre mask appearance. This seeming omen gives him the shivers.

Noticing the abrupt change in his demeanor, Julia says, "Jim, I think you need to go home and get some sleep."

"I probably do, but I can't help but feel something weird is going on." Finally concluding Julia is intent on doing it her own way, he reluctantly leaves, and Julia goes back to her room, locking her door behind her.

CHAPTER 16

A Telepathic Murder

Startled awake by an uncompromising struggle for air, Peggy Fortine sits straight up in bed, grasping at her neck, tearing at an imperceptible object tightening its grip around her throat, sending her whole body into a thrashing mode. Accompanying this strange phenomenon is the bad smell of alcohol and cigarette breath, along with the unmistakable stench of sweat and raspy, guttural sounds. All coming from her seeming assailant—only invisible. Her sympathetic nervous system sends her hands slashing out with the hopes of warding off this unseen assailant. Literally thrown from her bed to the floor, the dark of the room conceals what she imagines is the presence of her attacker. No sooner does she hit the floor when she feels the distinct sensation of a blunt instrument striking her skull and then another and another. She is surprised she is still conscious. With no notice, she is suddenly left alone. There is no sound to interrupt the silence other than her own heavy breathing. Not certain what she has just encountered, and not certain what she may yet be facing she musters the courage to turn on the lamp next to her bed. Even more perplexing, there are no visible injuries anywhere on her body. Her mind hits a dead end.

Not getting the satisfaction that her entire being is screaming for and finding it impossible to return to bed, she makes a cup of hot tea with the hopes this devilish experience will explain itself. There is nothing forthcoming.

Was this a dream? She attempts to reason through this seemingly unreasonable encounter. Everything in the bedroom is as neat as she had left it several hours earlier. Her clothing laid out for the next day is just as she had left them. Her dorm room door is still closed, and her window shades are still drawn, with no evidence anything has been tampered with.

With dawn approaching and a strong aversion to return to the bed that produced in her so much anxiousness, she chooses, instead, to curl up in her dorm room chair. She soon drifts back to sleep.

A full morning sun soon turns itself into a different reality. With the daylight easing her tension, Peggy's thoughts turn toward the here and now. She lets the early morning debacle remain as some weird unexplained anomaly.

*

The same morning arrives with Gil awaking, not sure where he is, he stumbles out of bed. No matter where he is there has to be a bathroom. Once his feet have hit the floor a number of things are beginning to look familiar. Staggering each foot side to side, but with enough forward momentum, he reels into the bathroom, barely in time to keep his shorts dry. While relieving himself, he struggles with remembering the circumstances that led him here. Alcohol blackouts are common with Gil; he can't account for whole blocks of time. Never totally comfortable with them; he fears the unknown surrounding them.

Finishing his bathroom calling, he attempts to clear his head enough to make it back to the bedroom without falling. The trek back requires he pass by the open stairway leading to the second story. What he sees is confusing. The dim morning light is casting a disturbing scene on a weakly lit stairway leading to the second floor. Julia appears to have fallen; she's lying headfirst halfway down the stairway. *"The little bitch probably got drunk and fell,"* is his initial thought. Curious, despite his foggy state, he makes the effort to negotiate the few steps to where her head lies. It's encrusted with dried blood; her eyes are half open with a blank stare. Lying on the step is a wrench he had used to replace some hoses on the Subaru. Picking it up, he uses it to nudge her.

"Hey, you!" he calls out, poking her at the same time. Failing to initiate a response, he pokes her again, yelling, "Wake up! What ya doin' sleepin' on the stairs?" Still not getting a reaction, he attempts to move her. She's as ridged as corpse. In his typical deranged manner, he takes it to the next level, saying, "What are ya, dead or somethin'?" When there's no response, he stumbles back to bed, but not before downing a half a pint of whiskey left over from the night before.

A few hours later, he comes to once again. This time, he considers it morning enough to get himself out of bed. Attempting to sort out his clothing that's in disarray all across the bedroom floor, the scene of Julia lying on the stairs comes through his thoughts. Not seeing Sylvia in bed he's hoping she's dealt with the problem. "I hate dealin' with that kid. She's a little witch." Feeling the effects of a hangover, Gil stumbles around looking for any drinks that may have been left over from the day before. Making his way out of the bedroom toward the bathroom, he comes across the scene he had left a few hours ago. This time, Sylvia is sitting on the stairs with Julia's head in her lap, stroking her hair. She has a vacant gaze. Remembering what he had hoped would not be here when he woke up is not to be.

"So, what's the deal, she and that punk boyfriend of hers get drunk?"

With the same, continuous stare, Sylvia states, "She's dead Gil." Her voice is empty of any emotion, as she further underscores, "My baby's dead Gil. What am I going to do?"

With the same deadpan look Gil gives almost all happenings, this is *definitely* not something he wants to deal with. To satisfy a searching, alcohol-soaked brain, he forces himself up the same steps he climbed a few hours ago. The scene is the same. Whenever he has an alcoholic blackout, he is never certain about anything. Seeing his wrench lying on the step makes him more uncertain. *"Did I have anything to do with this?"* is his singular thought. *"I never liked her, and I know damn well she couldn't stand me, but ... did I do this?"* is his continuous thought.

The fact that he can't remember causes him to have more guilt feelings. In a flash back to some thirty-plus years ago, he remembers his father going head long down a flight of stairs. An overwhelming fear he can't control is gripping his whole person. When this phenomenon takes possession of him, he flees. Without a further word to Sylvia, he is hurrying, terrified, out the door.

Sylvia hardly notices Gil leaving. She is in her own world. Still holding Julia's head, she begins to rock. Recalling the words to a lullaby sang to her as a child begins to take form. It's a song her grandmother sang to her before she went to bed.

"Sleep my child and peace attend thee,

All through the night.

Guardian angels, God hath sent thee,

All through the night.

Soft the drowsy hours creeping,

Hill and dale are slumber sleeping,

I, my loving vigil keeping,

All through the night."

In soft tones of a mother caring for a small child, Sylvia continues her bizarre behavior, stroking Julia's hair and gently kissing her forehead.

"O, why did this have to happen? It didn't have to be," laments Sylvia. Her derangement digs a deeper trench into her psyche as she wipes the encrusted blood away from her face and attempts to sit Julia's stiffened body on a step. "Come on sweetie, sit up for mommy."

Sylvia's mental regression is interrupted by the front door opening. "I just saw Gil tear out of the drive way, he nearly ran me over! What the heck is going on?" shouts Jim entering the house. He's come to pick Julia up for work but what he is confronted with goes beyond anything he could ever imagine. Seeing this off the wall behavior with Sylvia and the odd position Julia is in stops him dead in his tracks. This wacky scenario is too irregular to be processed as reality.

"What the heck is happening? What's the matter with Julia?

Sylvia pays no attention to Jim rather continues her effort to try and sit Julia upright. "Come on sweetie, help mommy you're getting to be such a big girl."

A flash of realism is quickly replacing his first impression that somehow what he is seeing is make-believe. Speechless, powerless, frozen in his tracks, Jim tries to develop some sense of reality with what's being presented by Sylvia and Julia.

Rushing to the stairway, he shoves Sylvia out of the way and grabs Julia. What he views and what he feels is not making any sense. The happy thoughts he was entertaining only minutes ago in anticipation of being with Julia once again have suddenly taken on a dark demonic perspective.

Still holding Julia's lifeless body, Jim's mind returns to Gil nearly running him over. He turns toward Sylvia, "He did this didn't he?" he shouts.

Sylvia is only able to mutter some unintelligible utterances. It's obvious that she is no longer in possession of her mind—at least in any rational way. Without a second thought, Jim is on his phone dialing the 911 number. His voice breaks as he reports the nature of his emergency. Closing out his call there is nothing left to do but wait. In frustration, he runs his hands through his hair, clasps his face between both hands with the hopes that this gruesome scene will somehow make sense. As this is all going on another strange phenomenon is unfolding. Julia's phone tone is sounding. It's coming from her bedroom. Jim steps over Julia's body as he makes way up the steps leading to her bedroom. Seeing the phone on the floor along with a room that appears to have had a tornado rip it apart, he answers the call, "Hello."

"Hello. Who is this?"

Jim immediately recognizes the voice as Peggy. "This is Jim, Peggy." They both pause for a second. Neither knows what the next words should be.

Peggy is the next to speak, "What's going on Jim?" He hears a tone of nervousness in her voice.

Not knowing how to respond; not able to form the words, he finally says, "It's awful Peggy, Julia is dead!"

The silence is resounding. Peggy responds saying, "It did happen! It is true! What I went through happened! I'm on my way home!"

By now, the sirens are in the front yard. It's made up of the full village contingency of an ambulance and Greeny's squad car. Within seconds both ambulance attendances and Greeny are reviewing the scene. Pictures are being taken from every angle before anything is moved. Along with the injuries on her skull, Greeny takes note of the bloody wrench lying alongside Julia's body and some unusual bruises nearly encircling Julia's throat. He takes several more pictures. Seeing things are out of his pay grade, he makes a call to the State Police. Another hour goes by, and they take over much of the investigation.

Satisfied the body can be moved, Greeny, in his official, investigatory voice, says, "We're gonna need an autopsy, so get her to the county morgue."

In as respectful a manner as possible, the attendants remove Julia to the waiting ambulance. Greeny proceeds with his investigation, ordering Jim and Sylvia to remain where they are. Entering the bedroom with the State Police crime team, Greeny is met with the same ghastly sight met by Jim on retrieving Julia's phone. Other than the clutter, he notices a long uncut piece of hose used to fix a faulty connection between a water pump and a radiator in an automobile and the heavy crescent wrench found on the stairway. Remembering the clutter of auto parts and tools strewn around the Subaru, Greeny makes a mental connection: *That piece of hose and wrench probably came from that bunch of crap in the yard.*

Greeny has some insight here that the State Police don't have. He knows who's responsible for all the clutter involving the Subaru. *"I know who's been working on that car, and I know the connection between that person and Sylvia."* He has only one person in mind: Harold "Gil" Gilles. He also notices, what he trusts to be a connection between the wrench that he believes to have caused Julia's head trauma, as belonging to a set left in the back seat of the Subaru. He also is linking the auto water hose found in the bedroom to the bruises around Julia's neck and the wrench with the Subaru.

With the State Police crime lab involved with the forensics, Greeny has already determined this as a murder. Turning to Sylvia and Jim—Sylvia first, he asks, "I know this is hard on you Sylvia but tell me how you discovered Julia?"

Sylvia is still sitting and staring blankly around the room. She begins her muttering again, "My baby didn't have to die. It's all his fault. I told him to leave her alone—don't go near her. I always knew he wanted her." Then she bursts into sobs, still muttering, "I told him to stay away from her. Just leave her alone. Now look what's happened. I love you, Gil. Why couldn't you listen to me?"

Seeing Sylvia is in no condition to give him the answers he's seeking, Greeny turns his attention to Jim. Jim doesn't waste a minute telling Greeny everything he knows along with his own hypothesis, "I know Gil done this. He couldn't get out of here fast enough. He's been a threat to Julia as long as I've had a relationship with her and then some."

Greeny continues with his investigation. Finalizing what he needs to finish here, he has already made a decision to track down Gil. Gil's trailer has been the focus of other investigations where it's questionable where some of Gil's "collection" of one of everything God and man has ever produced comes from. It lies in piles with blue tarps covering them.

Making the mile trip, Greeny discovers Gil's pickup is parked in the yard. "Well at least he's still here," say Greeny out loud to himself, satisfied he can get further down the road with his investigation. Bang, bang, bang. The sound emanates from the partially closed screen door slamming against door frame as Greeny continues to slap it. What is evident is Gil either inside preferring not to answer or is no longer here. After several verbal attempts to roust Gil to the door have failed, Greeny decides he's going to have to get a search warrant. This is going to take a few hours.

Late in the afternoon, the State Police finally finish with their investigation. By this time of the day, Sylvia is more withdrawn than ever. She has not been a dependable witness; she's always veering off into some pained diatribe no one could follow. Preferring not to stay with Sylvia, Jim leaves, wishing to be alone and sort out his own thoughts. He can't believe what has happened. It's still so surreal, as though somebody will come forth an declare it all a big hoax.

Peggy has made arrangements with a bus transit to get her home. Jim has made arrangements to pick her up at the bus station. They have kept in contact over their cell phones allowing them to establish a coordinated timetable. This busy work is welcomed by both them, as it doesn't allow for long uninterrupted thought periods. By early evening Jim has made the half-hour trip to pick Peggy up at the regional bus terminal. It's a strategically located to serve this section of the state. The meeting is clumsy at best. They end up trying to give each other a comforting hug which wakes up the grief they had been holding back until they met. Words are not needed for this occasion. It ends in both of them crying uncontrollably. They have a reason for waiting for this reunion. They were always drawn together by their love for the same person, and now they are drawn together by the loss of her. It's a feeling that declares if they can be together— If they can morn their lose together—it will prevent Julia from being quite as dead as she would be if they didn't. They both have a stake in hanging on to everything about Julia that smacks of life.

Time isn't stopping in the here and now. Soon, they make the next discussion about their personal involvements in the events leading up to this moment. Jim fills her in as best he can.

Peggy can't wait to replay her own experience that she shared with her sister's struggle with the murderer and murder.

"Jim, I was with her in the whole struggle, like we've always been with events in our lives—we've always fought them together. I smelled the foul tobacco, alcohol breath of the murderer and the smell of his sweat. I felt the tightening around her neck, the blows to her head, the fall down the steps—everything until she was dead. I dreaded thinking about it because I knew what must have happened. All morning I wanted to call. I finally did, and when you answered her phone, I knew something bad had happed to my sister. I hoped for the best, but all along, my heart knew the worst. God help me! What am I going to do without her?"

Suddenly there is a break in Peggy's thought process as she readjusts her disposition. It's not as emotionally charged, as some would expect considering the nature of her next question. "How's my mother doing in all this?" The question is one of concern but not much different than if she were asking how the house was handling it.

Jim notices the shift in her attitude with this question. "She's lost it mentally. It's hard to tell if it's because of the booze or the shock. Regardless, she's flipped out."

Considering Jim's assessment for a moment, Peggy begs for more explanation. "What do you mean?"

"It's weird. She'll have a blank stare, then suddenly she'll start blaming Gil for Julia's murder, then in the next breath she'll be carrying on how much she loves him. The police stopped questioning her because she was just babbling—none of it made any sense."

The trip from the bus station to town took about as long as the conversation lasts. With nothing more to say, Jim pulls into Peggy's driveway. The yellow tape surrounding the area carries a clarifying reality along with it; it brings home the permanence of their changing lives; that Julia is gone.

Both sit for a moment, staring at the house. Jim turns to Peggy. The look on his face has a lonely desperation. "I'd like to stay with you through this if you don't mind. I know there are going to be funeral arrangements to be made, besides, I'm not certain I want to be alone just yet." The tears are beginning to flow again with both as they clasp each other's hand for support.

The scene they encounter as they enter the front door is as disturbing as Jim had portrayed it. What is more disturbing than the mess is Sylvia's drunken image, towel in hand, angrily slurring her words, as she forcefully attempts to clean Julia's blood from the stairway. "You've gotten the house all dirty again, Julia. All you do is make more work for me."

Stymied as to what to do, they helplessly watch Sylvia go through a chilling reprimand toward her dead daughter. Peggy slowly makes her way toward the stairway. If her mother has noticed her, she hasn't let on as she continues her diatribe and scrubbing action. With her mother's back still toward her, Peggy places her hand on her mother's shoulder. "Mother?" There's more of a question in Peggy's voice than a salutation.

Sylvia's entire body recoils with a gasping sound at the touch. Seeing Peggy standing in front of her churns out another surprising reaction. "He best keep away from you, too. You don't need to die, too. It's all Gil's fault. I told him to stay away from you girls." Snaking her bony hand inside her blouse to adjust a strap that's slipped out and over her shoulder, she turns back to her scrubbing duties. Stopping short, she immediately begins another bizarre discourse, "Gil, you know I love you. I told you to leave my girls alone. You just don't listen."

After this unsettling encounter with her mother, Peggy turns to Jim, saying, "I can't stay here. This is too off the wall. My sister's dead, and my mother has lost her mind." Her eyes haven't dried since she arrived.

Placing his arm around her, Jim gives as much reassurance as he can. "We have an empty counselor's cabin at the camp. I know I can make arrangements for you to stay there."

"I just want to be alone, without a lot of people."

On the way to the camp, they stop by the funeral home and make arrangements for Julia after the morgue completes the autopsy. They also stop by the police station. Greeny welcomes them with as much sympathy as is protocol for a professional law enforcement officer. His tone is dutiful and respectful.

Jim can't contain his desire to find out as much of Gil's whereabouts as Greeny is willing to reveal. "I have a search warrant. The problem is the only thing that's left is all his junk. Evidently he left on a motorcycle he had stored in one of those junk sheds all over the property—at least, that's what the neighbors have told me."

"Hanging's too good for that scumbag. He needs to pay for what he's done, and it can start with a good beating," declares Jim.

Greeny listens respectfully. He may feel the same, but very seldom does he let out feelings that could compromise his investigation. "We've tagged him as a person of interest. It's gone out statewide. Hopefully, we'll get a response soon."

Greeny's way is to avoid the public as much as possible so as not to be put on the spot to answer questions. This short conversation is all Jim and Peggy are going to get from Greeny, as he has excused himself for another call, leaving the two of them with his female dispatcher answering the 911 calls. It just happens this young woman is Jim's first cousin on his mother's side. As soon as Greeny is out of sight, Jim's attention turns to his cousin.

"Lily, will you do me a favor and let me know anything that comes into this office of the whereabouts of Harold Gilles?" asks Jim.

Lily listens pensively, as she weighs what Jim is asking her to do, against what it can cost her if she gets caught.

"I know what Julia means to you Jim, and I feel bad for you, but you know what a stickler Greeny is about anyone knowing where his investigations lead him," answers Lily.

"I know I'm asking a lot of you, but if you change your mind, I'd appreciate a call," recaps Jim with another plea. Giving his cousin a sisterly hug, he and Peggy leave, left to rely on their own intuitions.

Chapter 16

A Steely Commitment

The next few days prove to be emotionally stressful for all involved. They've managed to get past the funeral. Jim was able to have his Presbyterian minister conduct the service. Sylvia wasn't able to make it. She managed to get her hands on several bottles of cheap wine and was in no condition to do anything other than drink, puke, and sleep.

The following afternoon, she missed her morning court appointment. Greeny has come to the house with a warrant. He finds her passed out—more dead than alive. After waking her, she begins her drivel, "Why don't you just leave me alone, I want to join my daughter. They want me. I've seen 'em. They're ready for me."

"Well, today the judge was ready for you and you didn't appear, so, now we have a warrant for you called "failure to appear." Greeny has already dealt with Sylvia's DT's and is readying himself to repeat the same scenario. Recently, it's as though Sylvia has crossed a line with her drinking and has established a permanent sense of community with her misery.

"Well, just haul me off Greeny, I'm all ready to go," she says, butting a cigarette she has just used to light a new one.

Taking her arms and placing them behind her back, Greeny places the required handcuffs on her wrists. The smoke from her freshly lit cigarette is finding its way into her right eye, causing her to squint. The whole scene looks like an episode from *Cops.*

"Get your smokin' done between here and my car, 'cause you ain't smokin' inside it," declares Greeny, leading Sylvia out by the arm.

As soon as Sylvia finds herself outside, Jim and Peggy are pulling in. Peggy, seeing her mother in handcuffs for the first time, jumps from the still moving truck. The panic is clearly seen in her.

"Mother, what have you done?" shouts Peggy over the roar of the trucks motor.

Greeny quickly steps between Peggy and her handcuffed mother. "I'm going to ask you to step back," orders Greeny.

"I'm not stepping back until you tell me why you have my mother in handcuffs—she's not a criminal!"

By this time Jim has his truck parked and has put himself between Peggy and Greeny. Having seen how belligerent Sylvia can be when she's drinking, Jim knows the outcome of this episode if she should get it in her head to resist. Greeny doesn't answer Peggy's question rather poses another question to Sylvia. "You got any animals you're leavin' behind?"

"Just that dog Gil, unless he's hidin' out somewhere up in the UP. He always runs there when he knows he's done somethin' wrong."

This is the kind of information Jim's been waiting to hear. He notices Greeny had a slight pause hearing the same evidence. Jim's mind is turning somersaults. With a slight head gesture, he motions to Peggy to get back in the truck. Once they're alone, Jim reveals the singleness of purpose he's been harboring. "Peggy, I believe your mother is on to something. I believe if I were Gil and wanted to hide, I'd look for a place I knew. It only makes sense that he'd head home."

Peggy senses the excitement in Jim's voice. "Are you suggesting that we know something we should share with the police?"

Measuring his words before he speaks, Jim says, "I'm suggesting we should follow up on that information and verify it before we go to the police. Whether it's justice or retribution, I want be the one who brings him in."

"I know Gil too. I've always sensed him to be a coward—a real bully. He never would have dared threaten either Julia or me when we were together," says Peggy, then adds, "What do you plan to do?"

"I'd like to make a trip to the UP and let Gil know that he may be in the woods—and should stay there—because he'll never be out of the woods with me. I'll hunt him 'til he has no more places to hide."

Peggy is listening to him. She knows Jim well enough to know his outward zeal only runs a second place to his inward fervor. Whenever he's committed himself to a project, it's never half measures. With a moment's thought, she asserts, "I want to be a part of this."

Jim looks at her with a look that is so blank that without words it can't be deciphered. His reaction is one of uncertainty. "Are you certain? Because once I start, I'm not going to stop until I'm satisfied he's gettin' what's comin' to him."

"I know that—that's why I wanna join—I feel the same way," commits Peggy. The strength of her commitment is not only in her words but can also be seen in a steeliness set in her eyes.

CHAPTER 17

Any Old Port in a Storm

He doesn't remember where he picked it up. It's an old motorcycle, but it's always been a good runner. Gil is familiar with the mechanics of both this old two-wheeler and the terrain. He crossed over the giant Mackinac Bridge an hour ago. He always looks forward to having that part of his trip behind him. It always brings with it a sense of being in familiar territory. This gives him a sense of refuge. If he doesn't want to be seen, he knows how to blend into the Upper Peninsula wilderness in such a way that only God knows where he is.

The purpose behind taking the motorcycle in lieu of his truck is simple economy. It requires a fraction of the fuel, and it's easier to maneuver around in off-road rough terrain in the event that he should find himself pursued.

Men like Gil are never secure in anything involving people—including themselves. Because of this glitch, his normal demeanor is to be defensive and stay as reclusive as he can. That is, until he starts drinking—then all bets are off.

At the present, he's charging across the Seney strip in Michigan's Upper Peninsula with the intention of making his way into the northern most part of the state known as the Keweenaw Peninsula. As a youngster, he and a cousin spent much of their time breaking into cabins to steal liquor, or anything of value that could be sold. The memories of these opportunities of yesteryear feed his idea to use these unoccupied tourist cabins as hideouts. There's usually a larder of canned goods in each one.

Before leaving, he drained the gas out of his reserve gas can to fill his bike fuel tank. Believing that every minute counts, Gil is too scared to stop in unfamiliar territory for fear his getaway could be thwarted; he is ongoing until the terrain looks like the stuff he knows something about. His gas gauge says he still has a quarter tank left. This information and the fact he's had clear sailing gives him the pluck he needs to stop at a gas station—hopefully one with a party store. As luck would have it, up ahead he spots a Speedway station with a party store. Gil's natural paranoia kicks in as he slows to a stop. With a wary eye that only the guilty have, he hurries through his shopping. Finishing, he's soon back on the road with a full tank of gas and a saddlebag full of beer.

The late afternoon wears into an early evening. It's beginning to cloud over and cool down. Michigan's Upper Peninsula is in an entirely different weather pattern than the Lower Peninsula. Its northern shore line looks like it could rain any minute. Gil has already turned off the main highway. His method is to begin to look for a drive way with a chain across it. This tells him there is no one there. Within a few minutes of cruising, he comes across what appears to be exactly what he has been looking for. There are two painted green metal posts with a chain draped between, with a sign attached to the center saying, "KEEP OUT" and a heavy-duty padlock securing one end to an equally heavy-duty ring welded to the post. On each side of the posts are woods. This is perfect to prevent large vehicles from circumventing the barrier, but totally inadequate to keep a motorcycle from merely going around and between a few trees. There are also no close neighbors to notice an intruder. It's a dirt two-track with uninjured grass growing in the track. This is a good indication that no one's been here since the spring grass began growing. Slowly making his way down the quarter-mile tree-canopied corridor, Gil keeps a wary eye open for any witnesses. As a young thief, he always prided himself on providing himself with an escape route. This is also his method for this gamble. The driveway is economic in that it is a straight shot sunk an eighth of a mile into the woods, where it suddenly breaks into a half-acre open field with wild grasses, a green tarpapered shack with a makeshift overhang above the only door, and a stack of fire wood. Off to the side, there's an outhouse covered with the same green tarpaper.

Stopping his bike at the end of the driveway, Gil takes stock of his chances of bedding down here for the night. There are no tire prints anywhere, indicating that this place is not frequently used. So far, it looks as though it meets his needs. Not one to let his guard down, Gil proceeds with caution ready to respond to any emerging danger. Straddling his bike with the motor still running, he walks it warily toward the shack. With each step, he gains a bit more confidence telling him he has chosen wisely. He is now within ten feet of the shack. Shutting the motor off, he remains on the saddle to reassess the possibility of some sounds he would have missed. It doesn't take but a couple seconds before he hears what sounds like the squeak of an unoiled door hinge. Surprised, he twists as much of himself around to meet an elderly woman with long grey hair and an ankle-length dress emerging from the outhouse. She is also pointing a rifle straight at him as she fires a shot. Gil barely has time to blink as he hears the whizz of the spent round speeding by his head. Frozen on his bike, the only reaction he has is the involuntary muscle in his stomach stuck in his throat. Before he can process any of this, he hears the metal-on-metal sound of the bolt of the rifle ejecting the spent casing and jamming another live round into the chamber. The next sound is from the lady herself.

"I don't know who you are or what you think you may be needin', but I'm here to tell ya, I'm only seconds away from a fit, and you're in the middle of my road. If you ain't off my land in thirty seconds, I'm gonna drop you like a bad habit!"

The chill of surprised fright has already climbed from Gil's ankles to the back of his head. There isn't a hair on his body that isn't standing straight up. Everything that's happened to Gil in the last few seconds has all suddenly turned to adrenalin. With barely any forethought, he has kick started his bike, has it turned around, in gear, and speeding down the driveway. In the split second after he had turned his head around to see what this lady is about to do next, he finds himself flying head first over his handlebars and into a thicket of saplings that are just waiting for the opportunity to make his life a bit more miserable.

Panicked and perceiving he has injured his foot, he nonetheless gets to his feet in time to hear another round whizz by his head. With all the mind and body strength he can muster, he picks his bike up. With a quick examination, he discovers the handlebars have been thrown out of line. There is no time to fix them, he struggles with the pain in his ankle to get his bike upright and restarted. Once back on the two-track, he can't get out of rifle range fast enough. In a matter of seconds, he has once again smartly circumvented the chained gate and is back on the road.

Still shaking from this experience, Gil has reignited all the fear he had engendered from this morning's incident. With no plan other than to escape, he rides blindly on, hardly noticing how the clouds have opened up dumping a summer deluge of water, creating a foggy mist as it hits the hot surface of the highway. Along with the splatter of each car or truck encountered, it all adds just another layer of misery to his already drenched mind, body, and soul.

Gil's thinking has clouded over once again. Barely noticing his soaked to the skin condition, swelling ankle, and twisted handlebars, he rides thoughtlessly on. As long as he's moving, he feels his fears won't push him beyond the brink of sanity.

As the rain subsists, it's quickly replaced by a cold front that's made its way across Lake Superior. With the fear of the earlier episode becoming more distant, the reality of Gil's physical condition is suddenly trumping his mental condition; he's realizing how cold and wet he is. With little choice as to how this is to be dealt with, his limited funds and his paranoia about getting caught, lead him to be on the lookout for "any old port in the storm." With the dimness of the evening giving a brief pause to the oncoming darkness, he notices an abandoned house along the highway with no paint, with trees and brush consuming its exterior, and an abundance of tall grasses for the surrounding grounds. Still smarting from his earlier experience, he takes an extra-long time to review this possibility. Had this been seen before the old-lady-with-a-gun incident, he would have ignored it, but at this juncture, it's reached the crisis stage. With the daylight waning, there are no other options—it's either stay here or spend the night in the open.

As he looks the old house over, his mind tells him this option is probably going to prove one notch above staying in the open and he better act on it while he still has some daylight. Opting to risk riding his bike through the tangled yard rather than try to push it with a swollen ankle, he gives it enough gas to power his way to the rear of the building. Satisfied he's concealed his bike well enough; he dismounts, dislodges his saddlebags, and makes his way to the entrance. What faces him is momentarily disconcerting. He's facing a back stoop that's has a tree growing through the center. The tree seems to be the main support for the otherwise tumbling down back porch with a full complement of rotting steps. Gingerly making his way up the three steps, he confronts the door. It's not locked, rather warped shut. A good stiff kick at the bottom springs it open. What he is viewing is what's left of a kitchen. There is the remainder of kitchen counters, a small inside hand operated water pump, a small wood burning stove hooked to the remnant of what appears to be a water heater, and lots and lots of dirt.

Anyone other than Gil would probably wonder what kind of families had lived here and what may have led to the house being unoccupied for what appears to be fifty years or more. But Gil's only interest is how its remains can service his needs. What catches his attention is the small wood stove. It still appears to be functional. "I ain't riskin' anybody seein' the smoke comin' outta this stove while it's still daylight," he muses to himself. Without hesitation, he begins to break up what's left of an old table, stacking the wood in front of the old stove and wait until dark.

Suffering through uncontrolled shivers brought on by his wet clothing and the pain from his swollen ankle, he manages to get a fire started. The fire inside is forcing its glow through the small cracks left in the stove giving just enough light to aid in stripping himself of his wet clothing. This proves equally as paramount as getting a couple of beers down and is done together. His supper consists of a packet of beef jerky and a couple more beers. Soon his clothes have dried well enough to put back on. He hasn't had a drink of alcohol since he stormed out of Sylvia's early this morning. His body tells him he needs a few more cigarettes, a couple more beers, and sleep will begin to replace his ongoing anxiety.

CHAPTER 18

Tractors, Trucks, and Yoopers

Meanwhile, Greeny is utilizing his search warrant to glean through Gil's belongings in hopes of discovering any clues as to where he should be directing his energies to bring Gil to justice.

"I've never seen the likes of this. I don't know how anybody can live like this. He's got junk layin' around everywhere," exclaims Greeny to one of his deputies. "If it's been cast aside by anyone, Gil would have imagined a use for it—and not necessarily any time soon."

Greeny is certain Gil is noncompliant for nearly every litter ordinance in the village.

The search remains fruitless. Everything Gil owns inside and outside his trailer is stacked at least waist high. The only mail Gil has received are late statements for everything from gas bills to his cell phone. His method has always been to never pay for things until he was put into collection. His idea was that by this time, his creditors would be happy with anything he was willing to pay.

His cell phone is the only thing that creates an interest. The trust is that he has it on his person, and if its use can be monitored, they can determine what part of the state he may be in. It'll take another legal trick to get that done. It will take some time.

Meanwhile, Sylvia finds herself back in jail. It doesn't take long before her health deteriorates again, and the decision is made to minimize any kind of civil lawsuit and place her back in the hospital. She's kept overnight. Once stabilized, she's sent back to jail. Her wait here is quickly translocated to the courtroom where the presiding judge is vigorously reviewing her record. Sylvia is left to stand alongside her court appointed attorney while this judge flips each document over until he's satisfied that he's finished studying its contents. Finally concluding, he removes his glasses, looks squarely at Sylvia standing in front of him, shackled in her orange colored county jail coveralls, and with a voice tinged with alarming concern, says, "Mrs. Fortine, I believe you have a drinking problem. The number of infractions that you've incurred, ranging from misdemeanors to felonies, are too numerous to discuss here." Still with a steady voice, he continues, "You are a danger not only to society, but to yourself. Instead of giving you the lengthy jail sentence each of your infractions ask for, I'm going to send you to an alcoholic rehabilitation center. This is not optional. If you violate this court order, I'll reimpose the sentence guidelines and you'll spend the time in jail until your sentence is completed. Do you understand?"

Sylvia looks at her attorney. He nods, indicating that this is the best she is going to get. She then looks back to the judge, answering, "Yes sir, I understand."

The judge accepts her answer. Not ready to stop yet, he continues, "You will be expected to stay the entire ninety days, and there will be court oversight to ensure that you aren't violating the mandates of your sentence."

Meanwhile, in another location, Peggy and Jim are straining at the leash to get after Gil. Their response to the loss of Julia is an intense feeling of hatred for this murderer— one Harold "Gil" Gilles. Peggy has heard him talk incessantly about the northern Michigan region he's from. Neither, she nor Jim have been to the UP and have no idea it's geography, other than its size.

In her desire to bring Gil to justice, Peggy is trying her best to put together enough of the details she remembers from over hearing Gil and her mother's drunken conversations. This is one time Peggy wishes she had paid closer attention to Gil's constant prattling, and especially about his cousin Ike. It seems they got in a lot of trouble together when they were younger.

In her investigative endeavor, Peggy is attempting to think like Gil. In order to do that she has to set aside her own moral compass and take on the mind of a criminal. In this case it's the man she is certain is responsible for her sister's death. "I think he'll head back to where he thinks he'll be safe," is her conclusion.

Without much of a plan other than to get to the get to the same region that Gil claims as his "hood" and play it by ear. Peggy and Jim compile a stockpile of borrowed camping gear from the camp, all the cash they have between them, and an unrelenting resolve to bring Gil in dead or alive. With Jim's truck packed, on this late July morning, they begin their campaign. A cold front with a substantial supply of rain greets them. The weather forecast predicts they will drive out of this mess before they reach the Mackinac Bridge.

There is an air of unpredictability about this whole affair. It's Jim's nature to have a plan in place before he gives it, his time and effort. In this case the only plan in place is to get to the area they believe Gil is likely to escape to. When that leg of the mission is complete, the next effort will be to hunt down this cousin of Gil's named Ike Gilles—providing he's not in prison—with the idea that somehow, he will lead them to Gil. That's the part that's still problematic for Jim. He generally likes things a lot clearer.

Peggy on the other hand is much more fixated and willing to take a chance and see how things work out. What can be said of each is they are equally obsessed with bringing Gil to justice. As is true with many situations like this, Gil's worth has to be reduced below the level of human in order to hunt him as one would a wild animal. How this is to be accomplished is yet to be worked out.

*

Gil is awakened by a sound he is familiar with: the throaty chirp only a racoon can make. After a restless night of trying to sleep on a bare, dirt-laden floor with the throbbing pain only slightly dulled by his continual consumption of the beer he had packed in his saddlebags, he finds he has invaded the home of a mother racoon with several kits. After a night of hunting, she is letting it be known she isn't happy to share her space with this interloper. She is visibly upset as she holds her ground, angerly bobbing her head and growling, hissing and a few other sounds Gil knows to be the sounds of an aggressive female defending her kits. Rather than risk being further incapacitated by a racoon bite, he wisely decides to vacate. With one eye on the screeching, very aggressive mother, he carefully picks up his saddlebags and shoes, slowly backing out the door.

The dawn has brought with it a dampness supplied by the previous evening rain. Gil is far from rested. The pain in his ankle is severe. Sitting on the step, he pulls his sock down to a swollen, yellow-green foot that rebels against any pressure. It's clearly severely sprained. With no other options, Gil replaces the sock and gingerly maneuvers his foot into his sneaker, tightening it as much as he can bear. With both shoes on, he gets to his feet to test his pain level. It's tolerable, but his steps need to be regulated, causing him to limp. With a deep breath, he makes his way to his bike. The only plan he has for the moment is to get back on the road. The skewed handlebar is still apparent, but he's met with an even more disconcerting dilemma—a flat tire.

"What the—!" is his only intelligible sound, the rest are a series of moans, and sighs. He has a patch kit, but no air pump to inflate the airless tire. His options are limited to only one thing—crawling. In a rage he tips the useless bike to the ground and begins a series of kicking it with his injured foot as though they both deserve more punishment. The senseless action leads him to rolling and moaning on the ground, holding his tortured foot. Exhausted, he lies flat on his back, staring straight into the open sky when he sees another debasing action heading straight for him. A starling has taken notice of him too close to its nest and is sending a missile of bird poop directly at him. Whether he has time to avert the inevitable or deservedly takes the load, only Gil knows. But the end result is the feeling along with the sound of a splat as it hits his forehead. Gil continues to lie motionless. After a few more deep breaths and a few more sighs, he resigns himself to his new atonement. His mind digs back below the several layers of bad luck to the one that still has him in its grip.

"I don't remember anything about killin' Sylvia's kid. I can't believe I did that. I know I thought about more'n once. I don't know.... I know I probably killed my ol' man, but I didn't think pushin' him down the steps was gonna kill 'im. I was only hopin' to break his leg or somethin'. Hell, I dunno, I prob'ly killed the little bitch, too."

Still on his back in the weeds, in the back yard of an unnerving old abandoned house some place in Michigan's UP, Gil remains transfixed with thoughts he can't resolve or make go away. He's tortured by the anxieties that make everything in his life uncertain. Men like Gil have always been prejudiced in their own behalf and have no problem turning themselves into victims. With no effort, his emotions take him to a familiar place where he wallows in resentments hating everything and everybody—including himself. It's a familiar place for Gil to be—so much so that it feels like home. He has no difficulty reviewing the methods he'd use to retaliate against everyone that's challenged his purposes. This is the stuff that drives him, giving his life motive.

Scrounging around, Gil examines his package of cigarettes that have dried out from yesterday's deluge. Cigarettes run through a rainstorm take on their own qualities. In this case, they are guaranteed to make the smoker feel as though smoking rope would be more satisfying. None of this can dissuade a committed smoker, who has to adapt to whatever variations his nicotine sticks have taken on. It's a simple thing to expect. They have taken on the yellow-brown color of a bad diaper. Nevertheless, out of desperation for the needed nicotine, he lights one. It tastes like his socks smell. In Gil's world, taste is secondary to effect—and that includes cigarettes. Without hesitation, he pulls the amorphous vapors to the bottom of his lungs to await the pulmonary orgasm.

With the fag hanging from his mouth, Gil exhales through his nose, adding another layer to his already nicotine-stained nostrils. His hands are busy opening one of his few remaining beers. It's warm, splitting its sudsy essence between finding its way down his throat and blowing out his nose. Convinced he thinks better after he's had a few beers, Gil settles into his usual morning routine of hacking, coughing, smoking, and getting a couple beers down. After the dark, rainy, dismal yesterday, the bright light in the sky is giving evidence to it being either the second coming of Christ or the sun making its way back.

Gil's thoughts soon turn to his next move. Since using his motorcycle is out of the question and not wanting to revisit the mother raccoon, he begins to search around the outside grounds for an adequate walking stick. His efforts soon turn up a weather-hardened hoe handle lying idle in the grass.

"Perfect!" he exclaims out loud. He meets this apparatus with the same exuberance one would a chauffeured limo. It's giving him something to lean on as he begins his *slow* but *determined* hobble down the road. As he begins his trek, it proves to be *slow,* but the determined part has worn slim after the first forty-five minutes. Leaning on his pole and out breath, he speaks aloud, "How'd I ever get in this mess?" At the same time, he takes note of a field on the other side of the road. It's a hay field. Not only that, there is a truck loaded with hay bales making its way out. Certainly not wanting to be seen by anyone that could identify him, Gil ducks into some tall grass and lies down, besides he's more interested in the tractor that's been left alone, than he is in hooking a ride with the truck driver. As soon as the truck along with its driver are no longer in sight, Gil, still leaning heavily on his staff, tentatively makes his way into the field where the tractor sits unattended. Cautiously, he looks in all directions to assure himself he's alone. Propping his walking stick against one of the wheels, he daringly climbs the several feet up into its cab.

"Well, I'll be—!"

He never finishes the sentence, but is overcome with delight when he discovers the key is in the ignition, just waiting for him to start it and steal it. Without hesitation, Gil snatches up his walking stick, turns the key, puts it in gear, and makes his way to the road. Without hesitation of mind or body, he looks to the right and to the left, opting to go to the left—the opposite direction as the truck. As usual, Gil pushes straight forward, always hesitating to look back over his shoulder for fear something or somebody is gaining on him. His hope is another door will open before that happens.

His eyes are never idle when he imagines it's just him the world is after and he is his only ally. With an eye open for another opportunity he realizes the tractor can only take him so far, besides it draws too much attention. It can only be a temporary solution.

Looking off to his right, he senses another door is about to open. There suddenly appears a restaurant. A large sign across the front denotes its specialty as "Home Cooking." These small, out of the way eateries tend to depend on regulars. Most are retired and gather for coffee and breakfast. He's not disappointed. Still at a distance, he speculates the place has at least a dozen vehicles in the parking lot. He knows the method of operation for these hangers on is to come early and stay late.

Gil guardedly enters the parking lot, always with an eye open for a quick escape route if needed. Watchfully parking the tractor in an out of the way spot so as not to be seen, he warily dismounts. Depending on his walking stick, he slowly hobbles between the parked vehicles. The habit of these "Yoopers" (upper peninsula inhabitants) is to have bragging rights as to how many trustful years they have left their keys in the ignition. Gil is not about to be disappointed. He's had his attention focused on a late model four-wheel drive Chevrolet pickup. This vehicle is common enough not to stand out, but able to navigate the back roads. Peeking through the side window tells him everything he needs to know. The keys are in the ignition and there's a gas credit card stuck in the visor. Hardly able to contain himself, Gil makes a quick survey of the door to the restaurant. "*Nobody comin'. Perfect!*" is the thought rushing through his mind. Inside of a second, he's opened the unlocked driver's side door, gotten behind the wheel, turned the key, carefully puts it in reverse and unobtrusively makes his way out to the road. With a keen eye on the road and an anxious eye on the rearview mirror, he speeds down the highway. Rather than risk being detected on the main thoroughfare, at the first opportunity, he opts to get off and onto the county roads.

With the reduced amount of traffic on these back roads, Gil's concerns about getting caught stealing a tractor and a truck are replaced with the terrifying fear of being apprehended for a murder he doesn't remember. Most of his life, he's lived with mainly a fear of the law. Now, becoming afraid of himself is only compounding his dread.

He goes over and over the circumstances of how he must have done it. It's true he had a love-hate relationship with Julia. To say that he didn't find her well developed, womanly body sexy and alluring would certainly be a lie, but to say he found her personality just as lovely would also be a lie. He'd pictured her dead more than once.

He's spent his entire adult life haunted by the fact he was responsible for his father's death. Much of his drinking is intended to dodge recalling the stupid, reckless things he's carried out only to find his dreams won't be fooled. Often awakening is the only thing that preserves him. He has lived his life dreading that one day there will be a knock at the door, and they'll ask him about his father. Somedays, he looks forward to it—it can't be worse than the demons that torment him day and night.

For the present, Gil isn't prepared to meet any reality. Once again, his alcohol companion is promising that it can champion him into a realm of nonthought if only he can get enough. The problem is, he has no alcohol with him. But he also betting that since this truck belongs to a Yooper that somewhere under or behind the seat is a bottle. He has already rifled through the glove box. The papers say the truck belongs to a Thomas Koskinen. With a name like that, he's a Finn for certain. This further verifies the likeliness of there being a bottle of cheap whiskey stashed somewhere in the truck. A Finn without a bottle in the UP is as unlikely as his Lutheran buffet without a hot dish. Without stopping, Gil manages to steer with one hand, allowing the other to freely search under the seat. "BINGO," he exclaims. Sure enough, he retrieves a nearly full fifth of Kessler's finest. With his elbows doing the steering, he holds the bottle in one hand and unscrews the cap with the other. The hot fluid bites at his throat; it's enough to make a dead man gag. Not to be disappointed, its warmth soon begins to sooth his frightful thoughts.

With a keen eye on the terrain, it's not long before he begins to realize he's in familiar territory. He can see the Porcupine Mountains off in the distance. These were his boyhood playground. Whenever thing went awry in his life, he could always rely on its wilderness to provide him with a hideout until the fracas blew over. He's hoping it's still up to its former reputation.

CHAPTER 19

Studs and Knobbies

Jim and Peggy have crossed the great Mackinac Bridge. As predicted, the weather has cleared with sunshine replacing a rainy, overcast sky. Little conversation has crossed between them. As many things in life that begin with ambiguity, like the first leg of an uncertain journey, the first thing required is to take the first step. Both are certain the end will be to their satisfaction—though if it isn't, it's not the end.

There is a gentleness about the road and how Jim's truck meets it. It's narrowly accurate that there is a contrast between their irreconcilable mission and the gentle trip. Within a few miles, a warm breeze has replaced the cold rain. Driving with the windows down, allowing the wind to cut billowing channels through their hair is enough to make them wish that their quest was of a kinder nature.

"You still with me?" asks Jim.

"Just for the record, I am, but I wished I didn't have to be," she says. "We don't even know how to start."

"You're wrong, Peggy. We've already started."

This is all Peggy needs to hear; she's back on the same page. "Okay, let's do it!"

Jim lets a few seconds pass, then he says, "Think about the last time you heard Gil talking about where he came from; what comes into your head?"

"It wasn't much different." Peggy gives a little shrug. "He and my mother would be drunk and arguing. Gil would always tell her his cousin killed his own dad and would take her out too if he was asked. My mother would tell Gil that my dad was in prison for murder, and when he got out, she'd have my dad kill Gil *and* his cousin. Julia and I would just stay in our room 'til they passed out."

"Do you remember any mention of a town?" Jim asks.

It suddenly dawns on her. "Yeah, I think it was something like 'Birdland'... and he'd talk about burying her in the 'Porkies.'"

Jim pulls his truck off onto the shoulder of the highway, opens his glove box, and begins to examine a map.

"Was it Bergland? I see a "Bergland," he says. It's difficult to miss his excitement. "It's over by the Porcupine Mountains."

"Yes, that's the place," says Peggy, just as excited.

"We're only a few hours from there," says Jim, refolding the map, placing it back in the glove box. With a new resolve, he puts the truck in gear and pulls back onto the highway.

"We're not going to be there before dark. See if you can find us a campsite," Jim asks Peggy.

Using her iPhone, Peggy begins the search. After several minutes, she reports, "I found an opening. They have one primitive site left."

Without taking his eyes off the road, Jim says, "Take it!"

Peggy's only response is the rapid use of her thumbs as she texts all the required information. In seconds the reservation is confirmed.

*

Gil has reached the end of his destination—at least for now—the Bergland Bar located in Bergland, Mi on the far west side of Michigan's upper peninsula. It's his home area. Parked in his stolen pickup in the bar parking lot, he's experiencing a mixture of excitement and reservation about being here. Since he rarely leaves an area under good terms, his first reaction is an attempt to recall the circumstances that led him to leave the last time. At least this will give him a heads up with any encounters he'll come across in the bar.

Looking around satisfies him things have remained just about the way he left them. Snow mobile trailers still dot many of the yards even though it's mid-summer. The same sedan is still in its place parked across the street. He takes comfort in the predictability of Bergland. He also takes stock of the types of vehicles in the parking lot. He recognizes many of them. To push his luck any further to continue in the stolen pickup could prove disastrous. Finishing the last drag from the last of his water stained cigarettes, he flicks it across the parking lot and makes his way to the door.

He knows exactly what he expects to see. The bar is still in the same place, the same chrome legged tables and maroon seated chairs are just as they always have been, as is the worn spots on the floor. Making his way to the bar, he orders a shot a beer and a burger. Finishing his burger and swallowing the last of his beer, he feels a tap on his shoulder. Swinging around on the stool, Gil finds he's confronting a determined looking fellow whom he immediately recognizes as his cousin Ike.

"Ya got the hundred bucks ya stole from me?" is Ike's only greeting. Gil is more accustomed to these kinds of greetings than he is to friendlier platitudes.

"What ya talkin' about? You lent that money to me," reports Gil without the slightest hesitation.

"That's right, lendin' without payin' it back is stealin' in anybody's book. So, gimme my hundred."

Gil has entered the familiar area of confrontation—it's where he is most comfortable.

"Tell ya what, Ike, as soon as your brother gets outta prison, he promised me he'd write me a check for the hundred he owes me. Soon as that happens, I'll turn that check over to you."

Ike suspects he's being played a sucker by his cousin. He reacts the only way a Gilles knows how, he takes a swing at Gil. It lands right on his left orbital. Gil can hear the bone around his left eye crack. His ready response is to grab his empty long neck and smash it over Ike's head. Ike goes down like a pole-axed steer. He's not moving. He's out cold. With all the attention Ike's getting from those who know him, Gil figures it's time to get in the wind.

Hobbling his way out, he focuses in on an older model, four-wheeled drive, maroon colored Chevy pickup with a grill guard for hitting deer or plowing through brush. He had noticed it earlier as still having the keys in the ignition. With no apparent pursuers; therefore no one to sound an alarm, he quickly dispatches this truck, sending himself down the road unnoticed.

*

Within seconds of Gil's disappearance, Jim and Peggy pull into the parking lot. Hungry and tired, they make their way to the Bergland Bay Bar entrance. Instead of meeting a welcoming environment, they are met with a chaos of apocalyptic proportions. A man is lying on the floor bleeding profusely from a gash across his forehead. There is a pile of blood-soaked bar towels lying beside him with a couple of the bar attendants administering yet another one. Another dozen standing around watching, each with a glass in their hand. It's the most entertainment they've had since Lattie Nienem stormed in and caught her husband Wes cavorting with the widow Klack and clunked him on the head with his own half-empty long neck.

It seems in this present situation there has been a disruption that Jim and Peggy could have predicted had they known who was behind it. With just a few questions, they discover the trip they've made is not in vain. Hoping to find out more, they determine if Ike is able to come around, he may be able to give them some clues as to where Gil may be heading.

Within a few minutes, Ike is coming around. Still dazed he struggles to his feet casting aside the fresh towel against his forehead. "I'll kill 'im! I should've killed the S.O.B. along time ago!"

Seeing he's back to his old normal self, the interest in his wellbeing quickly dwindles. With drinks in hand, the crowd is soon back to other interests. Jim and Peggy are the only ones attentive to Ike. Introducing themselves, they help him to a chair.

"Ike, my name is Jim Samples, and this is my friend Peggy Fortine. We're trolls. ("Trolls" is the name given to Michigan people living below the bridge in the lower peninsula.) We're interested in locating your cousin Harold Gilles. Would you be interested in helping us locate him?"

"'Harold!? I forgot that turd's name is Harold. We've just always called him Gil," replies Ike. "What're ya lookin' for him for?"

Jim pauses for a moment as he and Peggy exchange glances. "He killed her sister," says Jim.

Now it's Ike's turn to pause. "Ya don't say," he says, leaning back in his chair with a renewed interest. "So, the S.O.B. done it again."

Jim and Peggy exchange the same glance again realizing they may be getting Ike's attention, but now he has theirs. "What do you mean 'done it again'?" asks Jim.

Realizing what he has just revealed, Ike suddenly becomes much more guarded. "Oh, nothin'. I'm still goofy from that busted bottle over my head." Not wanting to engage in any further discussion with these strangers, Ike suddenly rises from his chair with the simple excuse, "I gotta go." With that, he's out the door. In less than five seconds, he's back in the bar, shouting, "The S.O.B. stole my truck!"

Somebody nearby asks, "Who you sayin' would want that piece of crap?"

"That idiot cousin of mine, that's who!"

Most people in this area know the Gilles family well enough to know that it's wiser to stay out of their family feuds.

Frustrated that no one seems to want to share his anger, Ike has a sudden change of mind. Turning back to Jim and Peggy, Ike declares, "You do the drivin', I'll help ya find 'im. But I'm just lettin' ya know, I ain't getting involved—all I want is my truck back."

Jim rises, grasps Ike's hand, and pulls a chair out for him, saying, "You got a deal."

Not about to miss an opportunity for a tourist tip, a waitress stands by, ready to take their order.

*

At the first opportunity, Gil chances a stop for supplies. Using the stolen credit card, he loads up with gear to be used in a wilderness environment. Since his experience with the woman shooting at him, and his encounter with the raccoon, he's given up on chancing another happenstance with surprise inhabitants of remote cabins. His plan "B" is going to take him to a very remote part of the region where on one of his earlier escapades with the law, he came across old abandoned copper mine. It's buried deep in the woods with an old forsaken trail that's barely assessable. Since it had served him well years ago, his expectation is that it will do the same in his present situation. For the moment, he feels all his bridges are burned, leaving him with this single choice. Well supplied with all he believes he will need to survive, along with the hopes he can clear out his head involving his role in Julia's death. Without an invitation, and except for every minute his head isn't full of the anxiety involving his escape, the details of her death roll around and around in his head.

For this time of the year, it's going to be dark in an hour when Gil arrives at the trail head. Nonetheless, this trail promises to remove him from the world that's pursuing him and lead him to a wild but freeing environment. In one sense he's happy to see how the snowmobilers and off-road vehicles have made use of the trail, keeping it open but in another sense, it suggests there could be people. Nonetheless, he's driven by enough of an engendered survival mode to risk the odds. With the truck's four-wheel system engaged, Gil begins his several mile trek deep in the woods. As wild and foreboding as it is, this is his kind of environment. Not to be fooled that natures beauty is without danger, like a beautiful woman, it has her wiles, so nature's beauty always carries with it an element of danger. From his youth on, he has always prided himself in being able to outwit his pursuers in this kind of setting. In some ways, being forced back into this kind of a situation is welcoming. Nature has always had a place for its wild ones—it has an element of tolerance for his kind.

• •

As he plunges deeper into the woods, he's discovering the brush has reclaimed some of the trail's edges, narrowing it greatly. His hand to eye coordination is being tested every inch of the way as he twists the large four-wheeled behemoth to avoid a tree growing here and there where one had not been the last time that he navigated this track.

It's barely dusk by the time he reaches the end of the trail. Rather than negotiate the short trek to the mines entrance, Gil thinks better of that choice. "Rather than riskin' seein' somethin' out there I don't wanna deal with, I'm gonna stay right here 'til daylight."

Not having had the time to forage through this latest "borrowed" four-wheeler, Gil opens the glove box to discover the papers indicate this vehicle is registered to Isaac Gilles.

"Well, what d'ya know about this? If this don't beat all. This here piece of crap belongs to good ol' Ike."

This is the first time he's felt this good inside in days. Rummaging through the rest of the crap under the seat produces a large hunting knife. Ike's been in prison, and being a convicted felon, he's stripped of his right to bear arms. But being a Gilles, these rules are meant to be broken. If caught with this concealed weapon, he'd surely get a penalty. Gil has also had his share of trouble, but never more than a series of misdemeanors. Nonetheless, he welcomes the big buck blade as another gift from Ike. There's also a large assortment of mechanic's tools he'll have little use for out here in the boonies, but they're still worth admiring as though they all belong to him.

Feeling the pain in his swollen eye, added to the existing swelling in his ankle, only serves to raise up a bit more animosity for what his cousin did to his face. With little left he can do to prepare for the oncoming darkness, Gil checks his phone. He has just about enough juice left to make one more call. Flipping it open, he scrolls down until he finds Ike's number. Not able to resist the temptation, he pushes the pads and holds it to his ear. It's ringing. He's decided on one more nastiness he can dole out against Ike.

Ike recognizes the caller's name and number as it flashes across his screen, along with enough animosity and loud enough to scare the rats out of a barn, he yells into the phone, "YOU'RE SO ROTTEN, HELL WON'T HAVE YA, GIL. YOU'RE A S.O.B."

Gil is fully aware he's hit a homerun with his call. "I just want to let you know if you're lookin' for yer truck, just look in the sky for the smoke, 'cause I'm burnin' it right to the ground."

"I'M GONNA HUNT YOU DOWN LIKE A DOG. THEN I'M GONNA KILL YA IN YOUR SLEEP AN' FEED YA TO THE PIGS," Ike screams into the phone.

Jim and Peggy are convinced beyond all doubt that they are dealing someone with the same Gilles family DNA as they have experienced with Gil and that said "someone" is riding in the truck with them. They are also becoming aware of a family rift whose root cause has become lost in the dynamics of their dysfunction. If they didn't need Ike's help, they would gladly add another lump to the one already on his head and dump him off to the side of the road.

Even without Ike's speaker app. on, Jim and Peggy can hear a diabolical laugh on the other end of the phone. Then everything goes quiet. It's obvious Gil has hung up or his phone's gone dead. With this last installment of meanness in place, Gil settles down for a good night's sleep.

There is no practical way of dealing with Gil any longer tonight. Ike is beside himself. In typical Gilles fashion. He continues to rant. "That scum bag ain't ever gonna change. He killed his ol' man when he was a kid, an' everybody knowed he'd done it. Now you say he killed your sister? I believe every word you're sayin'."

Ike lives close to the camp ground where Jim and Peggy are registered. It's agreed they will pick him up first thing in the morning. Ike's place is a typical backwoods combination of trailer and stick-built add-ons. He considers himself an independent, self-made man who lives his life the way he has chosen. Cutting and selling firewood is a mainstay for his existence. Since he has never had a wife, there is nothing around his abode to suggest a woman has been within throwing distance. The only items that have any semblance of order are the neatly stacked piles of cordwood all categorized by types and arranged for easy access and loading. In Ike's world, without a truck, he may as well not have a life. But then, in the Gilles clan, they're known for sabotaging their successes into chaos on a regular basis. Ike, in particular, has a great community with calamity.

Having all the details in place with Ike for the next morning, Jim and Peggy arrive at their own campsite. It's in the primitive section of the campground. Using the truck's headlights, they quickly set up their tents. No sooner does Jim hit his pillow and he's sawing logs; Peggy can hear him ten feet away. She, on the other hand, is having a tough time getting settled down enough to fall asleep. Things have been moving so rapidly she has hardly had time to mourn the loss of her sister. Her mind is going a jillion miles an hour thinking about the events in the past few days. Her family life has never been anywhere near what can be referred to as "functional," it's always been on the bottom of the scale.

Her thoughts take her back to the experience she had encountering Julia's murderer. Between her waves of grief that come over her like Lake Michigan's storm rollers, Peggy feels the strong presence of her sister in a way she has never experienced before. It's in an odd way, as though she is being prevented from understanding something important that Julia is trying to tell her; it's as though the gap between them is thwarting their efforts to remain together. They have always lived their own lives as though their telepathic relationship was a given; not to be understood, but rather experienced. Peggy still feels it. But now it's as though something not a given is thwarting her effort. Her mind and body are both exhausted and as happens with humans, sleep will sooner or later have its way. Even in her dreams, she sees Julia but it's in a haze she can't clear and at a distance she can't shorten.

Peggy awakens to Jim's clattering. It's barely daylight. He's prepared a camp stove already in the full process of cooking eggs, bacon and a pot of camp brewed coffee. By the time she returns from her morning visit to the outdoor commode the camp ground has provided, her breakfast is on a plate ready to be eaten. Within the next fifteen minutes, they have finished policing their camp and as agreed, they are on their way to pick up Ike.

They find Ike looking exactly the way he had when they met him the day before; same disheveled hair twisted under a hat with a grimy bill—except now his hat is tilted to one side to avoid the scab that's formed on his forehead, same shirt and pants with red suspenders, work shoes with the same socks lacking elastic allowing them to drift down around his shoe tops. Ike is the kind of man who puts together a seasonal outfit to wear for the entire season. Having Ike ride in the truck cab's close quarters is also a challenge; the musky odor of aged sweat is overwhelming. Jim can't get his windows down fast enough. The air has taken on an odor that feels like it is bonded itself to every molecule it makes contact with.

To suggest he should replace a knocked out front tooth brings the same response, "Yeah, I'm gonna do that. Had it replaced once, but I got drunk an' puked it out somewhere in Marquette." His nearly five decades of life have produced weathered lines crisscrossing his face, each entrenched with the grime from some past endeavor, all suggesting that bathing is what one does only before going to the doctor.

Nonetheless, at this point, Ike is indispensable. He is the only link between themselves and the whereabouts of Gil. Ike, despite the early morning hour is as animated about his cousin stealing his truck.

Jim's cell phone suddenly breaks into their conversation. Answering it brings about a moment of silence from Jim as he intensely listens to the caller. Closing the phone for a moment before he speaks, Jim breaks his silence, turning to Peggy, he says, "That was my cousin Lily. Remember she works in Greeny' office? She has just informed me they have traced a phone call made by Gil to a cell tower in this region and have alerted the authorities here."

Ike is all ears. "Hell, boy, you don't need those guys. Forget about them cell towers, I know where that bonehead is hidin' out."

Jim's concern is that he is going to have to deal with the authorities before he is able to deal with Gil on his own terms—his own way.

"All right Ike, you tell me where we're going and I'm right with you," resigns Jim.

"Pull over right here," orders Ike. He's half out of the truck before Jim can bring it to a complete stop. In the next second, Ike's on his hands and knees peering at a tire track leading down a two track. Coming back to the truck he hops back in.

"He ain't down this way," reports Ike. "There's another trail up a ways. There's an old copper mine at the end of it a ways back in the woods. Last time I was there was with that no-good S.O.B. cousin of mine. We was about fourteen. We'd been bustin' into some Troll cottages when the law figured out it was us." Ike lets this information sink in a little before he continues. "Gil come on an old abandoned mine after his ol' man caught him stealin' an' threatened to beat him to death. I remember he hung out there for a month."

Peggy is listening to this with a little more than passing interest. It's involving the method of operation by a man she has grown to despise. "What kept him alive? Like what did he eat? asks Peggy.

Ike looks a little shocked at the naiveté of her question. "Same damn thing the S.O.B. is eatin' right now. Your campground is only about a half mile behind where Gil is holed up. There ain't no doubt in my mind he'll be lookin' it over for some easy pickin's." With hardly a break in his conversation, Ike shouts as he points out the windshield at another two-track leading back into the woods, "Right there! Stop right there!"

Once again, Ike's out of the truck investigating the trail. This time still on his hands and knees with his back to Peggy and Jim. Suddenly, back to just his knees, he raises his arms with two thumbs up letting out a whoop. Peggy is still suspicious of Ike. She sees him as coming from the same moronic household as his cousin Gil. Turning to Jim, she says, "What's he doing on his hands and knees? He looks like he's attempting to pick up a scent."

In a matter of a second, Ike is back in the truck, all excited and shouting orders. "He's down here all right. This where he come in an' there ain't a bit of sign he come back out."

Peggy is still listening with the candor of one whose survival techniques are totally different. She again asks, "How do you know he went down this trail, and much less that he's still there?"

Once again, Ike looks at her with the same disbelief he had at her last question. "'Cause them tire tracks come off only one truck in this whole dang county, an' that truck happens to belong to Ike Gilles, an' in case you don't remember, that there guy is me!" Ike retorts, pointing two thumbs at himself.

Still reluctant to give anyone with the name of "Gilles" any measure of intelligence, she asks yet another question, "What makes you so certain those tracks came from the tires on your truck?"

"Well, little lady, it's 'cause I got one knobby tire on the right rear side an' a studded tire on the left rear side," answers Ike with the assurance of one who keeps track of the slightly different nuances he creates. "An' why do I believe he's still out there? Ike asks, repeating the same question Peggy had asked and ready to answer it himself, "'Cause they ain't but one set of them tires goin' in and none comin' out. If they was comin' out, you'd be seein' them knobbies crossin' over on them studs. Didn't happen—he's still out there."

Jim listens to this exchange between Peggy and Ike rather impatiently. He's chomping at the bit to get going. He's well aware of Peggy's dislike for Ike, yet he's hoping she doesn't tick this alligator off too much before they get through the swamp. Peggy is sitting in between Jim and Ike permitting Jim to give her a little nudge in the hopes she catches on. Indicating she understands, she gives Jim a little nudge back. It helps with his impatience only slightly. He definitely wants a confrontation with Gil—and certainly before the authorities get involved.

With the swirling finger gesture of uncurling a wagon train, Ike gives the motion to move forward. The trail is narrow, and the overgrowth on each side still carries the fresh wounds of broken branches, giving even more credibility to the fact that someone very recently made the same journey. Unable to relax during the jaunt, Ike is leaning so far ahead in his seat that his nose is nearly scrubbing on the windshield. Watching him reflexively throw his arm up as if each branch were coming through the windshield is more than Peggy can stand. *"This idiot is more of a Gilles than Gil,"* is her singular thought.

CHAPTER 20

Treed

Several miles down the trail, Gil has rousted himself out of Ike's stolen pickup. He's awakened to the pain of a swollen foot, an eye socket ballooned so bad that he can't see out of it, and if this isn't enough, he has the shakes. Rather than enabling his thoughts of what he intends to do next, they are flying in every direction. He's purchased several bottles of wine because they're much easier to transport than cases of beer. After consuming nearly half of a fifth, he thinks, *This must be what it feels like to be an alcoholic. Thank God I don't have to drink this rot gut very often. I'd probably end up an alcoholic.*

Once the shakes are out of the way, despite the pain of the eye and foot, Gil is much more able to focus on some sort of a plan. What he had recalled of this hideout has changed with time. Struggling to see something familiar, he finds nature is doing what it does best—it's reclaiming that which has been its own all along. The entrance shaft to the old copper mine is a bit more over grown but still carries enough recollection to be somewhat familiar. With the aid of his trusty hoe handle, he manages to hobble his way toward the opening. With his mind on his disability, his eye socket swollen shut, what he doesn't notice immediately is the two bear cubs staring at him from the mine entrance. As soon as this becomes a reality, he freezes with fear. As all upper peninsula persons are taught, when there are cubs, there is an angry mother bear not too far away. To get between her and her cubs is suicide. The inevitable is already in the works. Gil hears the all too familiar growl of this irate mother. With no time to hobble back to the safety of the pickup, his only other choice is to immediately begin to climb the only pine tree in the area—and thank God it's available with low enough branches to be assessable. Forgetting everything about pain, he climbs up and into this tree as though it were the stairway to the safety of heaven. The mother bear is not that far behind. She has made the same split-second decision Gil's made and is working her way up the tree in hot pursuit. Gil's mind is on one thing and one thing only: getting as far away as possible from this mother turned predator. It's soon apparent that he's quickly running out of tree. The only other option he has is to begin to rely on the buck knife he found in Ike's truck. Before venturing away from the pickup, he'd enough sense to strap it to his side. With an angry bear balancing itself on the branch below him and Gil with nothing but instinct, hangs onto a branch above him and swings the knife blade striking the bear behind the ear. It proves to be a good hit as the blood begins to soak her fur. It also proves to enrage her to where she strikes back and nearly losing her balance on the thin branch supporting her. With the instincts of a cat, Gil swings the blade in rapid succession, hitting her eye and nose. It's enough to cause her to give up the fight and scrambles to the ground only to look up and lick the blood pouring out of her snout.

Gil's sight is hindered by the thick branches of his tree and reduced to sight in only one eye; it's enough to where he has no idea where this mother bear and cubs have ventured. Not being a tree dweller by nature, it's becoming very uncomfortable and impossible to find a spot that doesn't feel as though he's sitting with only his bones against the tree's hardness. Willing to give it a few more minutes just for the sake of caution, he repositions himself with the expectation of some kind of relief from the hurt he's feeling.

It's in this process that he hears the familiar sound of a vehicle. Remaining dead still, Gil peers as best he can. His sight disadvantage is going to have to switch from seeing to listening. He can tell the vehicle is getting closer and closer as its transmission and motor give off a mixture of whining and groans as it powers its way through the changing parts of the trail. It soon comes to a stop. He's so intent on the changing sounds that suggest movement that for the moment, he's forgotten how numb his legs have become as a result of his abnormal seat. Even the other sounds of the forest are filtered out when he hears the distinct sound of a vehicle doors open and close. His primary focus is on who this interloper or interlopers may be. *"If it's the law and they got a dog, I'm done,"* is his first thought. listening intently with his attention riveted to what kind of voices he may hear that will give him a clue as to what he's up against. His heart is racing even more than with the bear; he feels much, much more vulnerable with his own kind than with animals. At least with the bear, he was afforded an escape route and a weapon. If this is the law, they will definitely have all escape routes covered, and his buck knife will give him zero advantage in a gunfight. This is all stuff he knows he can't rise above. Then he hears the first human sound. It's a voice.

"There's my truck. I told ya the S.O.B. is here someplace."

Gil immediately recognizes the voice of his cousin. It gives him immediate relief that it's not the law. Another spar with Ike is not something he is looking forward to, considering the condition he's in, but neither does he fear it.

Jim responds, "Yeah, you did, but all we have is a cold trail he could be anywhere."

Gil has heard that voice before. It takes a few seconds for him to put a face to it. *It's that muscle-head boyfriend Julia was hangin' around with,* is his immediate conclusion. *What the heck is he doin' here?*

"I don't care how cold the trail is. I'll hunt him if I have to follow him through the gates of hell."

Oh, my god, that's Peggy, is his next conclusion.

This latest voice gives him a cold chill. Not only is Gil's legs numb, his whole body is nearly catatonic with distress. All the running, being shot at, nearly breaking his ankle, punched in the eye by his cousin, chased by a bear, and now this. His distress is morphing into an alarm. *At least with the law, I'd get a fair trial—all three of these want to kill me without a trial.* The thought of this gives him a second thought about his cavalier attitude toward sparing with Ike again.

The distinct sound coming from Ike's exhaust pipes is the next thing Gil hears. Along with this, he hears Ike, saying, "You guys are on your own. I got what I come out here to get."

Peggy and Jim swing around in time to see Ike put the truck in gear and head back down the same trail alone that just moments before they had blazed together. The two of them stand speechless for a moment, processing what has just happened. Peggy is the first to speak. "Good riddance. I can't stand that guy. He reminds me way too much his idiot cousin."

Still contemplating, Jim finally says, "You know, Peggy, you're probably right. We can do what we have to with or without Ike."

"So, where're we gonna start?" asks Peggy.

Looking around, Jim says, "Here's as good a place as any. He couldn't have gotten too far."

By now, Gil is only twenty feet from them, as they are directly under his perch. He can see them with his good eye. They are the new enemy. Gil considers his options. It doesn't take him long to conclude that, *Next to rocks in my bed, I ain't got but one option—stay sittin' in this tree.*

"What are we going to do with him when we catch him?" asks Peggy.

"He's gonna have an accident. Then we leave him for crow bait," answers Jim.

The way Gil is beginning to feel sitting up in this tree, he's wondering, *Maybe I should just give up and get it over with. I can't sit up here much longer.*

Just as he thinks "giving up" may be his only option, the duo begins to move in the direction of the cave. Peggy is the first to note there is movement in the foliage. A loud growl follows. What appears next causes them to begin a slow backward movement. Directly ahead is a bear not more than

179

thirty yards away swinging its head with a simultaneous low growl. The truck is the same distance away as the bear.

"Oh, boy, we're in trouble now," she says as her face suddenly turns an ashen grey.

Jim isn't saying anything. He's looking straight ahead. Some of his survival training is trying to force its way past his terror.

"Don't look him in the eye. Back away slow," is his sage advice. The terror they're both experiencing is shouting for them to get away as fast as possible—to run as hard as they can, but so far, the bear seems to be satisfied with their acquiescence. With what seems like a lifetime of panic, they finally reach the truck. With a hundred feet of peaking fear, it explodes as they nearly tear the truck's doors from their hinges and catapult themselves into the truck's seat, slamming the doors behind them. Their hearts are beating so hard they can't speak. Without a word, Jim has started the truck and proceeds to turn it around. This is not the time to regroup and come up with a plan "B"; rather, it's time to get out while the going's good.

All the time this is happening, Gil remains safe but horribly uncomfortable in his tree perch. He has had a death sentence given to him by the forces of nature in the form of an irate mother bear as well as members of his own species— even this tree is making falling to the ground more appealing than attempting to remain in it. Gil has never had a good relationship with God. He's always been of the opinion God is for everyone else. In his mind, if he dared complain, asking God why so much of his life has been under duress, he would hear God say, *Oh, I don't know, Gil, there's just something about you that pisses me off.*

The way things are playing out, it's looking much like history is repeating itself, as usual Gil has more suffering to go before, he meets his next crises.

In their plans to eliminate Gil, Peggy and Jim are also skirting around the edges of disaster. They're hoping to convince others that Gil escaped into the big woods and never came back. Historically, taking the law into one's own hands has had its repercussions—external as well as internal. But those most guilty of this infraction always believe they had a just reason that should—but never does—exempt them. If they don't pay a penalty for externally breaking law, sooner or later, the law of conscience won't let them off the hook.

Gil is a living example of breaking laws and suffering their external as well as internal consequences. He is accustomed to living in a world where he considers himself the captain of his own destiny. Even after he's forced to examine his track record of failure, he remains faithful to his ego driven causes. The best one can say about Gil and his approach is, "He's committed."

CHAPTER 21

Food Raid

Jim and Peggy remain silent on their way back to camp. *This is not supposed to be this difficult,* is Peggy's silent perception. What had begun as a pursuit that in all fairness would end with justice served; Gil would be caught up with, she'd get her pound of flesh, and the authorities could have what was left.

Jim is getting over his feelings of defeat. His competitive nature is kicking back in. looking over at Peggy, he can't help but notice how her normal upbeat demeanor has changed to sullen and overcast. Rather than take a chance of losing her, he tries a locker-room half-time talk, "I believe we just suffered a setback, but I also think we can ferret Gil out with a little more diligence."

Peggy lets out a sigh, "Let's get back to camp, make some lunch and regroup. This last episode wore me out."

The longest part of this journey is the trail leading back to the highway. Once that leg of the jaunt is out of the way, the rest of the trip is a matter of making three turns around a square mile that puts them back in their campsite. As the crow flies, this places the last known evidence of Gil's whereabouts not much more than a half a mile from their campsite.

*

Gil slowly makes his way down the tree. His legs and body are cramped enough to force him to give up his perch before he gives into the idea of just falling down. He has one eye cautiously focused on the area of the copper mine and the other on where he's going to plant his next step. So far, he sees no movement or sign that this mother bear and her cubs are still in the vicinity. His instinct tells him that with all the activity they've moved out of the area. Finally reaching the ground with his swollen foot is one of his concerns, while the other is to keep a wary eye open for any impending dangers. Searching around for his hoe handle, he finds it twenty feet from the tree. Hardly able to hobble enough to retrieve it, he wonders how he had been able to run that distance without it.

Having lived most of his life with some kind of misfortune, thus far Gil has managed it. This is expected in his world. If his life isn't stressful, he'll find a way to make it happen. Taking stock of his present situation, Gil discovers his stash of food and booze had been left in Ike's truck. "If it weren't for bad luck, I'd have no luck at all," has been his leading mantra all his life. Remembering the fresh water creek that made its way through this section, he stumbles through the overgrowth dragging his bad foot in hopes of rediscovering its location. An hour later, with luck, Gil comes across his elusive creek. It's been thirty years since he's been in these parts, but it's much as he remembers it. The banks are lined with short grasses. The creek always freezes over in the harsh northern Michigan winter, causing flooding in the spring thaw. When this occurs, the foliage along the banks is swept away, leaving only what can survive until the next rampage of water and chunks of ice strip it once again. What he meets is a fresh water supply but he's not alone. He's expected to share with his old nemeses—the bear and her cubs. With a wary eye on her every move, she's upstream far enough not to be an immediate threat, but not far enough to be of no concern. With the fresh memory of what seemed like a lifetime in that pine tree, the last thing he wishes for is a repeat performance.

Gil is beginning to process how he's going to survive without his gear. It's getting late in the afternoon, he's hungry, the black flies and the no-see-ems are out in force, and he hasn't had alcohol since morning. His anxiety level is increasing by the minute. Nonetheless, when necessity becomes the mother of invention, Gil will rise to the occasion regardless of his condition. At the moment, he's at the mercy of his circumstances. Winded from struggling with his bum foot and in need of a cigarette and a beer, he finds an old tree stump just the right height to be commissioned as a chair. He begins to churn his circumstances around in his head. looking around at some of the familiar terrain leads him to speculate, *I ain't that far from that campground. Me an' Ike used it as our grocery store. I wonder if it's still there.*

*

Jim and Peggy have arrived back in camp. Jim is quietly going about busying himself with policing the area surrounding them. He's concerned with leftover food stuff bringing an unwanted bear visit; making certain it's all put in the bear proof trash containers. These have all been placed in a centrally located area. When he returns, he detects what sounds like sobbing coming from Peggy's tent. With nothing on her tent to knock on, he says, "Knock, knock! You all right in there?"

Even before she responds, he has a clear idea what her sorrow is concerned with. In spite of their setback and renewed attempt to reinvigorate their quest to ensure that Gil will have justice served for his vile act, they are finding the reality of Julia's death will not correspond with their schedule. It's catching up with them, and it's proving to have a stronger impact with the lapse of time. Neither of them has allowed themselves time to grieve. Instead they had turned their attention toward getting even with Gil. Hatred has replaced anguish. But without warning, heartache is overtaking them both. They had expected this mission to be a righteous undertaking and would be a slam-dunk, now they are finding the reality of Julia's death to be a crashing wave overriding their emotions. Despite their effort to postpone it, it has no intention of giving either of them that kind of indifferent luxury.

Unzipping her tent, Jim discovers Peggy rolled up in a ball. Peggy's response is clearly one of uncontrollable sobbing. It's not something he's prepared for. Nonetheless, he is not ready to ignore it. Seeing her in this condition triggers a response in himself that he isn't expecting. He feels a helplessness overtaking him as sorrow replaces all other emotions. Placing a hand on her in an attempt to comfort her, he begins to feel his own tears begin to well up. This joint display of emotion is not a first nor will it be a last for them. In a back-handed way, it brings them together in a different dimension. They have found little or no effort to become one in their anger; now they are sharing their grief as one.

Peggy's thoughts are disjointed and scarred with grief driven elements. On one hand she continues to lash at Gil. "I don't know why Gil wants to torture us this way. Why doesn't he just quit screwin' around? He's not going to win." In the same breath, she turns her thoughts to the sisterly devotion she continues to hold for her missing twin. "I miss my sister so much. I wish I could join her."

"I miss her, too. My heart aches for her," states Jim. By placing his arm around Peggy, he hopes to vicariously benefit from the atmosphere of comfort he's attempting to create. "I didn't how much her smile, her touch meant to me until now. She meant everything to me. She had become the purpose behind my life. I blame myself for leaving her that night. My gut told me something bad was going to happen. She assured me there was nothing new going on and she could handle it."

Peggy is listening to Jim's seeming over developed sense of responsibility for Julia's death. She has accepted Jim's kindly gestures of concern and in turn accepts as genuine, his love for her sister. It's in this shared expression of devotion for the same person, that the gloomy cloud of grief begins to part enough in each of them to let the sun peek through; it's creating a trust between them they had only previously shared in common with Julia.

In turn, something inside Peggy is composing a desire to comfort Jim's sense of loss. "Oh, Jim, stop! You can't blame yourself. I would have done exactly what Julia did. We did it nearly every day of our lives. I know how much she was beginning to love you and would never want you to spend your life blaming yourself for a choice she made."

Jim listens to her simple words. He holds them contemplatively for the moment. Within them he hears the sweet music of redemption. But then, the devil's lie of blame always tries to force itself between redemption and conviction.

"I wish it was that easy. She trusted me to look after her—I feel I let her down."

Peggy has a confession of her own. "Well, I've been blaming myself for leaving her home to contend with our home life by herself. What now feels like a selfish desire to play college sports, pales in comparison to what my sister and I have shared our entire life." Her tears begin to flow once again in convulsive sobs.

And once more, out of their shared memories of Julia, Jim is ready to set his own sorrow aside in lieu of Peggy's need for solace. "Peggy, my heart bleeds for what you must be going through. I know how empty I feel having known Julia for such a short time compared to your lifetime of togetherness."

In a strange way, as she hears Jim's words, Peggy is sensing the same tenderness in Jim that Julia had voiced. She is finding herself drawn to him in a similar way. In these extraordinary circumstances, she is giving him a comparable measure of the private type of companionship that she had previously only shared with Julia.

Things have also changed with Jim. Unlike his first date with Julia where he was hoping she would find his physical prowess attractive, the relationship he and Peggy are developing is one emerging out of a common affection for Julia. As of late, the chemistry between these two has been driven more by who is more adamant in bringing Gil to justice than by honoring the memory of Julia. That's changing. Both are seeing where Julia needs to be honored in not just the single dimension of justice but also in honoring her life in theirs.

Becoming more transparent with each other in their grief, they move from Peggy's small tent to their campsite's picnic table where they continue sharing and borrowing memories. Mentally, Peggy is fully aware her sister is physically dead but oddly, she continues to share a soul communication the two of them have always held.

"I know she's dead, but I also know she's all right; I feel her just like I always have—that hasn't changed."

Out of a genuine concern for Peggy, Jim has chosen to let her have the floor. Not that his sorrow is any less than hers, he nonetheless, senses her need to talk.

In this climate, he is curious and poses a question, "Explain that to me. I want to understand what you just said. Are you saying that the two of you still communicate?"

Peggy hears his question and knows what he's asking. "What you're asking is 'does Julia speak to me with words in my ear?', the answer is no. But we do communicate the same way we always have. We have always known each other's thoughts. I know for certain that she is safe, loved, and happy. I know it just as certain as I knew she was being murdered. That's all I can tell you."

Jim listens attentively. From the beginning, thru his relationship with Julia, he has always sensed that the sister relationship she held with Peggy was always going to be much different than the most promising relationship held between himself and Julia; he understood that his and Julia's bond would always pale with the consummate bond Julia shared with her twin.

With a deeper sense of thought, Jim poses another question, "What do you think she's trying tell you?"

"It isn't so much telling me something as it is sharing our spirits." Peggy pauses for a moment to better define this seeming telepathic communication. "It's almost as though she wants for me what she has."

Over a month ago, prior to his happenstance meeting with these twins, Jim would have given very little—if any—thought to what Peggy is relating. His life has definitely changed. This strange connection Peggy has with Julia is a networking Jim wants to encourage. Even if he has to live vicariously through their connection, it's better than no connection at all.

This afternoon, Jim and Peggy have set a new pattern. It's resulted in setting aside their obsession with Gil to include keeping Julia's memory intact. They're also of the same mindset in finding they're enjoying each other's company; satisfied for who each other is. In so many ways, Jim sees so much of Julia in Peggy and Peggy is discovering more and more of what her sister had seen in Jim. At this point, neither of them is emotionally prepared to explore more, but are comfortable with the tie they share for now.

After a joint effort of putting together a meal, they retire to the privacy of their individual tents. Left with nothing other than their own thoughts and an ample amount of fatigue from a full day's activities, they soon drift off to sleep. Peggy's is particularly stressful. She has a vision of Julia off in the distance with a full smile, waving at her. She is overcome with joy but then Julia seemingly drifts off. It happens several times—enough to become disconcerting. The last time is enough to bring her from a deep sleep to an awake state. Fully awake, she decides to leave her tent and revive the fire enough to sit near it long enough to hope to begin to drift off to sleep again. Once outside her tent her eyes catch a movement inside their truck. Looking twice tells her it's the dim form of a man. Believing it to be Jim, she draws closer.

"I'm glad you're awake. There's something weird I want to talk to you about." What she meets is far from being Jim and more than enough to startle her. She lets out a gasp. What she discovers is none other than Gil rifling through their food, stuffing his mouth with as much as he can. In hearing her, he involuntarily snaps his head around, coming face to face with her. He nearly chokes on the remains. It's obvious he is as startled as Peggy. Of all the campsites he could have rifled, this would be the last he'd visit if he had the slightest inkling who its occupants were. Before Peggy can get out any more than a gasp, he is out of the truck hobbling off into the darkness. By this time, the commotion has awakened Jim, bringing him head long out of his tent. His first thought is there must be a bear in the camp. His face isn't much more than a shadow, but his voice tells the horror it's holding. Seeing Peggy still standing next to the truck and the truck's dome light reflecting of a face reflecting as much terror as his own.

"What the heck is all this commotion?" he says, struggling to discover its source.

Peggy is still struck with disbelief. "It was Gil, Jim. He was in your truck, stealing our food."

Still listening to Peggy's near hysterical account, Jim bounds into his truck. His eyes are darting from one area to another assessing how much of an unwanted foot-print Gil may have left. Satisfied nothing is damaged other than a bunch of candy bar wrappers strewn around making a mess. Still silent, Jim's thoughts are off in another direction; he's assessing something else.

"He's gotta be getting desperate to make a raid like this. It means he has no food and is relying on stealing enough to stay out there. According to the people back at the bar, he's also got some injuries. They were saying he was limping pretty bad."

Peggy is regaining her wits. "He was running with what looked like a stick supporting him," she reports.

189

Jim is listening but simultaneously, his mind is also speeding at nearly Mach speed. "Which way did you say he went?"

Wanting to be of maximum use, pointing off into the darkness Peggy, says excitedly, "That way!"

"That's exactly the direction where we found Ike's abandoned truck," returns Jim.

With this sudden change of events, Peggy decidedly leaves out her seeming visit with Julia. *It'll keep for now* is her thought as they both agree there is little they can do tonight and head back to try and finish getting their much-needed rest.

CHAPTER 22

Medevac'd

Gil had been milling around in the darkness looking for any sign of the campground when he spotted the slight glow left of a campfire. Carefully watching for any signs of a possible human interference, he had slowly hobbled into the campsite. Seeing no signs of the campers, he was satisfied everyone was sleeping. His expertise as a juvenile delinquent was to break into a car so silently that he was never caught. In this instance, remembering their encounter with the bear, Jim had—to Gil's advantage—left the doors unlocked in the event they needed to make a quick escape. Gil was very happy to find this advantage and was certain he was home free when he was suddenly interrupted by Peggy. Overwrought with pain, with the desperation of a cornered animal, he mindlessly charged into the darkness of the woods.

At this point, unable to make a quiet escape in the darkened forest he has opted to remain still until he can see better. The terror of being discovered by the very people he fears will kill him, if they should be so fortunate to capture him, is over riding the agony of being eaten alive; the mosquitoes are having a feast along with every other night creature that find him juicy.

It's during these times of inactivity that his mind returns to that fateful night only a few days prior. Usually when he has had an alcohol blackout, within a day or two his unaccountable activities begin to sort themselves out, but not this time; nothing is coming to mind to vindicate him.

His mind also returns him to his most recent encounter with Peggy. *If I did murder Julia, I don't know why I'd let Peggy live. As pretty as she is, she's been a pain in my neck ever since I hooked up with their mother.* His mind then drifts to the incident he just experienced with Peggy. *That was my chance and I blew it. I could've clubbed her with my hoe handle and stole the truck and I wouldn't be lyin' out here in this godforsaken, mosquito infested hell. But what'd I do? I ran like a baby girl.* Unable to sleep, Gil spends his time loathing everybody and everything. Finally, enough light begins to rid the forest of its weird shadows to allow Gil to begin to move around. In spite of being totally exhausted, he manages to get to his feet. By now, his ankle has taken on a yellow-green-black hue. He's remains uncertain as to whether it's broken or merely sprained.

The last time he suffered this kind of injury was back when he was running with Ike as a young boy. They had broken into a summer cottage looking for booze when they were discovered by a neighbor left in charge by the absentee owner. He had chased him and Ike into the woods. At some point, the two of them had split up. The pursuer chose Gil to run down. Gil had a decent enough head start until he stepped in a rabbit hole and went down. The only thing that saved him was the ferns were so thick they allowed him to lie undetected. He was certain he had broken his ankle, instead it turned out to be a bad sprain. This recent injury looks and feels much like it had in his former ordeal.

Not certain what his next plan is to be, Gil heads back to where he is certain of fresh water. "I'd much rather have a beer than that damn creek water," are his words said aloud to the pathless tangle of vines and fallen trees. This whole fiasco of hiding out in the woods is much more difficult than he remembered it being back when he was young and restless. The only food he's had in the last twenty-four hours is what he's been able to cram in his mouth before Peggy interrupted. He feels the same depredation with his lack of booze. He's starting to feel light -headed, it's getting harder to convince himself that prison life doesn't beat this. "At least there, I'd be eatin' three square meals a day and drinkin' all the spud juice I could handle." His voice is flat and expressionless without enthusiasm. He continues to walk without a destination. It's a staggering gait, digging his hoe handle deep in the soft forest floor as he twists his body with each stumbling step. He's taken on a grotesque hunch as he lurches forward. His world is made up of the twenty-foot circle he manages to fix a gaze on—but within a few steps it's gone and replaced with an entirely different twenty-foot world surrounded with its own layer of vines, ferns, dead trees, and underbrush. It's as though everything is crushing in on him with indifference. Nothing looks familiar, he knows he's lost, but armed with nothing more than a cold attitude, and a disheartened outlook, he moves only for the sake of having nothing else to do.

Gil's wristwatch is telling him it's nine o'clock in the morning, and still no sign of physical or mental relief. His shakes are becoming more intense and he getting some dry heaves. Each retching incident puts enough pressure on his swollen eye to make it feel like his head is going to explode. He drops to his knees holding his stomach as if it were ready to feel it course through his throat and exit his mouth. Exhausted, he lies on his back, gazing up through the forest's canopy. He's hungry and thirsty, he's got the shakes, the pain in his foot is only competing with his pounding headache, and there is hardly a square inch on his body that's not itching from bug bites. A noise catches his attention. Rolling over on his elbow, he locates its source. It's a mangy coyote that appears to be as forlorn and hungry as he is. It's staring at him as though it's running through its mind the chances of making a buffet of this decrepit excuse for a human. More angry than afraid and gripping the knife he absconded from Ike's truck and his hoe handle in the other, Gil yells as loud as his condition will allow him, "Get outta here, ya mangy gully dog, 'fore I mash yer skull." The coyote's ears go up. After thinking it through, it decides this guy has more life than it first thought. It rears back on its heels, turns, and runs off in search of a more opportune meal.

He'd like nothing more than to get some rest, but he's driven on by a combination of hatred for his perceived tormentors and the physical and mental pain of his broken body. It seems even his blood has turned bitter as stomach bile from all his retching burns the tender tissue in his throat. At the moment, he feels lower than a snake's belly in a wagon rut—but then, this is Gil's life pattern—he's either being tormented or he is the tormentor—he's either seeking revenge or others are seeking revenge against him. It's as though something inside him is crying out for relief but when it comes, he finds his community is more with misery and he rebuffs it, returning to the anvil chores as a dog to its vomit.

With the afternoon sun high in the sky, his strength is withering. With the forest canopy holding the heat, his body has reached the point where it will take any kind of liquid—even water—rather than suffer the pounding headache preceding heatstroke. With blind luck or some guardian angel taking pity on him, he finds himself facing the freshwater stream. With little thought of anything other than lying his body into the coolness of the stream he lays himself on its stony bed allowing the water to cascade over his feverish body. After drinking his fill, he crawls to the shore more tired than refreshed. Lying once more, flat on his back, with his eyes closed, he can feel the warmth of the sun. Inviting its heat against his wet skin, he drifts off to sleep. A few hours later, he awakens. The sun is setting along with its warmth, leaving him chilled and sick. For the first time in his adult life, Gil begins to cry. At first, it's muffled sobs against his arm. But as he lies by himself, alone, hungry, sick, and cold, his sobs become louder until the forest receives them as part of herself, resounding them as far reaching as the green light for sound allows.

Accepting once again life's indiscriminate misery, he pulls himself together enough to build a fire. With his comfort expectations lowered to below basement level, this small amenity gives him a semblance of joy. No sooner does he begin to gain back a bit of hope that he's going to survive than he hears something foreboding—a clap of thunder. With no shelter and an open fire, his sense of wellbeing has been at best short lived. A downpour will surely be the end of him.

This is a signal for him to begin to look for shelter. Whether it has to do with his weakened condition or something more serious, he's finding a shortness of breath and a near cramping feeling in his chest isn't permitting him to travel more than a few yards before he needs to sit down, exhausted, and faint. A new sense of survival is greeting him. The morbid feelings of victimization are being replaced with a desire to live. Resting long enough to clear his head he opts to stay right where he is. "I'm gonna build me a shelter." This sudden epiphany of life is reinvigorating his psyche. Using his hoe handle as a cross bar between to small trees, he begins to hack the low branches of the spruce, hemlock, pine and branches from any other thick leaved trees in the neighborhood. Carefully stacking them against his hoe handle cross bar, Gil has managed to put together a tent-like structure he hopes will keep him dry.

*

After the encounter with Gil, Peggy and Jim have returned to their tents. Hours earlier, they had been wiped out from all of the day's fast-moving events. Now both find it difficult to get back to sleep. Jim is lying on his back, hands behind his head attempting to slow his mind down enough to be pragmatic about how to deal with their ongoing situation with Gil. The more he tries to shut down his crazy thoughts, the swifter they fly through his mind.

The next sound he hears is Peggy's voice. "Can I come in your tent for a while? I can't stay alone, Jim. I don't trust Gil. I know he's still out there. If he can kill my sister, he won't hesitate to do the same to me."

Sitting up, Jim responds. Still unzipping the tent, Peggy nearly plunges in on top of him. (They may refer to these as "two-man" tents, but it's stretching it when two full-sized adults attempt to roll in any direction without kicking, punching, or generally mauling their partner—or worse yet, destabilizing the tent enough to cause it to collapse.)

What thoughts may have been plaguing Jim have been suddenly trumped. The idea of Peggy being in the same tent as himself brings with it a whole new line of understanding. This is a situation he had never had to experience with Julia despite their more intense interactions. Now he finds himself facing a terrified replica of Julia—mentally and physically— under circumstances he'd rather not have to deal with at this time. Strangely, he has been able to separate them enough to maintain an allegiance to Julia as though she were still in his life. He almost feels like he's cheating by finding Peggy almost as though Julia is her.

Peggy on the other hand, feels she can now assume Julia's share of what they both had seen in Jim. She is not feeling as though she is cheating against her sister in any way. As a matter of fact, it makes her feel closer to Julia to be with Jim. She has already admitted to herself that she intends to pick up with him where Julia had left off—and as far as she's concerned, he may as well get used to it.

Jim's feelings are complex. He had not dated Julia for longer than a month but despite that, he feels an allegiance to their budding relationship. He had struggled earlier during the time they were making this trip with Peggy's habits. Her looks, her gestures are all as Julia's had been. He had found himself almost calling her "Julia" at times. Having separate tents was good because for him it put things in their proper perspective. *She's not Julia. And I haven't shared my life with Peggy. They're two-separate people.* This is Jim's narrative that he poses to himself and hopefully to Peggy. But now he feels the same closeness creeping in on him that he and Julia had shared. *This is too crazy* is his thought. *Julia, you're barely dead, and I'm finding you resurrected in a girl named Peggy that I hardly thought I knew.*

The morning comes with Peggy waking to the smell of bacon. Jim has been up attending to the details that kept him awake most of the night. He has already patrolled around their campsite for any lingering sign of Gil. Finding nothing other than a few pieces of upturned dirt where Gil's hoe handle had been plunged in his haste, he has turned his attention to more domestic undertakings. He has a pan full of scrambled eggs with strips of well-cooked bacon. Peggy congratulates him on his domestic prowess. Again, this is something Jim would have expected from Julia. Peggy's smile and demeanor are hauntingly those of Julia's. Jim is trying hard to keep a differentiation where there seemingly is none. They are finished with breakfast when Jim's cell phone signals a call is coming in.

"Hello." He's quiet, as the caller has his attention. "You're kidding me," are the words Peggy hears him say. This conversation now has her attention. "Okay, thanks for calling, I appreciate it."

Peggy is all eyes and ears as she stares at Jim waiting for some response. Instead, he stands silent with a pensive look. Not willing to wait out his silence, Peggy says, "So?" It's as much a question as a statement.

"That was my cousin in Greeny's office. She called to tell me that the state police have taken over this case and have pinpointed Gil in this region through his cell phone. Something we already knew. They're bringing in dogs and helicopters with infrared as support."

Jim becomes even more pensive as Peggy chatters on, "I don't want them getting to him before we do. I need to be able to slap and kick him until he can't stand up. He's worse than a dog."

Jim is half listening. He finally is ready to say something. "We have only one choice as I see it. We have to get Ike to agree to help us."

Peggy is attentively readjusting her entire body in response to this idea. She found Ike just as creepy as Gil. But she is ready do what it takes to get a stab at Gil. Hastily getting things in order they make the trek toward Ike's. They find him sitting outside smoking a cigarette and drinking a cup of coffee. Seeing these two coming down between his neatly stacked cords of wood gives him pause. Jim brings his truck to a stop and before he can exit Ike is on his feet, defiantly waving his arms. "If you two city slickers want anything other than directions to get off my property, ya come to the wrong place."

Seeing Ike's belligerence, Jim takes a moment to regroup. He's well aware from their previous encounter that there is no love lost between these cousins—they'll fight over everything and anything. "We helped you get your truck back, and we were wondering if you'd like to help us get a stab at Gil before they bring in the whole United States Army to track him down?"

Ike's listening. Jim can sense there is something on his mind. "That S.O.B. stole my good buck knife and a half pint of Schnapps outta my truck. Plus, he broke my side mirror, an' I came close ta runnin' outta gas 'fore I got outta them woods. He owes me!"

Believing he has the right thought to place in Ike's mind, Jim says, "Like you're saying—Gil owes you."

"Dang tootin', he owes me. I still ain't got the hundred back I give 'im a long time ago."

"Well I don't know if you can get all of that stuff back, but you can sure as heck get even," says Jim. He's been around Ike just long enough to see that Ike can put almost as much value in getting even as he does in getting a dollar value owed; ninety-nine percent of Ike's life is led by an immediate visceral reaction.

Ike's attention is keen when it comes to his victimization. He believes he's been "rubbed raw" by people. His daily life is led by counting the slights he's endured. Jim has zeroed in on the basic fabric of Ike Gilles. "getting even." In the next moment, Ike has butted his cigarette and is mentally "suiting up" for the next episode. His mind is already doing calisthenics in preparation for this upcoming ultimate cage fight—except there will be no cage, just a bunch of trees.

He is visualizing an invitation to have a "no bars held," "free for all" fight with his hated cousin.

"I'll beat him so bad, his grandkids'll feel it," declares Ike with a little satisfied chortle at his attempt to say something original.

Jim is satisfied he has gained Ike's support once again. At least, he is satisfied that Ike's hatred for Gil matches his own. And he's hopeful it will remain strong enough to find Gil. Exactly what entails after the fact, is still up for grabs. Peggy and Ike have already made their plans to beat Gil once he's found and leave his remains for law enforcement. Jim certainly wants to get a few of his own licks in but short of killing or permanently maiming him.

"I'm takin' my own horse so's I can leave if the law gets to close," says Ike referring to driving his own truck.

"That's fine with me as long as you don't take us some place, we can't find a way out," replies Jim.

"Naw! If a moron like Gil finds his way around, you folks sure can," is another of Ike's assurances.

"I hope you're right," says Peggy very happy she doesn't have to be crammed in the truck cab next to Ike again.

Ike is leading the way once again. This time he takes them to another two-track trail leading back into the woods. Jim would never put his only vehicle through such torture under ordinary circumstances but his desire to have his way with Gil before the law interferes is paramount at the moment; it trumps his penchant to use common sense. These grown-over old logging trails left by men of some bygone era are cut in straight lines, despite the terrain. The idea was to get timber out by the shortest route possible, even if it meant traversing a hill instead of circumventing it. Jim's truck groans as it navigates a grade it's never tried before. He has a gear especially designed to ensure it will succeed. What seems like a trip to the states outer limits has come to an end. Ike has stopped short of a creek. Climbing out of his cab, Jim and Peggy notice he has a holstered pistol hanging off his belt. They are left with stares for only a moment.

"Yeah, I know I ain't s'posed to have a gun since I got felonies but when it comes to them damn bears with cubs, I'd rather be tried by twelve than carried by six," states Ike, giving his forty-four a light pat.

To be truthful, neither Jim nor Peggy have any qualms when it comes to having protection against wild life—they just hope Ike isn't planning on shooting Gil. A good beating, yes—a shooting not so much.

They are all out of their trucks. Ike is giving some thought to this creek. "I know for certain, ol' Gilly boy knows about this creek. It's the only fresh water in this section. We gonna find him along it in the next half mile for sure. Ain't no doubt about it."

With that, he starts down creek. The banks are mossy and wet enough to give a sucking sound to each step taken. Eager to meet their objective, Jim and Peggy fall in line.

Ike has something more to say. He's taken a liking to the importance these two are giving his guiding experience. "If I were him, I'd stay on this side of the creek 'cause there ain't no place to hide on the other side—ain't nothin but hard rocks over there."

At this point, there is no reason to disagree. They trudge on. The bugs are getting bad, and Peggy is beginning to complain. She's slapping first on one arm, then another. Jim is plagued also but since Ike isn't whining, neither is Jim going to. Ike, on the other hand, doesn't seem to have any bug complaints. In the next moment, he's produced what appears to be a can of snuff.

"Here, put some of this stuff on ya."

Peggy takes the can, opens it and after a quick examination, realizes it's the smell of Ike's that she's been complaining about. She looks at the open can, then at Jim, and then at Ike.

"What is this stuff?"

Ike takes the open can from Peggy's hand. "This here is boiled-down coon fat. There ain't a thing this stuff can't cure. A good chuckin' of this stuff on a hemorrhoid, it'll shrink it down ta nothin. An' sure enough, I found it keeps the bugs off ya."

"I'll take the bug bites," declares Peggy, holding her hand up.

Jim looks at the can and smells it. He, too, hands it back to Ike.

With an offhand shrug of the shoulders, Ike retrieves his potion and puts it back in his pocket. Trudging on, he says, "Suit yourself."

The going is slow because of the up and down terrain along the creek banks. At his juncture, and with his most imposing voice, Ike says, "From here on, we go inland." He nods to indicate their direction. "He's gonna be somewhere in there."

The next sound is a clap of thunder. The concern about Gil's whereabouts is suddenly abandoned in favor of thoughts about where they're going to find shelter.

*

The sky has turned dark, dark grey, nearly obliterating normal daylight. Rain is beginning to pour in what Michiganders refer to as "raining in buckets." It's the kind of storm Michigan is used to—the kind of gale that can hardly come about by caprice. Over days, the clouds have sucked up water from the Great Lakes and are redistributing it inland in quantities that resemble a deluge of Biblical proportions. This is one of those storms.

Gil has finished his crude survival hut just in time to meet the storm's fury. He lies inside without movement, soaked with sweat from the day's heat saturating his miserable body and each of his hundreds of bug bites itching and burning from the salty irritant. *A miserable day*, he thinks.

Again, in the loneliness of his seemingly soulless mind, he replays the vision of Julia's lifeless body lying on the stairs. He curses its unwelcome intrusion. Wracked with pain, he rolls over on his side in an effort to escape the vision. "How could I have done that?" he asks himself for the thousandth time. Inside him, the ever-flowing river of fear and hate has become a hell on earth where no breath of heaven will come. He suffers alone. He's shaking now more from an internal palsy than from the lack of alcohol. There is life around him— healthy, strong life, very much alive, and he knows his sick demons are trailing him, knowing all along who is going to die first. They wait with wistful stares hoping to totally consume him. For the present, they are content to sit like crouching vultures with visions of a dying prey.

The rain continues, coming in torrents, defying his best attempts to remain sheltered. It's pouring in on him as though he had no shelter at all. His efforts to protect himself are completely compromised. He may as well have saved what energy he had left and met the elements unprotected.

As horrible as it is, he has become nearly immune to life's notions since he expects nothing more than to remain a plaything to destiny.

His thoughts change suddenly as he realizes the thunder storm has passed and it's replaced by a new sound of thunder, only this time it's coming from an overhead in the form of a chopper. He has an idea that it has a connection to him. Rolling with the consequences of being found and the penalties accompanying it with what's left of his mind, is blurred by delusions. His mind is becoming fragmented with disconnected thoughts where sanity is replaced with the insanity of his distress; where a moment ago the helicopter was in his reality, a moment later, it's part of a movie he's watching. Even his curiosity is dulled by his deteriorating mental condition. He's content to lie inside his rain-soaked shelter and chew on his shirt's cuff as though he were a defeated child.

He lies totally broken and unresponsive as he senses someone angrily speaking to him and kicking him at the same time.

"Come on outta there, ya S.O.B. You been found."

Amid his delusions, Gil recognizes the voice of his cousin, Ike. Ike has ripped the shelter apart and is beginning to kick his cousin without mercy. Gil feels it but has no feelings about it. The sensation of pain has left his compromised body; it's as though his brain has shut down his nervous system to let him die in peace. At this point, Gil has no reason to wish to live. He's been beaten to where he has no life left in him. He doesn't even have enough life to wish for a quick death; in many ways, it's as though he is already dead.

Ike continues with his singleness of purpose; to impose insufferable pain on Gil. Peggy is watching with new eyes. What she is seeing is a man who has already been beaten to a point where he will no longer feel her vengeance. It's as though he has died before she could get her licks in. The entire scene is proving to be a disappointment on the one hand, but it is a little satisfying to no longer see her nemesis as a threat.

Jim is also seeing a part of himself in Ike. It's a part he is finding he loathes. He is discovering in watching Ike continue to pummel a helpless man that, that it is himself doing this despicable deed as much as it is Ike.

Ike has the sick grin of a man enjoying the misery of another—even more so since his victim can no longer defend himself. The Germans have a name for it—they call it *Schadenfreude.*

This is not to remain the only sound in the forest, another sound is unexpectedly noted from another direction. It's the sound of a men's voices. Within seconds the awareness of these voices is apparent. There appear three uniformed Michigan State Policemen. All three have pistols drawn, including one with a leashed dog tugging at the restraint.

"EVERYONE, LAY FACE DOWN AND PUT YOUR HANDS BEHIND YOUR HEAD!"

Each of them, with the exception of Gil, are taken by surprise. Gil, aware of very little, is already face down as he teeters between consciousness and unconsciousness. On the other hand, the others are trying their best to process what has just crept up on their blindside.

Not satisfied with the gradualness of their responses, the same voice bellows out the same imperative.

"FOLLOW ORDERS! NOW! EVERYONE, ON THE GROUND, PUT YOUR HANDS BEHIND YOUR HEAD!

At this juncture everyone—with the exception of Gil who is already as prone as he can get—places their hands behind their head.

"EVERYONE ON YOUR KNEES!

Each of them is quickly on their knees.

"EVERYONE, LAY FACE DOWN!"

Without exception all four are lying face down. Within seconds all of them are cuffed and pulled to their feet. What they are observing is a squad of uniformed Michigan State Policemen. Little conversation is transpiring as each of these detainees are then searched.

The dog handler is the only one of the officers not participating in the pat down. Peggy is the only one not patted down until they can get a female officer on site. She is placed sitting with her back against a tree trying not to draw the dog's attention. Ike's prison involvement gives him a near reflexive action to the officer's requests. They are well aware of this kind of obsequiousness, as it only comes from convicts. Jim is next on their list to question. Then it's Peggy's turn.

Arriving in time to view Ike's free-wheeling exhibition in beating Gil, these lawmen are viewing Jim and Peggy with the same wary eye they are Ike. They are told they are being held as accomplices. Soon, each is allowed to give a rendition as to what has been transpiring.

These policemen aren't in the least bit impressed by this act of vigilantism—especially when they realize Gil's grave condition. He is in such bad shape they have to medivac him by helicopter to a hospital in Marquette.

Jim and Peggy along with Ike are all going to be held in jail for the allotted seventy-two hours to allow law enforcement to put together the charges they are going to be charged with so bail can be set.

CHAPTER 23

Life Summons

Sylvia is having her own issues. She's been ordered to an alcohol rehab but has been transferred to a psychiatric ward for the mentally ill for further evaluation. Her bizarre rantings have promoted a further evaluation of her mental deterioration.

Thanks to Jim's father, Jim and Peggy are out on bail. They had been charged as accomplices in an assault. Despite Gil's injuries, the family code to seek retribution in their own way and keep the law out of their family business prevailed, since Gil refuses to press charges against anyone. Nonetheless, the state is bringing the charges against Ike, Peggy and Jim, disregarding Gil's refusal to prosecute. Gil has been released from the hospital and is being prepared to be extradited back to his district in lower Michigan to face a possible open murder charge.

With all that's going on in Peggy's life, she has decided to stay home from college until her legal issues are settled. In the meantime, she needs transportation. Jim has agreed to meet that need as best he can, but Peggy has decided to get the Subaru back on the road. The only apparent problem with it seems to be that it won't start. It's been determined that when Sylvia had backed the Subaru into the ditch and Bob Zachar pulled it out and placed it back in the driveway, he had left the ignition key in a position that drained the battery. Jim—always prepared—supplies the needed jumper cables to recharge the battery enough to start the engine.

Hearing the familiar rough but encouraging sound of the Subaru's engine brings a satisfying smile on Peggy face. This is as elated as she's been in days. Before she can give this situation another thought, in her exuberance, she plants a kiss on the side of Jim's cheek. This causes both to come to a halt; it's brought about a reflexive pause. They both stand looking at one another. What they are unexpectantly dealing with is the culmination of spending days with one another where a new feeling for each other has developed. It had been manageable until this moment, when their feelings are fiercely overwhelming their managing skills. Their eyes are nervously trying to read the others facial language as they find they have interlocked with each other's fingers in a feeble attempt to hug without hugging. This action has brought another level to this relationship; it's a new link that has opened the door allowing a more intense connection. Jim is still battling some inside battle that on one hand knows intellectually this is not Julia but on the other hand this woman standing before him looks, acts, even reacts the way Julia did. He's not certain if his feelings are not much more than allowing Peggy to be the vicarious substitute for Julia or if he's really in love with Peggy.

While he continues to mull over his confusion, Peggy has taken it upon herself to move this connection to another level yet—she has planted her lips firmly on Jim's. In her heart of hearts, along with her continual bond with her twin, she has not the least doubt that she is fulfilling a relationship that had been begun by her womb mate. Jim feels the familiar flush of desire he had held for Julia wave over him like a heaven-sent sensation. The gates of his heart swing wide open, he feels his blood rushing to those places in his body making him light headed. Unable to contain himself, he gives in to this new encounter. With weak knees, a rapid heartrate, heavy breathing, he wraps both his arms around Peggy, drawing her, as if he dares, ever closer to his heart. Oblivious to the fact they are standing in the driveway until a passing car sounds its horn. Had this peck on the cheek been seen as they had been doing yard work or some menial task, this small sign of affection would have would have initiated no more than a friendly wave. However, in this case, being far from the initial little peck on the cheek, it had transformed into a full-blown display of affection that is oblivious to where they are, or who is paying attention, and how passionate *it* had turned into. The embarrassment of being discovered initiates a small chuckle between them.

Peggy is determined to pick up this relationship at the point where Julia had dropped off, whereas, Jim is slowly making an adjustment. It's not that he lacks feelings for Peggy as much as it is that he finds it confusing to set his grief aside for what amounts to hurling himself headlong into a relationship with Julia's sister.

"I know that you aren't Julia, but in so many ways, you are Julia. You leave me comfortable in one way and muddled in another," confesses Jim as they continue to explore their engulfing series of ordeals.

"Because I know how my sister treasured you, I share that feeling toward you with her. I am also attracted to you for the same reasons, in the same way," assures Peggy.

Never experiencing the kind of relationship Peggy had with Julia in life and now seemingly continuing in death, Jim remains tangled in his feelings.

"This whole ordeal makes me feel like a bigamist. Like I have two different girlfriends that are different people but in so many ways the same person. I'm attracted to you like I am to Julia. It's all very weird. It's like the boundaries of faithfulness have been removed to include you both," reports Jim, using his usual pragmatic reasoning.

"Julia and I have always thought of ourselves as two separate people, but that didn't prevent us from bonding in such a way that included an extrasensory connection to each other. We may have two separate bodies, but we share so much of the same mind."

Remaining with more questions than anyone can answer, Jim is relinquishing and is becoming more willing to let nature take its course.

Satisfied the Subaru will start, Jim reluctantly leaves Peggy to return to his job at the camp. Peggy is also ready to go back to work. Casually stopping by the Midway for lunch she hopes to re-establish her connection. With school out, this time of the year is busy, and they appreciate the extra help. Without Gil there, she's thinking it's actually not a bad place to work. Mandy is still the manager and has no qualms about hiring a seasoned waitress like Peggy.

"I want you to know how our thoughts have been with you since the loss of your sister. We all know how hard it must be for you to go through what you are suffering. There isn't anyone who wouldn't help put a rope around Gil's neck and let him dangle."

"Hangings too good for him," says Peggy in a flat, emotionless voice.

Realizing Peggy wouldn't need any assistance, Mandy gets the picture and is ready to change the subject.

"Since you know the routine, you can start tomorrow morning getting things ready for the lunch crowd."

Over the next few days, things are falling back into a routine. Within the week, Greeny has sent a deputy to the upper peninsula to bring Gil back after he spent the week recovering in the hospital. His sprained ankle and black eye proved to be the least of his injuries. After Ike had nearly kicked him to death, he suffered from bruised ribs, a cracked vertebra in his neck, plus all his contusions. The doctor pumped him full of enough pain medicine for the ride back to Greeny's jurisdiction.

Ike has managed to bail himself out. When he was told he would more than likely go back to prison, he decided to take his fate into his own hands. He tied one end of a rope to a rafter in his garage and put the other end around his neck. Standing on a chair, he kicked it out from under himself and began the slow process of strangling himself to death. The next thing he's aware of is being on a gurney with a uniformed policeman standing by him. The police had driven to his residence to serve a warrant. The garage door was open. Seeing him twisting on the end of the rope they cut him down, started CPR, resuscitated him and are now arresting him on his warrant and sending him to jail. Ike's luck continues in the direction it always has—down. The people who know Ike, often discuss his only glaring virtue. It's usually put in terms that bring on a howl of laughter. It goes something like this, "There ain't no way ya can consider Ike a total failure as long as he can be used as a horrible example." Unfortunately for Ike, his life course is well on its way to completion.

Sylvia is also having her difficulties. Doctors are trying to get a handle on her deteriorating condition. They fear she may have cirrhosis of the liver. Alcohol has not been a factor since it hasn't been available, although her physical and mental condition continue on a downhill spiral. Her face has gone from tired looking to taking on an almost crazed, jaundiced appearance. It's as though some outside demonic force has come to occupy her. She is obsessed with a continual tirade of frustration against Gil for his lack of accountability in Julia's death. "He couldn't leave her alone; he was always trying to mess with her," she repeats over and over. Her thoughts have turned dark, like she's ready to jump out of a window. Her sleep is sporadic and what sleep she manages is filled with horror where waking is an act of saving herself.

Peggy is struggling with herself in how she intends to relate to her mother. Her thoughts swirl around groups of convoluted notions, "*I really don't want to see her. I have nothing to say to her. And maybe I don't want to see her. Where I have always hoped she'd improve if she'd just quit drinking, now, drunk or sober she's even less capable of being a mother than she's ever been.*"

Whenever her thoughts drift toward her mother all her grief over the loss of Julia's physical presence turns to anger, which if dwelt on too long has a tendency to go to the next level—rage. Nonetheless, this morning as Peggy wakes, the thought of visiting her mother has become an idea that won't give her a way out. She has the day off from the Midway, Jim is working at the camp and the Subaru has been put back together enough to get her to and back from the stress center.

Readying herself, she stops at Russ's garage long enough to fill up with gas and have the tire pressure checked. An hour and a half later, she's entering the rehab center. Her thoughts are centered around all the events that have taken place over the past couple of weeks and how much her life has changed. Taking a moment to collect herself, she stands outside her mother's door. Taking a deep breath, she enters. What she meets is a total surprise. She finds her mother sitting in a chair, staring unblinkingly out the window. She is picking at something only she seems to be aware of on the blanket covering her scrawny legs.

"Hello, Mother," says Peggy with a longing look for something better than what she is encountering. The disappointment is written on every furl of her young brow.

Sylvia doesn't seem aware of her surroundings and that includes Peggy. Having followed in behind Peggy a nurse with a cup of what appears to be ginger ale is attempting to place the straw between Sylvia's lips. Looking at its color, she brightens up as though she is expecting something more potent than ginger ale. After tasting it, she pushes away any further attempts. Since little more than a few weeks have passed since Julia's death, Sylvia has rapidly gone downhill to a point where Peggy is struggling with what she is seeing of this woman sitting right in front of her. Whatever was left of the motherly love Sylvia had for Peggy two weeks ago has disappeared. Looking at Sylvia today, Peggy barely sees a remnant of the woman who she has called "Mother" for her entire life. Not able to contain her feelings any longer, Peggy can't take her eyes away from her mother.

"Julia and I have begged, pleaded, and threatened you to stop drinking," she declares. "But you wouldn't stop! You never cared what was best for Julia and me. You only thought of yourself, and how much you wanted a man in your life. For that matter, the men you brought into our lives were pigs.

They demeaned all of us. Now my sister is dead because of your stupidity. It was you who brought her killer into our home."

These last words should be a challenge to any person with a healthy attitude, but in Sylvia's case, they simply echo through her room without a response.

In the next moment, Sylvia's head drops, she begins to cry—not for Peggy or Julia but for Gil. "Oh, my poor Gil. You know how I love you. I begged you to stay away from Julia. You never listen to me. Now she's dead. You killed her, and it's all your fault. For God's sake!" she says, and goes back to her blank stare. Finished with her stare, Sylvia's mouth begins to move once more as if she had another thought. "I was always pretty. Gil used to tell me I was pretty." As if a second thought occurs, she adds, "He said Julia was pretty." After saying this, her mind drifts off to some other place.

Peggy sits staring at her mother as she desperately tries to process these words coming out of the mouth of a person who calls herself a mother. It's as though her outburst had been unheard and for certain disregarded.

Even though Peggy and Julia had always held out in hopes things would eventually change with their mother, Peggy is finally realizing her mother is who she is and will never be that butterfly emerging from a cocoon they longed for. Seeing her now, in view of the life she's led, Peggy knows she can never be any different; what you see is what you get.

Peggy is digging around in her purse for a Kleenex. She gently wipes the ginger ale dripping from her mother's chin. It's not a case of a role change—after all, roles can't change if roles were never established. This helplessness revealed by Sylvia has caught Peggy's sympathy. At this point, Sylvia is incapable of doing either a good deed or a bad one. Rather it's a case of one human seeing a weakness and showing kindness to that weakness. At one time, Peggy would have run. Today, she has an unwarranted compassion for this pitiful woman. At this moment, Peggy feels Julia's strong presence. It's as though Julia is sending a message in absentia to contribute her part of the concern for their mother.

By going to prison, Peggy's father disappeared and for any practical purpose has remained out of sight her entire life. He disappeared like Julia disappeared: both without a trace. Now her mother—whether good or bad—is slipping away. For the moment, Peggy is sensing a feeling of loneliness. Regardless, she has never run from anything in her life and isn't about to begin now. Life has taught her better. It is only when Peggy gets to the parking lot that she begins to cry. It's like a part of life has ended that shouldn't have. Despair, tragedy, gloom, desolation, and anguish would like nothing more than to have their way to remind her every day for the rest of her life that her present is her future, to just quit and join Julia. Having her cry out of the way, she takes a deep breath. Her mind drifts to the words of one of her coaches: "To get out of life all that it has to offer requires you to be all in." Letting out the breath, she feels a hand on hers. She knows it's Julia letting her know she isn't alone. With that, she starts the Subaru. It's time to get on with life.

CHAPTER 24

Drained

By now the regional newspapers are hot on this latest murder. According to one account, the last homicide in this county was twenty-five years ago. Greeny has gone through the process of extraditing Gil and has sent Jack Pattengale, an officer of the court, to make the trip to bring Gil back to his jurisdiction. Jack has also served as the code enforcer for the county and has had dealings with Gil over much of the debris surrounding his property.

Gil has spent a few days of recovery in the hospital. Other than bruised ribs, a broken nose, and less than life-threatening bruises everywhere on his body, Gil has been released from the hospital with the understanding that he's in sufficient shape to make the trip. They have posted a deputy outside his hospital door for security reasons. Not only is Gil considered a flight risk, but as a suspected murderer, he also poses a threat to the hospital personnel as well as other patients. As soon as he is released from the hospital, he is taken to the county jail to await his extradition.

This morning, Jack makes official contact with the jail after a good night's rest. He had arrived the day before but since it's nearly a six-hour drive, he had rented a motel room to ensure he'd be in a rested condition to make the return trip. On completion of the paperwork, all that's left to do is to bring Gil out of the waiting cell, exchange handcuffs, secure him in the backseat of the waiting sedan, and wave goodbye and good riddance to an expense this poor county hardly needed.

Jack's eyes are directly on Gil as he half scuffles, half limps his way to the waiting car. He's manacled on both wrists as well as both ankles. Waiting beside the open back door of his unmarked sedan, Jack sports a mocking grin.

Being the first to acknowledge Gil, he says, "You ain't lookin' so hot, Gil. You fall down some stairs or somethin'?"

Hearing the sarcasm in Jack's voice, Gil responds saying, "Yeah, somethin' like that. To damn bad you wasn't in front of me."

Jack is hardly willing to ignore Gil's rebuff. Even though special considerations have been made due to Gil's injuries to space his arms further apart by linking two sets of cuffs together, when the cuffs are exchanged, Jack makes certain he tightens them an extra notch. Gil's wince gives Jack a little satisfied grin. Eager to get on the road, Gil is quickly placed in the caged back seat of the sedan. Taking his place behind the wheel, Jack begins the long trek back to the Mackinac Bridge and down into the lower peninsula.

Once again alone, this time in the caged back seat of a police car, Gil is rehashing the actions that led to these unseemly results. He still can't get a handle on his part in Julia's death. *"I know I was drunk, but I can't remember anything."* This has been an ongoing conundrum for Gil since he stormed out of Sylvia's house the morning that he discovered Julia's body on the stairway. Jack isn't helping the situation. He's been in law enforcement long enough to know when people are struggling with something. Since Jack has a personal grudge against Gil for managing to circumvent his attempt to get what Gil convinced the judge was his "collection" under control, he's decidedly uncoiling his needling skills.

"You better hope you got a better lawyer than that flunky you been using to protect that junkyard you got going on."

Gil has no other choice than to listen. He's trapped in the back seat. There is something guarded about his silence. He doesn't trust Jack any less than Jack trusts him. In many ways, the two of them are cut from the same cloth; it's just that they're on opposite sides of the law. Gil's musings continue, *"I know the law ain't gonna give me no break.*

They're all against me. I don't stand a chance. I gotta do somethin'."

The miles add up. By lunch time, Jack has decided on a truck stop that serves, "The best damn pasties in the UP."

The restrooms provide an outside access, and Jack has found a parking spot nearly in front. Leaving Gil locked in the back seat, he makes use of the facility first. Finishing, he returns to retrieve Gil. Gil is required to remained cuffed, but his cuffs are rearranged so his arms are in front of him. This allows him to feed himself and, as Jack puts it, "I may be required to be in the room with you when you piss, but I ain't unzippin' your pants." Gil hobbles to the rest room with Jack in tow. Standing at the urinal, he makes a quick analysis of his surroundings. It's a small room. The door has a lock. Gil is prepared for any opportunity that will present itself. Jack is impatiently waiting. Gil takes a little longer than Jack likes, provoking him to say, "Quit playin' with yourself and get goin'."

On the outside, Gil is slowly going through the motions of finishing his business. Hardly able to contain himself at Gil's dawdling, Jack impatiently turns his back to open the door. In a flash, Gil seizes the opportunity. In less time than it takes to say "Jumpin' Jack Flash," Gil has leaped forward toward Jack's backside, his manacled wrists have wrapped around Jack's throat, pulling tighter and tighter as Jack helplessly tries to pry them loose. Gil can feel the excruciating pain in his bruised ribcage screaming as he tightens his hold on Jack's neck. Gil is used to pain, and at times, seems to welcome it—this is one of those times. His hatred for Jack is exemplified by his willingness to endure whatever pain it takes to even the score for all Jack's taunting in the past few hours. It's finally accomplished. Jack's body slumps to the floor. Knowing in which pocket Jack has placed the keys to his manacles, Gil quickly frees himself. His next step is to rid himself of his orange jail coveralls and replace them with Jack's civilian clothes. Quickly stripping Jack and re-clothing himself, he drags Jack's lifeless body to the toilet stall and, with what little strength he has left, sets him on the toilet. With the keys to the car in hand, a different set of clothing, and Jack's billfold, identification, and 9MM service revolver, Gil tosses his cast-off county-issued jumpsuit and manacles in the bathroom's trash can. He calmly locks the bathroom door behind him, gets in the car, and proceeds down the highway. The first thing he does is stop at the first store that sells cigarettes and beer. Within ten minutes, he has already consumed an entire forty-ounce bottle of beer and a cigarette. Once again, he's beginning to feel like his old self.

To put his pressing schedule into action, his goal is to place as many miles between himself and the truck stop as possible. It isn't relevant in what direction he travels, as long as he doesn't get caught. With the beer calming him down, he's decided on making a return trip to the lower peninsula. His next goal is to get to and cross the Mackinac Bridge.

Gil is aware that when Jack's body is discovered without ID, it will take a while to identify him. He calculates this bit of introspection into his escape equation. By late in the afternoon, he has crossed the bridge and is finding himself staring at a sun that's well on its way to dumping itself into Lake Michigan for the trillionth time. There suddenly appears a restaurant with a bunch of upside-down women's legs. Its name is, of all things, Legs Inn. After finding a parking space that does not expose the car to someone who's just passing by, he cautiously enters. Torn between using Jack's credit card and saving his cash, he decides to spend the cash. After ordering himself a steak and lobster dinner washed down with several of the area's microbeers, he returns to the parking lot to see a young man peering into his car.

"Hey, bud, what d'ya think you're doin'?" he half shouts, not wishing to draw any undue attention.

The young man is affable and simple enough in his answer. "I'm from downstate. I work in the car factory that put these cars together. The state wanted a GPS locater in each of these. It was my job to install them. I was just looking to see if this beast was one that I worked on."

This answer suddenly has Gil's full attention. This is information he hadn't been aware of. Cussing under his breath, he replies, "So, what d'ya think, kid? This one of those?"

The young man takes a second look. "Open the door, and I'll tell you."

Gil complies. Lying on his back on the driver's side, the young man begins an examination of the under portion of the dashboard. With his head still below, he announces, "Yup, sure is. The fuse I put in is right here."

Gil pokes his head in its direction with the intention of locating it and disabling it. Satisfied he can solve this problem in a few minutes once he's alone, he thanks the kid. Looking around more out of habit than actually suspecting someone to know his intentions, he locates the small fuse holder and pulls it out. Certain things are beginning to go in his direction. He gives himself a knowing little smile—that is, until he attempts to start the engine, and all he gets is silence. The removal of that little fuse is designed to cripple both the GPS and the engine. Sitting there like someone had burst his big bubble of satisfaction that things were finally going his way, he feels the cloud of frustration reforming as though it had never forsaken him. Not ready to give way, he quickly gives the car a last once-over. After grabbing the bag of things that he'll need to pull off his next angle, Gil abandons the vehicle as though it contains a virus. Slowly, with the purpose of a thief in the night, he begins his prowl among the cars in the parking lot, searching for the elusive driver who has left his keys in the ignition. These are always locals who brag about trusting their neighbors but are oblivious to the Gils of this world who are opportunists and rely on taking advantage of their trusting nature. Attempting to appear touristy, Gil makes casual sweep after sweep of these vacated cars, hoping to stumble on that negligent patron who will leave their car unlocked.

It's not happening, and Gil is beginning to get antsy about the clear-cut possibility of being found through his all-afternoon connection to this GPS. In the typical Gil way of doing things, he is contemplating going to a new level; he is ready to throw finesse to the wind and get back in the groove of doing things his way. Not willing to wait out the random negligent person leaving their keys and car together, Gil steps up his crusade. The next person coming out of the restaurant becomes his focus. In a very aggressive manner, he has placed Jack's service revolver at the head of this unaware patron. "GIMME YOUR KEYS, OR I'LL PUT A BULLET THROUGH YOUR MISERABLE HEAD!"

The terrified patron is taken totally by surprise. It's a young woman who on her best day would be no match against a man with a gun. The look on her face is terror. Without a second thought and still without enough time lapsing to begin to shake, she surrenders her keys. With keys in hand, Gil shoves her aside, knocking her to the ground. With the swiftness of one who is accustomed to this kind of violence, Gil is behind the wheel, reeling the car out of the parking lot. Once on the road and out of danger of an immediate challenge, his nerves settle down enough not to do anything erratic. It's just as well, because he meets four Michigan State Police cars coming in the opposite direction. His hunch is that they've found Jack's body and have been alerted, but it's actually the GPS in his stolen state-owned vehicle that has brought them swarming toward the restaurant. With a wary eye on his rearview mirror, he pushes the accelerator a little harder.

The twilight period of the evening is giving its last warning before darkness sets in. Determined to stay on as many backroads as possible, Gil presses on. His intention is to get to a hunting camp down near Arcadia before morning. It's never used during the summer, and it's well hidden at the end of a quarter-mile two-track. A look at the gas gauge convinces him he needs to look for a filling station—one that also sells beer. His prayers are answered; a Shell Mart is suddenly perched on the four corners in front of him. As he pulls in, he notices a county sheriff's car parked in front. Cautiously, he attempts to use a pump that is difficult to see from that angle.

His first thought is, "I need to be in a spot where I can drive off if I need to."

Keeping a wary eye everywhere, he watchfully makes his way to the inside. Scanning the store, he spots the two officers in a small deli attached to the mart. They appear to be sidelined, eating sandwiches and flirting with a cute waitress. Determined he's going to pick up a couple forty-ouncers, he attentively makes his way to the coolers and grabs his beer along with a jar of peanut butter and a loaf of bread. Making his way to the checkout counter, the clerk challenges him: "Card or cash?"

He's a bit rattled over the two deputies sitting less than twenty feet from him and trying to keep his attention in their direction, so the clerk has caught him off guard. Before he can think the decision through, he hears himself say, "Card."

Here and now, Gil has created a situation where he has to rifle through a billfold that he's unfamiliar with. Still concerned about the officers, he finally musters up a card. Handing it to the clerk, he hears the words, "We don't take Mastercard."

Straining to remain calm, Gil retrieves the card saying, "Cash," as quietly as he can. He notices one of the deputies glancing his way. The next question the clerk is concerned with is, "Would you like paper or plastic?"

Struggling with his demeanor, Gil puts on his most restrained face, saying, "Plastic."

He is terrified to look in the direction of the cops for fear he'll meet a gaze he hopes he'll not need to encounter. As purposely as he can under these unseemly circumstances, he walks out and circles his stolen car, which allows him to face the path he's just taken. Half expecting to see two lawmen on their way, he sighs with relief when he only sees a mother and child making their way to the restroom. Not willing to spend even another second in this less than comfortable environment, Gil gladly hits the road once again. Cracking open a beer, he takes as many gulps as his shortness of breath will allow.

It's dark as he passes through a small town: the village of Elberta. He calculates that he'll be at his destination in less than a half hour. His calculations prove correct. Soon, his headlights are reflecting off a green, antiquated sign announcing, "Arcadia Hunting Club." Taking a minute to slow down enough to look at the rusted chain stretched across the driveway, Gil can decipher by the lack of car tracks that no one is there. (The only reason he is aware of this place is because he stumbled across it a number of years ago, when he answered an advertisement for a motorcycle that was for sale. In typical Gil fashion, he stayed the night, but not without helping himself to whatever canned goods they had left in the lodge.)

In short order, Gil unhooks the chain, drives through, re-hooks it, and makes his way down the two-track to the lodge. His headlights hit the same green tar-papered lodge pieced together over the past hundred years to accommodate someone's idea of comfort on the inside at the expense of pleasing architecture on the outside.

Tired and less than happy about the way his day has ended, he breaks the same window to gain entry he had a few years previously. The place still has the same old, musty smell Gil recalls from the last time. He uses his headlights until he can light one of the Coleman lanterns left on a table. Holding the lantern above his head, he chooses one of the beds on one of the lower bunks. The bedding shares the same musty smell of the rest of the lodge—but then, Gil has never paid much attention to his bedding.

Quiet times have never been Gil's allies. This is when his past actions reappear in his mind. The mere recollection of Jack's taunts brings back his anger and reliving the action he took in chocking the life out of this nemesis. This recall is enough to bring about a feeling of self-righteous indignation all over again. With no one else to share his construed victory, he congratulates himself once more. "That S.O.B. got what was comin' to 'im. Wish I could kill 'im again."

After killing off another forty-ouncer, Gil settles down enough to fall asleep. His rest is never the rest needed to refresh oneself after a hard day's work; rather, his is the restless kind where he wakes every few hours. Daylight is never the best part of Gil's day—nonetheless, it's here for him to deal with once again. After his usual hour of hacking, shaking, smoking several cigarettes, and finishing off the last of his beer, he's ready to meet the day.

It's time to let the day unfold. Riffling through the cabin, Gil comes across a pair of binoculars. Focusing across the couple acres of treeless field, he spots a wooden structure. On closer examination, he concludes it's a deer blind. It's pretty fancy. It's up in the air on stilts, but has a set of steps ascending to a door but not until it stops at a small porch. Musing over this wonder, he moves the binoculars slightly over head. What comes into view causes him to snap the binoculars down and head for the car. What he has sighted is a drone. He isn't really familiar with their use, but he's certain it has something to do with him. The first thing he notices when he enters the car is a small purse tucked between the driver's seat and the console. He's overlooked it in his haste and the darkness. He stares at it for a second. His mind believes it's something that he should have seen. Tenuously, he pulls it free. Unzipping it brings to view the very item he was hoping it wasn't: a cell phone. He slams it to the ground with his eyes snapping upward, rescanning the sky for the drone. "How could I be so stupid?" are the only words he's able to complete. In the next second, he's thrown the phone to the ground. It's apparent this device has a GPS and is the signaling contrivance alerting the law to his whereabouts. His mind has no other message than to escape as quickly as possible. Tearing down the two-track at a speed designed for a less formidable road, he is banging off the side trees and spewing a rooster tail of dirt behind each rear wheel. The chain crossing the two-track is looming in front of him. With no mindset other than to flee, he doesn't bother to stop and remove it; instead, he charges through it, snapping it loose. The indescribable sound accompanying the chain scraping across the hood and meeting the windshield of this Chevy sedan leaves its evidence with a cracked windshield. The other episode awaiting him are the presence of two very blue Michigan State Police cars. They have set themselves in a position to overtake him before he can get to the road. Seeing his less than desirable conditions, his only option is to return back down the same road he's attempting to exit. Meeting his circumstances, the "Gil" way, he slams on his brakes, throws the car into reverse and backs at a break neck speed back down the two-track careening off the same trees he had attempted to extract in the other direction. The two police cars are in sudden hot pursuit. With the end of the drive is the open field. Yet again, he slams the brakes and turns the wheel in such a way that the car is replaced in a forward position. Smashing the shifting knob down into drive, Gil floors the accelerator. The car's rear end is fishtailing as he begins to circle the house. The two patrol cars are not about to let this maneuver through them off; each of them is determined to overtake him. What they haven't calculated is when he circled the house with each of them following, he is once more in a position to bolt down the two-track with them behind him instead of in front. Gil sees the opportunity and blasts forward. Once he hits the road, he feels he has a fighting chance to make a getaway. His speed is quickly exceeding one hundred miles per hour when he suddenly has a car in front of him and another coming toward him in the opposite lane. His derelict thinking has no concern for his own safety at this juncture much less the wellbeing of the occupants of either of these cars. Without a hesitation of thought, he charges around the car, traveling in his lane only to risk a head-on with the oncoming vehicle. Fortunately for Gil, the oncoming car swings off the road, plunges down into a ditch and flips over. Looking in his rearview mirror, Gil sees the flashing red light of only one of the police cars still in pursuit; the other has stopped to give aid to the persons in the flipped over vehicle. Congratulating himself on the outcome of this maneuver, Gil continues his reprehensible disregard for lives.

He begins to notice there are no oncoming vehicles. "This can only mean one thing; they've got a road block somewhere down the road. There are many side roads leading off the highway, but with no time to make a turn, he hauls forward. He rounds a curve, when he spots exactly what he had suspected—a road block. There in less time than it takes blink, he is given two choices; stop or smash into the cars creating the road block. Suddenly another option opens. On one side of the road block is a stand of brush that with enough force can be plowed through. With the reflexes that only insanity can create, Gil chooses this third option. As the car plunges through this seeming barricade, the airbag goes off, immediately blinding Gil. The interruption is enough to disrupt his acceleration. Once he realizes his forward motion is at a stop, his flee mode continues to serve him. Managing to get out of the car and before the mob of police officers can reach him. He is out of the car disappearing into the brush.

Within the few minutes it takes the police to respond, they find an empty car. Regrouping, they call in the dog handling team. It's another hour before the dog team has put together a comprehensive strategy. The chances for a gnat to breach their dragnet are better than Gil's odds.

Meanwhile, Gil is plunging through brush and fallen trees. Without a clue as to where he is, or for that matter where he's going. The same mindset he had when he was a young boy is still alive and well. When it comes to fight or flee, flee is always the option that Gil operates from—after all, it comes with no mental effort.

So far, he's had at least an hour head start. At this point, he's much like the optimist that has fallen from a ten-story building and as he passes the second floor, his defiance tells him, "So far so good."

Within this hour, he's had time to reflect on his actions. Rather than seeing a straight line to defeat, he imagines he's on his way to freedom; all it's going to take is a couple of good breaks. On the other hand, one obstacle to working his plan is his physical condition. What he's put his body through the past few weeks is telling. His sprained foot is far from healed. With every step, he feels an excruciating shot of pain. Since Gil's lifestyle has always had pain as its byproduct, he defines his life through its presence. Running with pain, attempting to elude his pursuers is the single kinship he holds with this entire fiasco—to what end remains elusive.

Up until this very moment, all his efforts have been directed toward putting some distance between himself and the law. Suddenly, Gil breaks out of the woods, and everything changes. Before him is a welcome cluster of buildings. Included in this collection is a house, a car in the driveway, and a barn. Without a pause, he is already working out a plan to hide in the barn long enough to assess how he is going to steal the car. The barn is the old hip-roofed structure with the guarantee of a hayloft filled with enough hay to hide him and his whole family.

Gil hesitates for a moment to make sure that he can make it to the barn unseen. There are enough loose boards in the back of this building that he can squeeze through unnoticed. Without a moment of thought, Gil is prying the hundred-year-old weather-worn barn boards apart far enough to get inside.

Once inside, he takes within his purview all the contrivances that he can crawl into until things begin to calm down and he can execute the rest of his plan. He chooses to crawl under a canvas tarp covering a power boat. It's setting up on a trailer. After crawling inside, he's in total darkness except for the corner he had pried loose to gain entry. It's also the only place he can feel air cooler than the air he's experiencing under the canvas. For the moment, like many already in hell, Gil would settle for enough cool water to cool his lips.

He doesn't have to wait long before he hears a voice. It's not a normal sounding voice, rather it's enhanced like it's coming over a loud speaker. It takes him only a moment before he realizes the voice is accelerated by a bullhorn.

"Harold Gilles, this is the Michigan State Police. Surrender, or we'll send the dogs in." They are making it clear they are not going to risk coming in after him because they don't know his location and they do realize he's armed.

Gil's defiance tells him to remains quiet, as though if he didn't say anything, it will give him a few more minutes of freedom.

When they realized they are not going to get the response they had hoped for, they give him his last warning.

"If you don't appear at the door in two minutes, we will allow the dogs to find you!"

The allotted time runs out with no response from one Harold Gilles. The handler turns the dog loose with the expectation of the next sound being that of Gil screaming for someone to call off the dog. Instead, they hear a pistol shot and the weak yelp of an injured dog. The handler is to his feet with the selfless intention of rescuing his injured dog. The poor beast has been shot in a front haunch by Gil as it attempted to enter his canvas cave. In turn, it has managed to limp its way to the barn's open door. With a wary eye on the door, the handler is quick to remove the injured dog.

They don't know where Gil may be hiding, and there's a wounded police dog. These are game changers. Their hope of capturing him in the open has passed. A SWAT team has been ordered and within a half hour, they're in place. The conversation on how to handle this situation among the lieutenants is varied. One, in particular being the SWAT team commander would like to have the feather in the cap of his team, says, "We can have him out of there in ten minutes, just give the word."

Less anxious is another commander with a different idea. "It's eighty-plus degrees out here. Wherever, he may be holing up in that barn, it has to be ten degrees warmer. I think if we can wait him out—especially since we don't believe he has water."

In the end, the later idea is initiated.

Gil is far from comfortable. The perception by the police that it will be much warmer inside the barn holds doubly true inside a canvas covered boat inside an already overheated barn. Added to this, Gil has broken an eardrum caused form firing his pistol in such close quarters—he has blood trickling down the side of his neck. His former feelings of freedom are quickly being replaced by a sense of desperation.

"I don't know what I'm gonna do. These guys got me boxed. I'm gonna die under this tarp, or I'm gonna die from them shootin' me."

There is fast approaching a time when Gil realizes he must make a decision. In the meantime, the loss of hearing, the dehydration his body is undergoing, and a feeling of nervousness is bringing on a wave of drowsiness. He can hardly keep his eyes open. It's definitely the effects of a heat stroke over coming him.

On the other side of this debacle are a group of lawmen who are anxious to get this fiasco behind them. The SWAT team—a very disciplined unit—are also wearing down from the afternoon heat. Since there has been four hours with no further communication with the perpetrator inside the barn, a decision is made to slowly and purposely move forward. In a very professional and coordinated movement, the SWAT team begin their action. Step by step, they stealthily gain entrance to the barn. They immediately realize the problem they're facing. They are looking at an overwhelming number of hiding places and their own vulnerability. Compared with the outside, the barn has its own character. The difference is, the strange quietness the building holds. As each of these men find a position of cover, they begin the process of acquainting themselves with this out of the ordinary environment. All that is heard is an earie kind of creaking of timbers caused by the heat expanding their fibers. There is another steady sound disrupting the barn's natural resonances—it's the sound of a human. But it's not the sound of a voice, rather it's the tones of one snoring. The breathing is by any account shallow and nearly imperceptible—but it's for certain it's human. Signaling to each other, the SWAT team begins to cautiously make their way toward the short, snort-like explosions. The closer they draw toward the boat, the more convinced they become that they are in the orbit of their perpetrator. One at a time, they advance forward until they are crouching at the side of the boat. With a hand signal, they coordinate their next move. In a flash they have the boat covering ripped back away. What they are staring at is a filthy, stinking form of a human barely able to breath. It's apparent he's debilitated—more dead than alive. In another flash of energy, they are in the boat further incapacitating the still subconscious culprit.

Gil's normal demeanor to flee in the face of danger is totally compromised, as he is barely able to move. Realizing there is minimal danger to themselves, the SWAT team has sped up their mission. Once inside, one officer is forcing him onto his stomach in the already cramped area between the boat's seats, another has his boot stepping on the side of head. Gil can't determine which ear hurts the worst since both ears are being crushed—one by a boot the other against the floor of the boat. He can feel the heel of the boot pinching against his lip. Another officer has Gil's arms twisted behind his back and is applying handcuffs. This is not to mention the already disorienting feeling from his steadily deteriorating physical and mental condition. He is hardly cognizant of his legs being untangled and pulled to his feet.

"You ain't gonna try an' run, are ya?" asks one of the officers. It's clear in his tone he's annoyed and is willing to go to any length to even the score for putting him through a hot wait in this stifling, dusty barn.

Gil tries to speak, but his throat is so dry that his words get caught. This results in a gasping kind of noise. Unable to get to his feet, he can feel faceless arms tightening around his waist, struggling to support him. He can barely stand, much less respond to any kind of command. Instead, he goes limp and passes out.

The next awareness he has is of waking up strapped to a gurney with an IV plugged into his arm. He's aware of an undulating red color bouncing off the rear windows. From a past experience, he believes he's in an ambulance. *"They ain't killed me,"* is his first, reassuring conscious thought. There is also a police officer riding along in the transport's jump seat. As soon as the officer is convinced Gil is conscious enough to hear and understand, he reads him his rights. Still groggy, not certain if he's "afoot or horseback," Gil is attempting to put two and two together as far as what is happening to him. The words he hears from this police officer are barely registering, but instinctively, he is aware of what's happening. All Gil is certain of is that he is exhausted—drained mentally, physically, and emotionally. At least for the moment, he's finding his circumstances reassuring; he had fully expected to be shot and killed.

CHAPTER 25

Heaven

Jim and Peggy have spent the better part of a week living in less than ideal conditions. Both are happy to actually sleep in their own beds. Since returning home, they have resumed their regular work routine; Peggy is back working at the Midway and Jim is finishing out his summer job at the camp. There lingers an awkward attraction between them that is demanding attention; there remains a persisting force within each of them to overcome its tensions. It's as though Julia is shouting at each of them to set her person aside and only use her insightful intuitions to build their relationship. It's as though she is calling from the grave, "Only see me as a reflection in one another."

There has been a sense of urgency within them in determining the circumstances surrounding Julia's death. It's as though they have convinced themselves that she is demanding they bring justice to her death; as though she can't rest in peace until her demands are met. Whether, real or imagined, this has become a very real perception in both Jim and Peggy.

Jim has received the latest update on Gil from his cousin, Lily and has met with Peggy to discuss his findings.

"I don't get it. This guy's got more lives than a cat. He should have been dead ten times over," declares Jim.

Peggy is listening with one ear, but her face tells another story. The little blood vessels running along her forehead are thumping as she strains to separate her thoughts. It's obvious there is something pressing on her mind. "What I don't understand is how sick-in-the-head my mother is—this guy has murdered her daughter, and she's still fawning over this piece of crap like he's her knight in shining armor," hisses Peggy. "If it were up to me, he would have been rotting in hell a long time ago."

The road traveled has had its challenges, and the road ahead appears to be just as challenging. Their mutual hate for Gil and contempt for Sylvia makes up a good portion of their relationship. There is another thing they are becoming aware of is that somehow, they are stronger together than apart. It's as though they have found a way to be much more resolute with the support of each other; each of them has had flashes of strength they've seen in the other even if they haven't seen it in themselves.

Jim stays awhile, but like he had with Julia, when he senses an odd kind of distance developing between them, he knows that Peggy prefers to be alone, so he takes it as his cue to leave.

Things in Peggy's life have flipped upside down. "I wish I had said something to Jim about this. He can think this stuff through better than me." Unwilling to cook for just herself, she has brought a burger home from the Midway. After Jim has left and she's cleaned what little there is to clean up after herself, she lets her thoughts begin to drift, *"Maybe, I'll take the Subaru and go visit my mother."* (Since their return home, Jim has spent some time tinkering around with the Subaru and attempting to make it safe enough for Peggy to drive the few miles to visit her mother.) She's grappling with what is normal—right now it's all she can think to do. There is a tenseness that accompanies this idea. It's like she's torn between love and hate for her mother. At what point she thinks, *"I wish I had Julia to talk about this. She could always think this stuff through better than me."*

There is something different this time about this decision Peggy is attempting to frame; there is a strange kind of pull she can't put her finger on; it's not anything she can explain—it's just there. After a short period of mental debate, she finalizes her decision to make the short trip.

The old Subaru is ready and waiting to make the journey. It may be old with a well-worn appearance, but it has always come through after a little coaxing—whether with anger or affection. The hill Peggy is concerned with is quickly approaching. The little Subaru move towards it as it always has with a bit of trepidation. Peggy has learned when she needs to put the transmission into a lower gear to assure the best performance. Despite her precise timing, the Subaru strains like it always has on this slope. Talking out loud to encourage its performance has been commonplace with any of its drivers, and Peggy is not to be the exception. "Come on, baby, I know you can do it!" Never one to fail, it finally crests without incident. Letting out a gracious, "Thank you! Thank you!" to any power in hearing range willing to take credit for the demonstration.

With the hesitation of one who is torn, she slowly makes her way to her mother's room. She finds her in the same spot she left her on her last visit—still sitting in a rocking chair with her back to the door, making little muttering noises, staring out a window with the same large leafed tree blocking any semblance of a view. Making her way to place herself in the path of her mother's gaze, Peggy tries to put on a good face, a little wave of the hand, and a cheerful voice, saying, "Hi, Mom."

Sylvia maintains her blank stare but stops her muttering. Her stare is directly at Peggy now. A little frown comes over her face as though she has just had an epiphany. Her mother's next action catches Peggy off guard. Reaching up from her seat, Sylvia begins to caress Peggy's face and hair, saying, "Oh, Julia, it's all Gil's fault. He always said you are the pretty one. He couldn't keep his damn eyes off you. Now look what happened." Her stare persists as she returns to her quiet mutterings.

Peggy is taken aback by her mother's mistake in believing her to be her murdered sister. Her emotions are upside down, inside out. Hardly able to contain her feelings, she bursts out of the room. Throwing the doors leading to the parking lot, she barely notices a pounding thunderstorm has blown in. By the time she reaches her car, her shaking is so out of control that she can barely get the key in the ignition. Succeeding, she manages to get the car in gear.

At this point, she is in the midst of what can only be described as a panic attack. Her mind is racing with only one thought—to get away as fast as possible. With no attention as to where she is going, she unconsciously begins to retrace her path back home. With uncontrollable crying and tears blurring her eyes, along with the pelting rain beating against the windshield, the Subaru begins the long decent of the tedious grade it had less than a half hour ago ascended. Peggy is, unable to get the insensitive words of her mother out of her mind. "Why do I keep coming back to her, she's a wretched excuse of a person—much less my mother?" she screams at herself.

With the rain running of the asphalt road in streams, Peggy pays little notice as to how fast she is traveling down this grade, she feels the Subaru begin to hydroplane as though it prefers to make the descent sideways. In a moment of clarity, Peggy applies her brakes. Quickly adding to her anguish, she discovers the brakes are failing. This, in turn, causes the car to continue its sideways projection. With no other thought in mind other than sheer panic, she continues her useless pumping the brakes. A sick feeling of hopelessness waves over her as she feels herself lifted as though she is airborne.

Her next sensation is one of total confusion. It's a feeling of being jostled around. There is a distinct feeling of pain. There are voices. "How are you doing, Miss?" is one voice she is hearing. "Hang on, Miss, we're getting you out of here and to a hospital as quick as we can."

Peggy is having trouble remembering anything other than the sensation of being airborne. *"I must have hit something,"* is the only thought she is considering. At this point, she feels very sleepy and drifts off to sleep. The next event she is sensing is a moment when she finds herself being jostled about and wheeled into what she believes is a hospital.

She is finding herself airborne once again, only this time, she is seemingly floating above a group of what appear to be hospital workers. *"Now what's happening? I just felt myself leave my body. This is really weird. I don't feel any pain."*

"We've lost her!" is one of these new voices calling out to the other attendants. With a closer look, she realizes that it is her body they are working on. Hearing them demonstrate such concern over her has her mystified.

"What are they talking about, I have never felt more alive. This is great," is her only thought. As she looks at her bloodied body lying there, Peggy's next realization is *"That really is me. How can I be here and there at the same time? I wonder if I'm not alive."* From her ceiling corner, she can't help but watch these people frantically working over her body. It suddenly comes to her, *"This must be what it's like to be dead."*

Seeing that broken body that is unmistakably her own generates within her a different awareness of herself and where she is. Looking at her hands first, she realizes they appear to be real hands. She then rubs them over what appear to be her legs—they seem to have a consistency. She is aware that she is not using a brain, nor thinking in a language but it is more real than anything she has ever understood. Everything tells her this is the *real* her and the form lying on the gurney is not the *real* her. Her next consciousness is revealing. *"I don't know why I'd want to return to that broken heap. Where I am now is more real than anything I have ever imagined."*

There is an instantaneous realization that this is beyond human making. *"I'M IN THE SPIRITUAL WORLD!"* is her overwhelming conscious awareness.

This transfer came with no thought, it merely came as a natural occurrence. These awareness's Peggy is experiencing are staggering. Never in her mortal life has she been so conscious of everything. Everything now is relative to eternity—there is no time in this plane; the awesomeness of this eternal awareness of no time is flabbergasting in that it reveals that nothing dies. Her earthly reasoning and logic have disappeared and has been replaced with knowing that she knows with constant new revelations all occurring at the same time. All this new consciousness is astonishing. Every color has taken on a brighter edge, things are sharper and perfectly distinct. Even her feelings and emotions are heightened. Everything is instantaneously understood. It's as though getting language and a brain out of the way has made things much clearer.

"I know I'm in the spiritual world. This is the real world. I can't believe I'm in it. This is incredible." Is Peggy's astounding perception.

Her consciousness has brought Jim to her forefront. Without any further perception about "How," she finds herself flowing through solid walls into the emergency waiting room. There she sees Jim among the many people crowded into the area but very much alone with his thoughts. What Peggy discovers is that she knows the thoughts of everyone in the room. She hears Jim's prayer asking God not to take her from him, too.

Her next awareness is a sudden perception of traveling. What's surprising is how she is able to see in every direction at once as she feels herself being pulled through each floor of the hospital, then through the roof, out into space. There are heightened emotions accompanying this event, it's a mix of fear, exhilaration, and apprehension. Things are changing rapidly without Peggy's consensus. It's as though some power greater than her has taken over. On impulse her mother comes into her consciousness. She immediately finds herself staring at her sleeping mother. The only emotion she can readily identify is how happy she feels to have her mother and her problems left behind. Not knowing why, Peggy opts to say, *"Goodbye, Mom."*

In another second she finds herself in another familiar place—the Midway. Like many small towns, news travels fast. They have already heard of the accident and who it involved. There she sees Ben, the day cook, praying for her. What is even more odd about this encounter is she can actually see his prayers streaking off to heaven as one would look at the light trail of a comet.

With no warning, she finds *herself* being drawn into a tube-like structure with black sides. They're sweeping by as though they are fluid. It's the deepest black Peggy has ever experienced. It's a kind of darkness that is not seen through the eyes but is a darkness illuminated by a supernatural consciousness; she knows it to be a darkened eternal void that is unmistakably clear to her enhanced perception. This experience is causing Peggy's emotions to create energy at a level never known to her—it can only be described as a *fear* energy battling against an awareness of a *love* energy. Aware of this anomaly as a disparity, she's thinking, "*This must be where I'm meeting the reality of God.*"

As this blackness is sweeping by, her uncertainties are heightened by the knowledge that the purveyors of this darkness have focused on her. She can feel their evilness. She immediately has a foreknowledge of what this is. The dreadful reality of a hell is the certainty of this experience. She recognizes this as a forever, nonnegotiable, eternal void, with an eternal life of horror, forever cut off from the eternal Source of Love. The more she looks at it, the more intense the reality of its nature become. She can feel how powerful its desire is to have her. "*I would be cut off forever from the source of goodness and life.*" The horror of it gives her pause, "*I could never wish this on anyone!*" Demon after demon stares longingly at her as she is towed through this darkness.

As the certainty of their purpose intensifies, her fears finalize in an agonizing outburst of horrific terror, "*Please, Please, don't let them get me! Save me, please save me! Let me live!*"

Looking ahead a new and different scene dominates her consciousness. What she perceives is a white, white light—whiter, brighter, and purer than any light she has ever experienced—more than any amount of suns she can imagine. In spite of its brightness, she is surprised how easy it is to look directly at it. At this point, she becomes even more aware of her movements. It's as though she is being towed by a force that can't be resisted. What is apparent is that the darkness seems to be racing ahead of her cutting off the light. It's as though this darkness is omnipresent and is actually a gate purposely closing shut on the light. All that's left is just a little crack of disappearing brightness. Peggy's whole person is left with no doubt that where she is at this very moment, is the ultimate reality. Her spirit consciousness makes her aware, *"I'm standing at the threshold of either eternal darkness, and horror, or eternal life."* In her terror, she screams once more, "Please forgive me! I'm sorry. I want to live with You!"

Just as the gate is about to close, Peggy feels something behind her so beyond measure, so infinitely wise, so colossal but yet so personal. It astounds her. Not certain of her standing, she is remiss to turn around. She recalls when she was in high school how she and Julia had gotten involved with Crusaders for Christ. For some unknown reason, she recalls how she and Julia had agreed to be baptized. For sill unknown reasons, she wonders if there is some connection with this experience and now. *"I wonder if this is Him?"* is her thought. All her short comings and unworthy feelings are flooding over her like a dark pervasive blanket. As she slowly makes the turnaround, she finds herself standing in the presence of something much greater than anything she has ever experienced. From deep inside her, she hears her name called. It's in a different way than she has ever heard it. It's as though it's coming from deep inside her but without a language or sound but it's like the living Creator of everything is in it. It's not just her earthly name she perceives but the name of her very being from all eternity.

"This is so wonderful; I can see everything; I know everything. I am part of everything. This must be what God is." is Peggy's singular thought. God's love is pouring through her like she and God are of one nature. Her sense of wellbeing is heightened to a point where expressing it has no language, no era, no tradition, no gender, no race. Her only expression is, *"I have never been more alive than now."* This is all experienced in the depth of her being.

A new knowing that affirms a knowledge of all that ever was as well as all that ever will be engulfs her. At this point, she is astounded at her knowledge. *"I am part of everything; everything, every person that has ever lived, or will ever live has become one with me. I am all of creation,"* is her new awareness. There is no consciousness of a past or a future, only a now. *"I am,"* is her only awareness. There is no language because there is no need for language. Being at one with the entire realm of eternity that ever was or will be, is a natural manifestation of this realm.

Without the sense of things being in sequence, her life is immediately in review like one would see a tapestry, but it can be seen all at once. With her spirit mind reviewing her life brings moments of cringing as the enhanced emotions are reexperiencing the events. Not only is she seeing her life's review through her own perspective but also through the perspective of everyone's life she has ever touched. The vision she is seeing in this review is as though her life's events were ripples that may have gone unnoticed making their way into the lives of all those she has touched with her decisions. The consciousness that nothing in life goes unnoticed is a recoiling revelation.

While this review is streaming through Peggy's awareness, her full attention is on *those things* she has said and done that were hurtful to others. This review is meant to involve her into the hurt and disappointment she made that person feel. *"Oh, why did I do that, I wish I hadn't done that, I'm so sorry, please forgive me,"* is her sorrowful response to the reel that is playing itself through her person. What Peggy is seeing is her actions and memories much sharper and clearer and more intensely lived than anything during her earthly realm. She is being shown how all her decisions are her own to make, but whatever choice she makes will make their way through the lives of others—good or bad. There are also many areas of her life where she does some unselfish deeds for the good of others. She finds little relief in this as her selfish deeds continue to come forward. Her thoughts have turned to her lowliness and unworthiness to be in the presence of this pure light. Her consciousness screams out, *"Oh no—I hope He forgives me!"*

With that thought comes a warm feeling of perfect, unconditional love. It's as though there are divine warm arms that have come to hold her and emanate the message, "My child there is nothing to forgive."

· This perception is striking her like nothing has, *"God is loving me right through all this."* With all the Divine assurance this Authority can emanate, It tells her, "Everything you have ever done no longer exists, it's all gone, all forgotten all forgiven and you are worthy to live in My Divine presence of absolute, unconditional love forever." With a sigh, Peggy is at complete peace.

All this is to lead her to understand how her life has been a life of wrongly lived self-centered actions. She's become aware of this —not by words—but by a consciousness that is her essence. *"If I spent any part of my life handing out pain and suffering to others, then, I am going to have to feel it much more sharply in this eternal realm than in the faint, dim, anemic world I had lived in."* This stunning fact has become her reality. What is over taking her entire person is how desperately she wants to integrate these truths into her very person.

Other than her brief contact with the Crusaders for Christ movement, Peggy has never been a church person. This isn't an issue. There is no religion in this realm, there are no priests, pastors, rabbis attempting to see clearer through the earthly mirror that's clouded with dogma and notions—there is only eternal Truth. With all the understanding that has become hers, Peggy sees clearly that it isn't about doctrine and books, rather, as she is led to understand that it's all unconditional love and compassion that comes from God.

From this standpoint, she fully understands how Divine Love *is* the actual spirit making up this light; how Its essence is a golden river of unconditional love that is flowing in, around, and through her without making judgement—like the living God is in it. The only judgement is coming from herself. This judgement has manifested itself in her life's review as a wish that when the realization of her many unkind actions were brought to the surface that she had responded kindly. *"I wish I hadn't said that, or done that,"* is her sincere desire.

What she is experiencing, is how her soul image of God created within her is judging her lower earthly nature, and is shown to her for a reason. It easily conveys the message without language or voice but nonetheless heard. "You go through these reviews in your life to become teachable—so you can see with new eyes the difference between good and bad."

It has also made known to her that at any moment, she has made mistakes based on what she had available to her and did the best she could do with what she had available. This is also forgiven.

In this realm, she is discovering a certainty clearer than any dream she has experienced. It's an eternal mindfulness. It's without a brain, without a heartbeat, no race, no culture, no time, no space. Despite this, she is more conscious, more alive, more perceptive than she has ever experienced before. It's as if all of these earthly things were in the way of clarity.

Since there is no sense of time and everything happens in the now or at once, words fail to give this experience its real element. In that vein, Peggy immediately finds herself facing a shimmering crystalline building. The brilliance of this structure is a radiance that cannot be explained with human language. While standing alone and awestruck at what she is perceiving, a ten-foot luminated person all dressed in a dazzling white robe—white beyond any white she has ever seen on earth—takes her by the hand and leads her into this marvelous structure. The gates are of a translucent light such that when she touched it, it was as if it were living and the whole of life flowed through her. It's as though the living God governed in this light and she continues to be part of its whole. It isn't a physical effort that opens the door, it's a consciousness. Once the doors are opened, the sound emanating from its walls are the sound of pure love. Every person who has ever lived is here. They are all stroking the shimmering, crystalline walls as though to absorb its glory. And they are all singing, "I love you! We love you!" It is making the remembrance of music she had enjoyed on earth sound like the flat, dull sounds of a shallow gong. Each swell of music is pouring into Peggy and through her like a wave of love and acceptance.

It's in this "Now," Peggy is understanding how there is nothing that doesn't have purpose and how every molecule of everybody and every thought and every emotion is interconnected and has impact on the soul of another even if they lived at different times on earth and have no seeming connection.

Peggy is absorbing the impact. This is her resonating perception, *"This is the most beautiful music I have ever experienced. I can hear as well as taste it. It makes me feel as though I'm not God but that I truly am one with God. I know I'm still me, but I understand I'm as much a part of "we" as I am "me" and that we are all God but not God."*

In this revelation, Peggy realizes she has a God like consciousness. She understands the universe—things that should baffle her. It's as though the entire creation were one with her and every other human but yet she is separate. And all are worshiping as one. Worshiping one another as a part of

God and God as a part of each other. It is all about love. All existence is emanating from this shimmering light and everything is reflecting it as pure love. All she is experiencing continues to take on dimension after dimension so as to include the parts of the whole in each exchange.

At this point, Peggy is so captivated by the music and what it is doing to her that she finds herself adding her own fundamental and unique note singing, "I AM." Not as a declaration of her ego but one of overwhelming gratitude for her being; beyond a "self" to simply "am." Her sound, along with all the other worshipers are reverberating their song through all existence.

Continuing in the actuality of the eternal now, Peggy finds herself in an ultra-fertile valley the most beautiful lush gardens she has ever come into contact with. Life is everywhere, gorgeous butterflies, brilliant colored birds all moving in rhythmic, swirling patterns as though this were a huge symphony of life. The grasses and the tree are brilliantly green, flowers are huge and of a brilliant color she has never or could ever imagine. They're all large and what is distinct about each of them is that each is a living thing. As she touches each of the them, their life flows into and through her in such a way that she knows their life as part of her own. The flowers have deep fragrance that emits a scent that words cannot describe, and a kaleidoscope of colors never seen on earth. There is also a cool breeze accompanying this symphony of movement that causes each of these plants to dance with the joy of life; as each sway, it's exchanging its life with another. Intermingled in this synchronization is the congruence of souls, chanting, HOLY, HOLY, HOLY in perfect harmony with frolicking, rambunctious children jumping and playing with bounding dogs. Able to see in all directions at once, Peggy intuitively knows the Source of all this joy and happiness is emanating from a radiant orb of light above, in and, around all the activity. She also is aware of other golden rings or spheres of perfect love flowing out and into all the activities. All this is the most real form of life she has ever experienced.

Peggy is certain beyond everything that she has experienced on earth that none of this is being heard with the ears or seen by the eye—it's much greater than either of these puny earthly sense organs can record—it's all become her, and she has become all of it. Along with these phenomena, there is a design that is making its way into Peggy's consciousness saying, *"So this is how all of this works, it's all so simple. There is no other Source of love than this and this Love is the Source of all energy."*

There is no doubt accompanying the ultimate veracity in or with any of these events; everything is clearly understood—unconditional love has the power to create and heal is the prevailing reality.

The tall divine being that has not left her side is demonstrating itself to be her guardian angel. The splendor of this being is unrivaled. Considering Peggy has not had the mindfulness of this angel presence with her on earth, in this realm she has a clearer, sharper, discerning powers, *"I feel like I have known you all my life,"* is her response. The angel gives a deeper assurance, "And, I've known you since you were in the mind of God."

With that established, this presence motions to Peggy to become aware of another phenomena. The angel has instructed her to turn around. Standing before her, all dressed in white, is Julia. Peggy's is stunned. Her joy at seeing her twin is so far unmatched. The voiceless communication between the two is immediately taking on a familiarity. They had always possessed an earthly telepathic bond that was unique but here it's common to communicate in a clairvoyant manner. They are perfectly content be in the other's presence.

Peggy is the first to communicate, *"I've missed you so much. To see you like this in this beautiful place and you so beautiful and peaceful fills me with nearly as much joy as just being with you once more."* To which she adds, *"After you were* murdered, I thought about ending my life so we could be together again."

Julia is just as elated to see her sister. The whole of the experience is something that is driven very deeply within her. "I am overjoyed to be together once again and will be beyond joy when we can be here together for eternity."

This last communication is leaving Peggy with her first vagueness since she has arrived. Observing, Peggy's uncertainty concerning her status, Julia continues, "Your work isn't complete on earth yet, dear sister."

Completely absorbed in the possible meaning of this seeming unbelievable transmission by her beloved twin is leaving Peggy even more stunned. It's created an instant insecurity. It's causing her to have a pensiveness that to her is totally out of place in this realm. This beautiful place is where she wants to be but is now facing the threat of having to leave.

Julia's face is more radiant than before as she continues, "This is a place of unconditional love and forgiveness. I have experienced this as you have. Since I have been loved and forgiven, I have also forgiven my murderer the same way I have been loved and forgiven. With all the encouragement, strength, and hope of heaven, I have done that unconditionally. You dear sister are going to have to do the same if you want what you have been allowed to taste. Yes, you, as I already have, need to forgive my murderer—not for murdering me, as only I can do that, but forgive for what that loss has done to you."

Fully aware of what her sister is communicating, Peggy is ready to interconnect with what she is asking. "Julia, you're asking a lot from me to forgive Gil for taking you from me. That is going to be very difficult."

Julia already has anticipated Peggy's response to Gil. "Dear sister, Gil will be the easiest to forgive—it's our mother that needs the most forgiving and will be the most difficult to forgive."

As soon as this communication is received, it begs a response. Stunned more by this revelation than anything so far, Peggy is left with little more than conveying her upsetting reply, *"Our mother murdered you?!"* Peggy's tone reflects as much a question as a statement. Julia's face assures Peggy she meant what she communicated.

Just as suddenly, Peggy feels herself slamming back into her body. Her first feeling is one of pain, devastation, and disbelief. The disappointment of being rejected, as she believes is the reality of her situation, has quickly become her overwhelming certainty. There is no way she wanted to leave her sister or that beautiful place of perfect peace, love, and forgiveness. Her earthly mindfulness—made even more acute by the pain of broken bones, a split spleen, and a swelling of the brain—is unwelcomed.

"She's back!" are the words of relief from one of the many people working frantically on her serious condition. With this announcement, Peggy's only response is to cry out in pain. Morphine is ordered. She feels the sharp prick of the needle and the sensation of the medication beginning to do its job. Her next sensation is waking up with little awareness other than she is in a bed. Her first thoughts are thoughts of hope that by a second miracle she's been returned to be with Julia and her rightful home in heaven. It's soon learned this hope is not to be so. The sounds she's hearing are the annoying sounds earthly gadgets make—hospital PA systems and the ever-present electronic beeping of monitors.

As for the present moment, she's well aware her person is firmly fixed back on the planet earth as she attempts to differentiate the irritating beeping noises emanating from these unseen contraptions behind her. She is also aware of an achy feeling in her arms. It turns out she has undergone hours of surgery and is in an isolated hospital recovery room, stuck with IV's in both arms along with every contrivance known to modern medicine, either pumping something into her, or monitoring every breath and heartbeat her broken body can generate. As the minutes tick by, she is becoming extra aware of her different areas of distress. Her right leg is covered with a cast and is suspended from a pully system over her bed. Her spleen has been removed. Her left wrist also has a cast surrounding it, and her mouth feels as though it' been used to store cotton balls. This is all in the first few seconds of consciousness.

With the very limited mobility she is discovering some unknown surgical dressing is immobilizing her head and neck. Out of the corner of her eye Peggy spots a nurse. She's busy changing out an IV bag of something that is hopefully helping to heal her broken body. Realizing her situation, Peggy can't help but wish she were back with Julia. With all the strength she can muster, she attempts to lick her lips followed by a nearly inaudible request. "Could I please have some water?"

The nurse is quick to respond. Placing the straw between Peggy's parched lips, the nurse is sporting a big satisfying grin. "You are one fortunate young lady. We thought you were leaving us for good when by a miracle you came back."

Peggy is very grateful for the water but couldn't disagree with the kindly nurse more adamantly.

CHAPTER 26

Dazzled

Peggy's stay in the hospital is by hospital standards lengthy. Her discharge day has finally arrived. Jim is faithfully here to pick her up and take her to her house. He has not missed one day of visiting her—often several times a day. He has spoon fed her until she healed enough to feed herself. Now, with Jim's promise to help her at home, she is entering the doors for the first time in ten days but for all that's transpired, seems like ten years.

She is hesitant to share her "heaven" experience with anyone. She considers it is totally out of the reach of anyone who has not experienced the occurrence and what's more, it has become so personal with her that risking anyone attempting to dissuade her would be in the same category as a profanity. All in all, she is reticent to share with anyone any part of her encounter—and that includes Jim. This, however, doesn't mean she has set it aside. Her thoughts are centered around the experience and how it is impacting her life with nearly every breath. As she mulls over even the smallest of particulars of the experience, she can't get past the imperative she was charged with to forgive her mother. *"How can I forgive that woman for the most heinous crime any mother could commit?"* is a near constant intrusive thought. She has become more pensive as a result.

Jim has noticed this change in Peggy but is inclined to fault it on her physical condition. His tenderness toward her and her condition has been his main focus for several weeks. He has moved into Peggy's upstairs bedroom allowing her to occupy her vacant mother's downstairs bedroom. This has allowed him to answer any of her needs through both day and night.

A few weeks have passed, and Peggy's physical condition has greatly improved. At Peggy's request, Jim has fixed her a breakfast of bacon, eggs, and toast. Noticing her mood seemingly taking a turn, reaching a level he is more familiar with, he chooses this opportunity to update her on Gil's charges of murder and the continuing investigation of his responsibility for Julia's murder. Peggy listens, as she silently continues to eat her breakfast with her eyes fixed in a down position. When Jim has finished, she continues to stare silently at her empty plate.

Jim is not unaware of her mood change. Puzzled as to its cause, he hesitates to go any further. In turn, he also remains silent, patiently waiting for Peggy to give a clearer significance to her reaction.

Still quiet, Peggy realizes she can't live any kind of a life with this secret part being unshared. She is going to have to find a way that will enable her to share what she has been exposed to. This means she is going to have to forget her misgivings and try to find a way to begin.

She has examined Jim with a deeper sense regarding his trustworthiness than she has with any other part of their relationship. Always a bit reticent to become transparent with anyone other than Julia, Peggy continues to monitor Jim's reaction to different subjects she brings up. On this particular morning seeing Jim sitting at the same table, opposite from her with an unmistakable look of concern prompts her to break her silence.

"Jim, all that you see of me is not as it may seem. I've had more happen to me than the accident."

This statement is mystifying to Jim but also hopeful. He is always ready with an attentive ear for Peggy to share something about herself that he hasn't known. Consequently, she has his entire attention. Sitting on a kitchen chair directly across from her, arms folded resting on the table with all of the facial signals he can give that tell her he is prepared to listen.

Seeing his receptiveness is not making it easier for Peggy. For her to have to put into human words an experience, that by its own description, defies an earthly language is at best a challenge, nonetheless, she begins.

"Jim, I've been someplace no other person I know has been and come back."

Listening intently, Jim agrees, "I know baby. You've had a tough go of it but even the doctors are amazed at how well you've progressed without any special therapy."

Pausing for a moment to regroup, Peggy ignores Jim's musing, continuing with her own account, "Jim, I visited Julia." She lets this blunt statement settle with Jim for a moment, allowing him time to digest what she is getting at.

Jim is rightfully even more puzzled than before. "I don't doubt with the number of drugs you've been given you've visited Elvis," is his explanation of her account.

Peggy is gaining more composure. She is ready to become as defensive as she has imagined she would need to be.

"No, Jim, drugs had nothing to do with it. This was during that period where I had died and before I was revived."

Once more, she lets this account settle with Jim. Peggy is undaunted by Jim's limited mental ability to grasp the spiritual nature of her story. It's evident he is completely perplexed. His eyes have taken on a stupefied expression as he is struggling for how much logic he can give to her recent report. With no arrows of logic remaining in his quiver, Jim is left to listen to Peggy's seeming illogical story that has culminated in an even more specious meeting with a twin that has been dead and buried for more than a month.

With a clarity that has never left her encounter, Peggy continues. She is very specific in all her details, beginning with her experience of floating above her dead body as the physician and hospital personal continued to attempt to revive her. Her tunnel of darkness with her seeming escape from evil into the waiting light.

"Jim, that light can only be described as a living perfection of love. I have never felt such total forgiveness. It gave me a sense of acceptance and love that escapes any words I can think of to describe it."

Jim is listening with a part of his person that has been dormant. He is very accustomed to the physical and mental rigors of life, but this unworldly account has caught his spiritual side on its blindside. Even so, Peggy's has hit her highest point, and she's more than ready to make him understand. She has also noticed that where Jim may have been inclined to give her a logical explanation, he has become unusually attentive. He has never heard anything like this before in his life. Peggy knows she has captured a dimension within Jim that is receptive to this kind of conversation.

Emboldened, she continues with her near-death descriptions. She describes all of the light, love, forgiveness, her guardian angel, the divine presence of God, the indescribable music, the beautiful gardens of flowers, and last but far from least, her moving visit with Julia and the imperative she was given to forgive.

Still attentive, Jim's facial features have taken on a blankness that Peggy has never seen in him. She knows she has hit an area of Jim's person that has not been kept fit. She has viewed him work out to keep his physical stature in good shape. She has also been familiar with his cognitive skills, as he is more than willing to take on a new mental challenge, but this spiritual dimension—other than the times his parents required him to attend church services—has laid dormant for a number of years. Jim has often spoken of his church confirmation as being his last regular acquaintance with anything spiritual. Since his father has been cheating on his mother with the choir lady, his entire family has dropped all association with the church—with the exception of Julia's funeral. Consequently, Jim has done nothing on his own to familiarize himself with his spiritual self. He finds himself sitting and listening to a person who he has never known to tell a lie, much less have a creative bent to fashion an untrue story like this for any reason. He's discovering her account is resonating with an inner part of him he hasn't used since he was a small child, when his grandmother made him aware of his own guardian angel.

With the same clarity she had with her near-death revelation, Peggy is satisfied she has revealed its elements to Jim exactly the way it all happened.

CHAPTER 26

Hate Rots the Soul

Jim's first response is an exhale followed with a, "Wow!" He's not confused, but he needs a moment to process. Lost for words, he isn't aware of his incessant blinking. Still in a state of spiritual overload, he clears his throat with the hope that a few words will find their way into his mouth.

Peggy, on the other hand, has integrated this experience into her person even more than one would a wonderful vacation. It's become an integral part of her that she accepts as her normal. "I didn't share this happening with you to convince you of its truth, I shared it because I need a trusted friend as an encourager to fulfill the orders it demands."

Jim is always more responsive when he knows he's needed. "I'll do what I can, but asking you to forgive your mother isn't something I can yell at you to do. It's something only you can work through."

Peggy interrupts, saying, "I'm not asking you to do anything but support me through this." Pausing for a minute, the tears are beginning to fill her eyes. Grabbing a nearby dish towel, she dabs the drops before they run down her cheeks. Pain and anger are drenched in each tear. "My mother is despicable. At this moment, I can't stand the thoughts of her name or her person. I hate her with all the hate I can muster. And now I'm being told I can't be with my sister unless I forgive?!"

Realizing Peggy's tender spirit, Jim rounds the table to place a comforting arm around her. In the beginning, they each tried to conceal their romantic feelings for one another, content to have their relationship center around their common feelings over their loss of Julia but now they have accepted their mutual attraction to one another.

Cautiously choosing his words, he says, "I can say this, I can identify with your hate because of my feelings toward my father for what he is putting our family through, but I also know it comes at a cost—hate rots the soul. I'll help you if you'll help me."

Looking up at Jim, Peggy feels his words lessen her anxiety. "Maybe that old adage about 'a problem shared is a problem cut in half' is true," she says, half crying and half laughing.

Jim continues to hold her. His feelings for her have intensified over the past month. Lifting her chin to place his eyes to hers, he very tenderly kisses her lips. In a near whisper, he adds, "I love you, Peggy."

Peggy is moved beyond anything that this earth has produced in her life. There is nothing guarded about her. Up until this point, their unspoken regard for each other had been enough, but know the spoken word is needed to seal it. With a cast on her leg and wrist, a brace on her neck, and a tender incision where the surgeon had removed her damaged spleen, she feels a flush overtake her entire body. Without hesitation or evasion of mind, she repeats back to Jim the most powerful words in all eternity: "I love you, too. I saw you in the emergency waiting room, praying for me. I deeply appreciate you asking God not to take me from you."

By now, Jim can't be made more dumbfounded than he already is, and is not surprised at anything Peggy has left to throw at him. "I thank God every day for answering that prayer," confesses Jim.

Their passion for one another is linked directly into an overwhelming desire to extend it into a lifelong pledge to each other. Savoring the moment, they sit silently in one another's embrace. After a time, as in all things earthly, it's time to do something. Jim breaks the silence with the more immediate concern.

"Where do we begin?" is his question. This is typical of Jim. Once his mind is set, it's time to begin the process.

Peggy is still enjoying the moment of near oneness with each other. Not quite ready to switch gears, she stumbles for the words. "Begin? Begin what?"

"Begin to figure out how we're going to deal the assholes in our lives," states Jim with his usual pragmatic approach to life's problems.

Peggy listens but with a different mindset. With her, it isn't merely a matter of "dealing" with these unlovables; it's a matter of forgiving where it is hardly imaginable.

"What I am certain of is I was totally forgiven in my near-death experience. I know Julia is also where she is because not only did she graciously accepted her own forgiveness, but she also graciously extended that forgiveness to our mother."

Jim is mulling this over in his head. "I don't know if I could do that. I feel that not only did she murder Julia, she further deceived us into believing Gil was responsible—she even deceived poor ol' Gil into believing he had killed Julia. What the heck, she had us running all over the state, endangering ourselves every step of the way."

Peggy is taking note but is also taking charge of her own feelings. She's been aware of a change within since she's come back. It's the kind of change that creates an inward desire to take an inventory of her behaviors and change any shortcomings for the better.

"Jim, I know what you're saying. That's the problem, I know I dislike my mother with no effort. Hate isn't an emotion I have to struggle to put into my life—it's coming with absolutely no effort. The question I have for myself is, 'What is preventing me from forgiving this contemptable woman?' This is what I need to figure out. I think once I can begin to answer that question it will make a difference in my attitude."

Jim is mindful of what Peggy is saying. He is also noticing a change in her since her injuries. There is more and more a growing hesitancy in her decision making as though she is having a second thought—especially when thoughts of her mother begin with revulsion and drift into how she needs to change this attitude.

There is another little incidental he's noticed—first with Julia and now with Peggy. He has always been amazed at how quickly they have been able to adapt to a change in circumstances. Living in the same house with Peggy, and especially using her and Julia's bedroom, has given him an extended insight on how close these girls are. They shared nearly everything. It's much liked to an archeological dig in that it contains their entire life. There are neatly catalogued pictures, scrapbooks, clothing, dolls, and sports trophies. Painting after painting of brilliant butterflies, adorning the walls—each with one or the other of the girl's signatures. It's evident, as Jim sifts through their archives that they led their lives wrapped in their interests. This proves to be a defiance to live their lives as far apart from the chaotic life led by their mother as they were able.

Jim can't help but admire her resolve—he sees it recorded in her life's achievements as she overcame a dysfunctional household and now how this same resolve is recounted in her most recent dilemma. The more he is able to observe Peggy's actions—and especially her reactions—the more convinced he is that this is the person with whom he wants to spend the rest of his life.

*

The day arrives where Peggy's injuries are healed enough to allow her to get out. Jim has rented a wheelchair, allowing her to become mobile. She and Jim have decided to have lunch at the Midway. She's met by a sympathetic and welcoming staff.

"I can't believe what you've been through and you look this good—very happy to see you," is the resonating greeting among the well-wishers. Peggy is beaming during this interchange. Under normal circumstances having lunch would be a common, even mundane event but today this is a monumental milestone in her recovery. Her thoughts drift off to the heavenly angels she had encountered in that other realm and how she appreciated them and here in this realm how much she appreciates these earthly angels that have skin on them. Her reaction is one of gratitude and thanks. Ben the cook is nearly on a full-court press to welcome Peggy. "Dang you, girl! You scared the crap outta us. All I could do was pray for you."

Peggy's reply surprises even herself. "Yes, I know I saw you. I want you to know how much I appreciate that."

Hearing this statement, Ben looks at her with a wondering look and makes his way back to the kitchen. He doesn't understand what she went through and because of her condition, he is willing to let the near spooky reply slide.

In-between sips from her soft drink, Peggy says to Jim, "I think I'd like to visit my mother."

Jim has noticed a heaviness surrounding Peggy. He's suspected this time would come and has prepared himself for it. "It's probably time. However, I'm not certain she has the capacity to understand what you've been through."

Considering Jim's point, Peggy says, "I know. I don't intend to bring her into it." Pausing for a moment, she adds, "I think I need to listen to her with different ears. I've been mulling around in my mind what she's been saying about Gil and Julia. I think I've been missing something.

When lunch is finished, Jim stops a Russ's garage to fill his gas tank. Russ suddenly appears at the passenger side of Jim's truck wiping his hands on a red colored grease rag. He's signaling Peggy to run the window down all the while shaking his head. "You know I warned you about driving that thing. It was no more than a wreck waiting to happen."

"It's one of those times I should have listened isn't it?" is all she can think to say.

Russ is pointing with his thumb back over his shoulder with the following report, "The county had Bob Zachar haul your mobile coffin to my place. It's out back. What d'you want done with it?"

The last thing Peggy wants to do is deal with the Subaru. It carries with it all the memories she is willing to forget. "Give it a decent burial, Russ."

A little smile comes across Russ' face with the words, "I can do that."

Presenting her with the car's title found in the glove box, Peggy signs off leaving Russ to say, "Consider it done."

They are soon on the road, making their way to meet Peggy's next challenge head on. Within the hour, Jim is wheeling Peggy through the doors and into her mother's room. Sylvia is sitting in her usual chair staring out the same window at the same tree, except the leaves are showing a hint of the coming fall season. Peggy has motioned for Jim to stop. With her wheelchair brought to a halt, she sits, staring at the back of her mother's head. Something she had never noticed before is the color of her mother's hair. It's graying and is pulled back into a simple bun, pinned together with bobby pins. "*She looks so old and sick*," is her thought. Her thoughts are suddenly interrupted with the vision of her twin sister. It's nothing more than a momentary flash, but it's a powerful pictogram. Julia's demeanor is the same brightness and purity that's burned into her memory. Peggy sees it as a sign reminding her of the imperative she had been given to forgive her mother.

Motioning to Jim to move her wheelchair, Peggy positions herself directly in front of her mother. "Hello,

Mother. How are you?" Her tone is amical even as she struggles to make it so.

Sylvia looks at Peggy with the same vague look Peggy's become accustomed to. It's a stare as if she's attempting to decipher something that's puzzling her.

"Peggy. You're back," are Sylvia's words.

"Yes mother, I'm back. I'm sorry I haven't been here sooner, but as you see, I've been a little under the weather."

With the same vague look, Sylvia continues, "You came to me in my sleep and told me goodbye."

Peggy is listening with great interest. "Mother, are you speaking about the last time I visited you on my day off?"

"No, honey, it was when you were dead. I knew you were on your way to be with Julia."

This revelation sets Peggy back some. Jim is sporting the same dumb look he had when Peggy first revealed her near-death experience.

It's now Peggy's turn to be flabbergasted. She makes a quick evaluation of what her mother is saying. She remembers coming to say goodbye to her mother in her spirit state, but she wasn't aware her mother had heard her.

Seeing an opening, Peggy decides to push further. "Mother, why did you kill Julia?"

Sylvia takes the question as if someone had asked her why she had to eat or drink. "I had to. Don't you see it?"

Peggy is shocked, stunned, staggered, and even devastated all over again. First, she didn't expect such a direct confession, and second, she didn't expect such a glib answer.

"What do you mean, you 'had to'?" further questions Peggy. Her voice reveals that this deranged confession of her mother's has thoroughly shaken her.

"If it hadn't been for Gil fawning over her like she was some kind of princess, I wouldn't have had to do that. I'm just as pretty." She pauses as if to remember more. The look on her face has turned from the previous vague look to one of stern seriousness. "Gil wanted her. Don't you see? I had to kill her. I'm pretty, too. Gil is mine. Julia had no right to take him from me."

Peggy is left speechless. She doesn't know how to react. It's never been a secret that her mother's self-centered thinking was a major part of her personality, but to have it end this way is unthinkable. Peggy's initial idea to search out a way to forgive her mother is now buried even further into her trauma.

Not much more has to be said. Another voice behind them is says it all. "I figured all along that was the way it happened!" It's none other than Greeny. He's gotten Gil back and has had ample opportunity to interrogate him regarding all the charges against him, including Julia's murder. In their continuing investigation, he has come to see what kind of response he could marshal from a fresh look at Sylvia's earlier statements. By a lucky happenstance, he came at just the right time.

Looking at Peggy, Greeny sums up what he has suspected, "I never was convinced ol' Gil was responsible for your sister's murder. Now your mother has put another option on the table."

All this is leaving Jim and Peggy dismayed beyond belief. Greeny makes no apologies as he steps around each of them and reads Sylvia her rights. His next step is to place her under arrest and place her in handcuffs. His following reply is in keeping with the situation. "Sylvia, you and I been hangin' around each other enough lately that people are gonna start talkin'."

By this time, the facilities personnel have been alerted. Not certain how to handle this sudden change in Sylvia's status from patient to prisoner, they scurry around, dumbfounded. Meanwhile, Greeny has placed Sylvia under arrest and is ushering her out of the building. When challenged, Greeny, in his usual casual way, says, "I'm just doin' my job. If you bureaucrats don't like it, get yer paperwork done."

This was not in Peggy's plan and it's leaving her just as taken aback as everyone else. There is no question that Sylvia's dysfunction is caused by years of alcohol abuse. But to see her this way—being led out mumbling to herself in handcuffs—is disconcerting to Peggy, to say the least.

Peggy has lived with her mother her entire life and not in her wildest dreams did she expect things would end this way. She is hurt beyond description. Turning to Jim, she blurts out, "Why do I need to be punished for my mother's sick mind? It's not fair. I hate her even more than I did before we came. Just take me home."

It's another dark day for Peggy as the tears flow down her face. Not willing to wait for Jim's help, she struggles with her broken wrist to turn her chair to the door.

The trip home is silent. Jim knows her well enough to let her have her time to work through her emotions without interference. Peggy's mind is far from silent. She's struggling against a part of her that would like to see herself as a helpless victim whose life has been destroyed by a wicked, evil mother who lived a self-serving life. Then there is another side of her that can't prevent the apparition of her sister from coming to mind, all dressed in God's glory, compelling her to have a change of heart toward their mother—it's all maddening. What she wouldn't give to have that peace she shared with Julia return. Her anger turns from her mother toward God. "Why do I have to do this crap? I don't have the slightest idea how to even begin to do what I've been asked to do."

Jim remains silent. As much as he would like to be of help, he has no answer. This helplessness prompts him to regretfully declare, "As much as I want to take away your pain, I know I can't. If you believe in all of what you've told me so far, it seems like your answer is buried somewhere in the circumstances."

"You're probably right, but I'm so exhausted over my mother's last fiasco, I can't think straight," laments Peggy. Her face is taking on a strain that's giving her a headache.

It isn't long before they find themselves parked in the driveway. Jim shuts the engine off to face Peggy. "I think you're being unnecessarily hard on yourself."

She hears him but it's obvious her thoughts are trapped in her own head, banging off the walls of her mind. The result of this process ends in more frustration along with the beginnings of a migraine. "At this point, I don't care. There is no way I can imagine just forgetting everything my mother's ever done. I mean—what am I supposed to do?" With a pause only long enough to blast out one more epitaph, she blurts out in an unmistakable sarcastic tone, "Just say, 'Oh I guess I've been just a little too sensitive' and let it go."

Jim is attentive. "Maybe you don't understand the difference between 'forgiving and excusing'."

"What do you mean?" she quires.

"I mean I don't believe anyone other than God can forgive unconditionally," declares Jim.

Peggy's head pops up. What Jim has just voiced has definitely struck a chord with her. She immediately recalls her conversations with her angel and Julia. It was along these same lines.

"You're not trying to play some kind of mental gymnastics with me, are you?" she questions. There is a definite reservation in her voice.

"No, of course not. I just don't think we are being asked to put up with someone's harmful, or hurtful behavior for a lifetime. I don't believe that is what it means to forgive."

Along this same line, Jim takes a moment to further organize his thoughts.

"Putting an end to a person's mean, hurtful behavior is different than forgiving the same person for being a screw up.

I believe the deed is not the same as God's created person and the two need to be kept separate."

Peggy's attention has piqued. "Let me think that over. That never occurred to me to see it that way."

"You're the one who received this 'forgive' imperative. I'm not here to water down anything you consider a part of that," concedes Jim.

During her near-death experience, Peggy was given a personal interview with what she knew to be either "God," or "of God." This has become another consideration her experience has left Peggy to ponder.

"What is so difficult is to refer to God as This or That when I saw God to be in everything," submits Peggy. "God was the light, the music, the flowers. I mean there wasn't a thing I experienced that was not God—even though Julia was still Julia, she was also God. Everything was so clear there—now it's all muddled again."

"I'm surly not here to tell you anything involving your experience—that's definitely between you and God. I only know, as you explained it to me, earth is a different deal and when it comes to a lot of this stuff, we don't see things as clear as you did while you were in that realm. But now you're back with both feet fastened to this world. All I can say is, with what you've been given to work with, do the best you can and ask for mercy for the parts you fall short with."

Peggy has needed this conversation and is truly thankful to Jim for his input. Her demeanor has improved a hundred percent. Her frustration level is dropping to where a greater degree of clarity is returning.

"Something, I remember during that experience is when I was given a life review, I saw an incident where I had been hurtful to a girl in eighth grade because Julia was being nice to her and it made me jealous. I made up stories about her and told others these lies. Well, after God let me feel that girls hurt, He assured me I was forgiven."

In reliving this account, Peggy recalls how terrified she was to have to live up to this and many other short comings after already tasting a bit of paradise.

"Jim, you don't know how relieved I was to hear those words: 'You're forgiven.' I truly felt like I was going to be kicked out—or worse, have to deal with that evil realm I saw chasing me along the tunnel."

"I think you already have been given your answer. I believe the only thing missing is how to loosen enough of God's stuff out from under our own crap and to put it into an action," submits Jim.

"You have a way of making this sound like a cake walk but don't forget, you've got your own issues with your dad," reminds Peggy.

"Well, you're right. I probably have no business telling you what you need to do until I measure myself with the same stick."

In Jim's well-intentioned insight that Peggy is going to have to work through much of this alone, the last thing Peggy wants is to lose Jim's support. "Why don't we see if we can work this out together," proposes Peggy.

"I'm all for that," agrees Jim.

Neither are certain when and particularly how this is going to occur but, they have the assurance they are here for each other.

"I know that on my own I have a greater chance of getting things screwed up than if I have your input to temper my goofy thoughts," confesses Peggy.

Jim makes a little chuckle. "I want that to work both ways. I know how squirrelly I can get dealing with my dad's BS. You'll let me know when I need to back off, won't you?"

"You mean that, don't you?" asks Peggy.

"I do," answers Jim.

Peggy could never be pleased her sister was taken from her but to have inherited this bastion of support Julia had found in Jim is a blessing.

There is a smattering of rain. It's likely the kind that sets in and makes a day of it. Whether it is the softness of the cool rain or the compatibility these two are discovering in one another, there is a renewed sense of closeness. They find it easy to set aside other thoughts and to concentrate on each other. Jim has been particularly concerned with Peggy's physical condition, and now he is expanding that to include her mental and spiritual issues.

The close quarters they have found necessary are, in turn, contributing to other tensions. They have, until recently, been able to escape these by living separately. Now it's in their face. They may have chosen to have separate bedrooms but with the increase of their interaction, it's creating a situation that's difficult to ignore. Peggy's physical condition is the main factor postponing taking this development to another level. Both are certain they have come a long way in learning of one another and aren't fearful of the possibility of yet some new discoveries.

With all of the tensions of the day beginning to settle into this unspoken area of their relationship, they fumble about with how to manage it. Jim, being who he is, can't resist the moment to move the conversation to a loftier level.

"Peggy have you given any thought to what you would say if I asked you to marry me?"

In truth, Peggy has not made this jump. Up until now, she has been content to let their relationship take its course. Nonetheless, this question has indeed, moved her thoughts surrounding their relationship into a different chapter. She's not reacting as to be "shocked" at such a suggestion, rather under the present mood, she is discovering this is probably a good time to feel out this possibility.

"No, but I'm not opposed to discussing it," she states trying her best not to appear taken back. "I know I want to be with you but then, I look at the mess our parents made of marriage; it makes me equate marriage with them. It's something I want to avoid."

Jim is quick to react to this borderline reaction. "Yeah, I know how you feel. I get discouraged when I think of it that way myself."

Both are quiet for the moment. It's okay if they have hit an impasse for the time being.

CHAPTER 27

4:00 pm

It's been a week since the ordeal with Sylvia and Greeny. Due to Sylvia's willing confession, she has been charged with open murder. Sylvia's incoherence during the first round of the investigation had placed her out of the loop until they had exhausted interrogating Gil. Greeny wasn't surprised when Sylvia blurted out her confession. He was never totally convinced that Gil had been the culprit. He had always known Gil to be satisfied with being merely a voyeur of women—though, as he's come to learn, Gil didn't demonstrate the same deference toward his male victims.

Life is still trying to find its track with Peggy and Jim. Other than her cast chafing her leg, Peggy's injuries and surgeries are still an issue, but progressively getting better. Jim is winding up his summer job at the camp and in is no longer in limbo as to what he's going to do this fall. He's chosen an apprenticeship with an electrical company. This direction will allow him to stay in the area. Peggy is also uncertain how and when she'll be able to go back to college. They both still face some unresolved charges as accomplices in the upper peninsula fiasco when they were arrested with Ike. For the present, they're content to take life one day at a time and not get caught up in its uncertainties.

For apparent reasons, Peggy has found she functions better if she can get an afternoon nap. This routine has provided some much-needed relief for her injuries. Even without Jim being present every minute, she has found ways to manage. She has come up with the ingenious method of tying a series of lines around the house to the various places she needs to get to, then uses her good arm to pull herself along to the bathroom, kitchen, and so on.

Today is such a day. Jim is running his errands, leaving Peggy to her own devices. In this case, it's the bedroom she's pulled herself to. After placing herself in position, she's able to stand on her good leg and role herself into bed. It's always a good feeling for her to lie in bed and stretch out the kinks she accumulates after hours of sitting in her wheelchair.

The clock on her nightstand says 4:00 p.m. Closing her eyes, preparing to get her half-hour nap, she suddenly finds herself standing in front of an eight-foot giant figure dressed in brilliant white. She immediately recognizes it as her heavenly guide who had identified itself as her guardian angel during her near-death encounter. Her first thoughts are, *"Oh my God, I've died again."* Realizing she had not fulfilled her imperative to grant her mother reconciliation, her next thought roars in, *"Now what am I in for?"*

The apparent difference between this encounter and her near-death experience is that in this incident, the energy of peace and love is not felt. It's definitely other than an earthly experience, but far from the perfect sense of joy and perfect wellbeing her heavenly episode provided. Also, the same telepathic method of communication used in her first experience is being employed once again.

Suddenly, Peggy finds herself looking at a school room. It's a kindly scene of a kindergarten class. She smiles at its familiarity. It's full of happy-faced, noisy kindergartners interacting the only way they can. Then her eyes scan to a little girl sitting alone, with scruffy clothing and unkempt hair. She has a blank look. It's not a sad or lonely look—it's just blank. Turning to her guardian angel, Peggy's question is answered before she can ask.

"The other children refuse to sit with her because they say she stinks."

For an unexplained reason, Peggy has an immediate connection with this little girl. There is something strangely familiar about her.

Since angels move at the speed of thought, their next stop is at a home setting. It's a young girl—maybe eight or nine. She looks similar to the kindergarten girl, but a few years older. She is crying. Again turning to her angel, Peggy looks for an explanation; the answer is prompt.

"Her father's drinking and beat her mother during an argument. When she tried to protect her mother, he beat her, too."

Peggy immediately identifies with this scene, as she has experienced this very thing with her mother and her mother's boyfriends.

The angel's speed is leaving Peggy confused. She isn't able to process these events before she is faced with another episode. This time it's seemingly the same girl, only twelve. She's not alone; there is a man with his hand over her mouth. Peggy is horrified as her eyes focus on the widened eyes of this young girl. Only terror can initiate this look. She is being raped by this man. Catching on to the routine, she automatically turns to her angel with a horrified look of her own.

"It's her father. He's drunk and is raping her."

Before Peggy can respond, she's already viewing another scene. She realizes this is all the same girl, and she is receiving remnants of this person's life. In this instance, the girl is in her teens. She is in a car with a boy who is gripping her by her hair with one hand and punching her with the closed fist of his other hand all the while, shouting, "You're nothin' but a dirty whore. You been cheatin' on me, an' now, ya rotten bitch, yer gonna pay for it."

This time, Peggy sees the face of this horrified girl. She is struck by the image. "What!" is her singular expression. Not ready to acknowledge the image she is recognizing, she gasps out the word, "Mother?" Once again, stunned beyond belief, Peggy turns to her angel.

"That's your father. He's in a jealous rage over things only his own mind created. I might as well add that this is the night you and Julia were conceived. In a jealous rage, he sought to punish your mother by raping her with no protection."

The bite of an ill wind begins to stir inside Peggy. "Why are you showing me this? I already have enough resentments without piling on fuel for more."

Her angel is seemingly unmoved by her question as they are immediately transported in yet another troubling situation. The scene is Sylvia as a young pregnant woman. She's in a setting that is not readily recognizable to Peggy. But what is apparent is that because of her condition, her mother is barely able to get up from her chair. It's obvious that her pregnancy is nearly full term. Soon, a nice appearing lady emerges from another room. She is explaining to Sylvia that her request for housing has to be appropriated through a panel before her case is reviewed.

"My boyfriend has been sent to prison and I've been evicted for non-payment of rent. I'm on the streets now," she laments.

The lady has a kind but firm tone, saying, "I'm sorry. There is nothing I can do. The board has to approve your situation, and they don't meet again until next week."

Peggy is observing the look on her mother's face as she meets yet another depredating attack. It's the same blank look she recalls on the stinky little kindergarten girl, and it's the same blank expression she had when she explained why she needed to kill Julia.

Lost in her own thought, Peggy is transported to another scene. In this instance, Sylvia is no longer pregnant, but is in a bar. It's difficult to analyze what is going on. This is the first time in all of these situations that Peggy notices her mother has a smile. She's actually attractive. She's sitting at a table with a man. As she is leaning in toward him, he pulls her closer, kissing her firmly on the lips. She complies, and with a silly little grin, she says, "You're a silly man. We need to get out of here."

Once outside, Sylvia leads him to a darkened part of an alley. Peggy is not allowed interaction with any more of this liaison except for the discussion of the prearranged twenty-dollar exchange the two have agreed upon.

Stunned beyond anything she has previously experienced, she turns to her angel. The quizzical look on her face already has initiated her angel to form a response entering her thoughts. As a result of her exposure to her mother's past, she has been tenderized sufficiently to receive some thoughts previously not available.

"I may not know how I'm going to forgive my mother, but I have at least been given a reason why I need to."

Her thought processes are noticeably taking a new course. New insights are overwhelming her. Her struggle eases somewhat as the truths provided by this divine being begin to skirt her soul, seeking an entry. Finding a receptive portal, they begin to formulate in Peggy's consciousness.

"Only God and Julia can forgive Julia's murderer—that's impossible for me to do. I can only forgive what has been done to me. The hurt, the sadness over the loss of my sister is the only thing I'm left with to forgive. How often I choose to replay all the hurts my mother initiated against me is my choice.

"I'm also coming to realize that the laws my mother violated are not here to protect me against the hurts she instigated against me. Rather, when she broke the law and was caught, the laws required her to pay back to society what is owed to them, not what is owed to me. It's up to me to clear up what is owed to me—if anything."

Turning toward her angel, she is amazed at how much insight this Being is willing to impart. An immediate awareness she is receiving is that her session of learning and insight isn't finished.

Without warning more things are rushing into her thought processes—things are becoming clearer to her. It's occurring to her that she would rather rage against her mother than face the feelings of how she's been victimized. It's as though raging is the cure, and by it, she needn't examine too closely her own wounds. The angel is quick to point out that getting the rage outside herself is good only to a point; rage is good to trace it back to let the wound identify itself. To rage without boundaries only lets the real wounds fester unchecked.

For Peggy and Julia, all the way through their sports careers, to complain about a hurt was forbidden; "suck it up," "adapt and overcome" was their mottos of choice. Facing her own wounds is a concept that has never sat well with Peggy. It's much easier to continue an attack of hate toward the perpetrator than to deal with the emotional wounds accumulated through the experience.

The angel is still not finished. Peggy's thirst for vengeance is not overlooked. Thought after thought is bombarding her psyche as a star shower bombards the galaxy. A truth that is suddenly made clear is that vengeance has never met its promise to eliminate a hurt—to free oneself from the hurt through vengeance, is the devil's lie. In truth, it always ties the hurt person to the hurter with an even tighter bond making it more difficult to forgive and digs the wound deeper. Her angel is adamant about this in reminding her of an old adage that has been over used to the point that in many circles it's become trite, but when used properly, it's very powerful. "When you hate someone, the effect is as devastating on your mental, physical, and spiritual condition as if you take poison and you hope the other person will die."

Peggy's next awareness is lying on her bed and opening her eyes. Her feeling is that she's definitely been somewhere. The clock still says 4:00 PM. What she has just experienced in the "no time" of the spiritual realm would have been at least a day to experience in earth time. No longer surprised at anything that is happening with her, she begins to mull over all those insights she has been exposed to. Without invitation, her mind begins to drift. It's weaving her back through the labyrinth of her vision. Each event in her mother's life is running like a movie reel through her thoughts. She is reviewing parts of her mother's legacy that she had never seen that made her mother who she is.

The higher thoughts initiated by a Higher Power through her angel to help her see her mother's past are running head long into those originating within her by some lower power. This entire fiasco, if nothing else, is leaving Peggy feeling like a riderless horse waiting for some outside force to mount her—either her guardian angel or some lower powered fallen angel. She has never felt more powerless in her life.

Within the hour of Peggy's vision, Jim returns. What he meets is an upset girlfriend. She appears to be on the verge of some kind of breakdown. Her expression is hard to define. It's one of frustration, anger, fear all twisted into one look. Jim can tell she's hurting. Peggy knows this. When she's hurting, she knows she isn't always seeing things clearly. Jim has a hunch something beyond his experience or understanding has occurred again, nonetheless, he's always willing to take time to listen.

Peggy knows she's at a point where the pressures of her out-of-body encounters are demanding that she make determinations. Julia had always helped her sister with making decisions but with her gone, she has come to rely on Jim. Without a second thought, or a reservation of any sort, she blurts out

"Jim, I've had another out of body experience, only this time I didn't die. But it wasn't any less intense." She's saying this like these spiritual encounters have nearly become normal enough to enable her to rank them.

Jim has learned enough from Peggy's previous near-death encounter to only be a listener and not attempt to analyze what has become a unique experience designed for her alone. As best he can, he gives her the look that tells her he's prepared for everything she's going to try and overwhelm him with.

"Jim, I met my mother."

Jim is less than overawed with this declaration. It could be an everyday comment since Sylvia isn't so far away that Peggy couldn't have gotten a ride to visit her again.

"Okay," he capitulates.

"No, I mean, I met my mother when she was a child," Peggy restates.

This declaration has piqued Jim's attention as well as his curiosity.

Seeing that she has Jim's interest, Peggy continues, "All I did was lie down for a nap. The next thing I knew was I was watching my mother's life begin to unfold."

In Peggy's case, Jim is way beyond being surprised. Instead he prepares himself for another incredible account from a realm he has never been given an invitation to visit.

"Remember me telling you about the angel that identified itself as my guardian angel—well that's who met me and introduced me to all the different segments of my mother's life—starting way back when she was five years old."

Jim is paying close attention. Not certain where he is going to fit into his understanding, nonetheless, he remains available. Peggy is sitting across the same table as she was when they had the last conversation centered around her mother. In this case, things have definitely been updated. Adjusting to these new insights into her mother's life has changed Peggy's demeanor. Using English to attempt to label a single emotion she's experiencing is futile. There's excitement, sadness, unrest, and many more without names, all adding to the turmoil.

"Jim, I watched her struggle with all of the adverse situations in her life. Her life was like a slow death with each event being like another nail pounded in the coffin carrying her soul. It made me so sad. I wanted to hug her and tell her that I loved her."

"Was that possible there?" asks Jim.

"No, it wasn't, but it was so clear that was what I was supposed to want to do. Somehow I got the message that I would have to do that in this earthly realm as an act of forgiveness."

"Is that still your plan?" further inquiries Jim.

Peggy is silent as she peers out the window. "Oh look, the butter fly is dancing on the window. It's beautiful."

She pauses for a moment, as though her thought is suddenly interrupted. "I've been seeing that butterfly often lately. It acts like it's trying to say something to me. I don't know—it's kind of weird."

Her attention returns. Remembering Jim's question regarding her forgiveness, she takes another moment to put into words a holding she still has. She says, "Everything is so clear while I'm there. The problem comes in when I'm sent back to this earthly realm. There's something inside me that wants to struggle."

Jim wrinkles his forehead in a quizzical manner. This tells her he is totally befuddled with her contradictive answer.

In an effort to clarify herself, Peggy says, "While I was there, everything was so clear and easy to understand. As soon as I found myself back again, the resentments picked up where they left off. If I were to go through the motions of forgiving her, I feel it would only be a shallow effort. There's something missing and I can't put finger on it."

The weeks continue to drag by for Peggy. The last time she was at the doctor, he was concerned with her progress. Looking at her bedraggled countenance, he asked, "You're not healing like you should be at this point. Are you doing more activity than you should be? You appear to be exhausted and your tests indicate your immune system is not up to par."

Peggy isn't surprised at this diagnosis. She's been feeling a kind of depression.

"No, I haven't been doing anything at all. I can't seem to get a handle on things—nothing seems to give me joy. I'm in some crazy kind of funk. I've never in my life felt like this."

Since the doctor is an integral part of the community, he is aware of Peggy's trauma surrounding the loss of her sister and the arrest of her mother for the murder. Taking the time once more, he gives her a long look, he then pauses for a moment as if he's come on something requiring a different thought pattern. He finally speaks.

"I see the beginnings of a depression in you. It's not exactly a clinical depression yet, so, I'm going to prescribe a light antidepressant. I strongly suggest you follow the prescribed dosage. Let's see if we can get ahead of something that could become worse if it's not treated."

Another month goes by. Peggy has returned to the doctor to hopefully get her leg cast off. It's taken an extra two weeks longer to heal than normal—this is true of all her injuries. Entering the examination room with charts in hand, the doctor gives her another long, hard look. "Last month, I prescribed an antidepressant. I'm curious to know how you think you're doing?"

Realizing her need to be transparent, she willfully bemoans, "Truthfully? I'm still having more down days than good days. It seems all of my life has piled in on me like a big wave, and I can't breathe. I wish I could put my finger on it."

Not taking his eyes off her, the doctor says, "I'm going to increase the strength of your prescription, and I want to see you in a month. But in the meantime, let's get this cast off. That in itself should give you a boost."

Leaving the doctor's office with crutches is not only lifting her spirits; it's also having a positive effect on Jim's psyche. To celebrate, they decide to stop at the Midway for a lunch.

There's nothing like a lunch away from home to give a little extra lift to the day. Peggy's decision to not return to school this fall is going to open up a lot of extra time that she needs to fill with something constructive. Mandy is once again asking her to consider returning to the bar as a server.

"Let me get healed up and I'll be back," Peggy assures.

Jim is happy to see this upward change in Peggy. It's enough to prompt him to ask, "Is there anything else you'd like to do today?"

They have chosen a table by a window, allowing the sunlight to brighten their meal. Clearly ignoring Jim's question, Peggy is drawn to another phenomenon. It's the butterfly dancing against the window again.

The spectacle only takes Peggy's attention away for a moment. Her face has taken on a more serious expression. "Today is Wednesday. It's visiting day at the jail. I'd like to see my mother."

This request has caught Jim unawares. Thinking of Peggy's bout with depression, he quickly challenges her wish. "Are you sure that's a good idea?"

"I'm not sure of anything lately," says Peggy with a sigh.

In his attempt to be Peggy's main morale booster, Jim adds, "It's not something you have to do. If you want to wait until you're better, I'm certain she'll still be there."

"No, I'm certain I want to go today. There is a strong feeling that won't leave me alone. It keeps pushing me toward my mother. I think Julia has something to do with it."

Once her mind is set, Jim knows better than to try and talk her out of it. Without another alternative, they finish their lunch, say goodbye to everyone and make their way to Jim's truck. Very soon they are in the parking lot adjacent to the county jail. Peggy has been very quiet. She is staring straight ahead without a blink. Finally, she lets out a sigh that indicates she has resolved to face this undertaking head on. Jim would rather sit this one out, but his concern for Peggy's ability to navigate alone with her new crutches brings him to her side.

Once inside, they approach the area housing the jail personnel, which is enclosed with bulletproof glass. After identifying herself, she is put on a list and told to leave certain items that are considered contraband. Someone would come and bring her to a holding cell used as a visitor cubicle. After a few minutes, a matron appears at the lobby door asking for a Peggy Fortine. Struggling to raise her hand, stand, and arrange her crutches she nearly falls. Jim is there to catch her. She is Sylvia's only relative on the list of visitors allowed in to visit. Since Jim has no use for Sylvia, he's just as well to be left behind. After assisting Peggy as far as he's allowed, he returns to his seat in the lobby. Just as he's about to reclaim his chair his eye is led to a movement on the window. On a closer inspection, he is shocked to see the same butterfly appear. It seems to have been stalking them. Its technique is the same. It continues to romp in the same well-coordinated, dance-like movement that it has on the previous occasions. Jim begins to view this spectacle as some kind of omen but is left to ponder what kind of omen it is—good or bad?

This jail was built at a time when there was less regard for space per prisoner. Claustrophobia is the best way to describe Peggy's feeling for the moment. The hallways are narrow and foreboding. She is led to a solid steel door with a small window operated from the outside. It's one of those steel windows that slides open and closed. It's there for the convenience of the guard on duty—not the prisoner. The matron on duty, applying a key, opens the door.

Sylvia is sitting in an eight by eight cell with no link to another world other than the door's ominous sliding steel slot. Even the lighting is from recessed lights designed to be unreachable by inmates. She's perched on a fold down steel stool at a fold down steel table. Her hair is pulled back into some kind of bun that Peggy had seen her mother wear many times. If it weren't for her orange colored coveralls, Sylvia would look similar to herself in other environments.

Peggy's first response upon seeing her mother in this environment is to try and not have a first opinion. She's decided to not let what she is viewing have a monumental effect on her emotions. As much as possible, she is attempting to make her celestial experiences come alive in her everyday life. Her overwhelming yearning to have a repeat performance of the love, forgiveness and peace, is undeterred. Since her near-death experience, she has become more aware of her spiritual nature. It hasn't resulted in her becoming more religious in a church sense; rather, it's made her more aware of her forbearance—especially when it deals with her mother. With this in mind, it's her intention to try and have a mother-daughter conversation regardless of the environment. Both of these choices originate from her ongoing battle against the disdain she continues to hold for her mother.

There is no doubt in her mind that her sister and all the company of heaven want her to forgive. The problem originates with the point that no one there told her how— they left her to figure it out on her own.

Eager to follow through, she has gotten several self-help books on the subject. These are written by well-meaning authors, who attempt to meet an unreasonable malady with a reasonable approach—generally in a series of steps. As with most of these, there are some well-crafted arguments as to *why* their approach is going to bring with it a successful conclusion. Peggy has remained faithful in her resolve to stay on track with her obligation to implement as much of these techniques as it takes. Now it's time to consider where she stands in a practical sense with each of the authors.

Maybe her insistence to visit her mother is to measure in herself the amount of empathy these exercises have produced. To do this, she has spent much of her time remembering how sad she felt for this poor girl before she realized it was her mother. From time to time, she would test herself with different scenarios. *"Would I have more empathy if I thought I was reviewing someone else's mother's life? At what point did I bring my resentments into the setting?"*

These, and other questions that she has not been able to resolve are the solid reasons why she is ready to meet again with her mother.

"Hello, Mother."

"Hi, sweetie." This has always been Sylvia's standard greeting for either of her daughters. It parallels the Biblical axiom, "They honor me with their lips, but their hearts are far from me."

This is the first obstacle confronting Peggy. She recalls how she and Julia used to mock their mother's hypocrisy by referring to one another as "Sweetie." Attempting to get past this, considering it as a minor annoyance, Peggy asks, "How are you doing here? Are they treating you okay?"

"Oh, I'm doing fine," she replies. "I do miss getting my nails done though. I've had to start biting them to keep them trimmed."

This small talk on the surface sounds okay but it doesn't match Peggy's inside stiffness. She's finding it difficult to find enough in common to have a meaningful conversation. For years, their lives have been *around* each other but not *with* each other. As a result, they may as well be strangers. Nonetheless, Peggy holds to her resolve to have enough interaction with her mother to say she did.

Sylvia is nattering on about her cell mate not taking advantage of the days they're allowed a shower. "She stinks so bad I can't stand her. I've even told her she stinks."

This immediately brings to Peggy's mind her mother's instance where her schoolmates segregated her because she stunk. This further cements the truism that "hurt people, hurt people."

Things are beginning to soften a bit for Peggy to begin to see more of the hurts her mother had endured during her vision and how they continue to morph into her everyday conversations. Matters continue along a civil line as minor daily events are tossed about.

"Oh, I want to tell you how thrilled I was yesterday when I saw Gil. They were transporting him to court for something, and we exchanged glances and waved to each other."

When the conversation reverts back to Sylvia bringing up something as despicable as Harold Gillen, Peggy's patience is at its end. Despite the gains Peggy may feel she's made, everything comes to a screeching halt. *How can she even bring up that pig's name in my presence?* Still trying to be civil and plan her exit before she no longer is.

"Well, Mother, I have somethings I need to take care of. I'll try and stop by next week." With that said, Peggy gives her still seated mother a quick peck on her forehead, gives the signal required for the matron to unlock the door—it can't come soon enough.

Hobbling her way back to the lobby, she finds Jim still waiting. Peggy can feel the tension coming over her. Once again, with no effort, the overwhelming feeling that she has fostered for years where she has let herself be a victim is quickly racing to the forefront. Trying to remember what her studies say about this situation is further adding to the tension. Add to this that her expectations for her mother's behavior are still not being met. Whatever studying she has done to prepare herself for this liaison is buried under the ever-pervasive layer of resentment. These and a few more waiting in the recesses of her mind are back as the main themes.

Peggy remains silent on the trip home. Jim lets it slide for the first half of the drive. Never wanting to overstep his importance but wanting to remain helpful, he waits until she has had ample time to replay her and Sylvia's liaison alone.

"So how did it go?" is his opener.

"About like it always does," is her curt answer.

Now that Jim has an idea of the nature of their meeting, he has something to deliberate on.

"In my own searching, I've come to some conclusions for myself."

Peggy is still in her own world, playing and replaying her life encircled by her mother. She is ready for something to pull her out of this obsession. It's very exhausting.

"Oh yeah, what did you come up with?" Her question is out of curiosity rather than expecting anything monumental.

"In my case, I think the reason I don't forgive my father is because I don't want to reward him in any manner for what he has done to our family."

This single statement has awakened another recess in Peggy's psyche. "I never thought of that, Jim but it makes sense. I'll have to give that one some more thought."

"I've got some more to go along with that. If I get really honest, I have to admit as much of a tough guy as I portray, my life decisions are based on a lot of fear."

Peggy gives him the wrinkled forehead look that doesn't require words. This is signal enough for Jim to qualify his statement.

"I mean, I fear the consequences of forgiving—I fear I may not be as comfortable as I want to be. What if I have to go out of my way to be civil, or I may fear if I forgive, I'll be expected to hang around somebody I don't trust."

"Jim stop! You're giving me a headache. I can't deal with all that!" cries out Peggy placing both her hands over her ears,

"I've heard enough. All this talk wears me out. Now I know why people start drinking."

Jim takes the cue and resumes his driving. Peggy spends the rest of the trip buried in her own thoughts, looking out her side window watching the butterfly's wings flutter as the sixty-mile-per-hour airflow attempts to tear its stubborn grip loose from the window frame.

CHAPTER 28

A Letter

Within a few more weeks, Jim has helped close the camp for the season and is working on his electrician apprenticeship full time. The pay is better than he made at the camp and he is able to help Peggy with the expenses they need to remain in the house.

Peggy is also getting closer to being healthy enough to return to the Midway. Her incision has healed, her wrist is back to normal and she no longer is required to use her crutches. She has not been back to see her mother in jail but did show up for her court appearance where she was bound over to a higher court on first degree murder charges.

Peggy's obsession to replay over and over all the hurts her mother has bestowed on her is exhausting. These grievances have been so deeply entrenched in her that to isolate each one and try and forgive it, is a lesson in futility. She is beginning to realize that her self-help books, along with Jim's analysis, and not to dismiss her own will power in an attempt to dash to pieces her apparent unwillingness to forgive her mother have done nothing but bring more unresolved conflicts to light—with no solutions.

After Sylvia's court hearing, Peggy has come to at least one conclusion. "I really don't want to set outside her cell and watch her suffer. I believe I've at least grown past that."

There is one more arrow in Peggy's quiver that hasn't been utilized—she elects to write her mother a letter. It's a thought that has not occurred to her until she became aware of the butterfly dancing on the window again this morning. Wanting to do this task without any outside influences, she waits for Jim to leave for work. Not exactly certain how to write this, she attempts to organize the chaos involving her mother that has occupied her brain for a lifetime. After getting herself dressed, she begins by searching around for a pen and paper. Thinking about its content is already causing her to perspire—maybe a mixture of anxiety and excitement. *"I believe this is the rightest move I've made since I began this whole struggle,"* is her singular thought.

Glancing at the window, she notices the butterfly seemingly staring at her. It's no longer dancing, it's still as though it's anticipating something. Looking back to the blank sheet of paper, tapping the tip of the pen on the table, she struggles on formulating even the greeting. *"Should I say, 'Dear Mother' or just 'Mother'?* Some place in her mind the thought to use the less hostile greeting takes precedence.

Dear Mother,

This is a letter I should have written years ago. I'm not certain how to start other than I know I need to. The purpose needed for me to write this and address it to you is twofold. The first reason is for me to relate to you how your actions have affected me. The second reason will wait until I finish the first.

From my earliest recollection, your absence due to having to work was at least something that had legitimacy but your absence while not at work is a hurt that is burned into my soul. It left me with the feeling that you didn't love me nor want me. Your time spent at the bar always worried me because I remember when you would come home with black eyes where some man had beat you. I remember the time you passed out on your bed with a lit cigarette and caught the mattress on fire. If I hadn't gotten up to go to the bathroom and smelled the smoke, you would have burned the house down with all of us in it. You also brought man after man into our home with no regard as to how they scared me. If it hadn't been for Julia and me literally locking ourselves in our room, one of us would have been raped—this occurred more often than with just one of these men. I feel it was your lack of concern for my wellbeing in order for you to fill your desire to always have a man in your life to replace me.

My point is, you were never the mother I could go to, and expect you to react any different than you always have. The result has been, I've been dragging you and me all twisted up around for too long. What you did to me in my life is not okay and will never be okay. Your actions in my life have given me resentments that are rotting my soul. In the prosses, I lost myself. I have always hoped you would become the mother I anticipated you would eventually become. But for me to wait for you to change or your apology is proving to come at too high a cost.

At this juncture, I want to tell you, you don't owe me anything. The reason I can say 'I forgive you' is because dealing with my resentments toward you have worn me out physically, mentally, and spiritually. In other words, it's become easier to forgive you than to live with the hate. I wish I could forgive because of the nobler reason being that I'm forgiven, but I can't. That kind of unconditional forgiveness is too difficult for me to fulfill in this world—I can only leave that in God's and Julia's hands. But like I've said, you owe me nothing and I needed to wear out all my ill feelings toward you—I had to, or I never could have forgiven you. I hereby give up the right to hurt you, because you have hurt me. The benefit is, I've been set free.

Your daughter, Peggy

Finishing the letter, she addresses it and takes it and places it in the mailbox. Peggy looks up to notice the butterfly is perched above the mailbox. With a little sigh and a slight smile, her singular comment is, "Thank you Julia."

With that, the butterfly circles around Peggy as if doing a ballet and disappears into the heavens.

End